DATE DUE

Other works by the same writer include:

The Canon in Residence (1904)
The Canon's Dilemma (1909)
A Downland Corner (1912)
Thrilling Stories of the Railway (1912)
The Templeton Case (1924)
A Bishop out of Residence (1924)
The Adventures of Captain Ivan Koravitch (1925)
The Crime at Diana's Pool (1927)
Shot on the Downs (1927)
Mixed Relations (1928)
Murder at the Pageant (1930)
Murder at the College (1932)

THE DEAN AND HIS DOUBLE

by

V. L. WHITECHURCH

University of Chichester
2007

The Dean and his Double
was originally published in 1926 as
The Dean and Jecinora.
It is now reprinted with a revised title by permission
of the literary heirs of the author,
and issued to coincide with the publication of
Otter Memorial Paper Number 22:

CHICHESTER DEANS -
Continuity, Commitment, and Change
at Chichester Cathedral 1902-2006

ISBN 978-0-948765-77-3

Cover design by RPM Print & Design
Printed and bound in Great Britain by
RPM Print & Design
2-3 Spur Road, Quarry Lane, Chichester, West Sussex
PO19 8PR

THE DEAN AND HIS DOUBLE

CHAPTER I

JULIAN BRUCE STANNILAND drove his car up the long, gradual ascent on top gear and at high speed. That was Julian Bruce Stanniland's manner of life when he was doing anything—top gear and high speed. When he was not doing anything he was as inert as his car was in the garage—for that was Stanniland's manner of life when he was idle. He was as thorough in his idleness as he was in his work. Just now he happened to be driving his powerful two-seater, and he drove it as he drove his own brain when that powerful organism came under his will, drove it furiously, and yet with the alert caution that was also his characteristic.

Stolid contrymen in carts, slowly pulling their left rein at the sound of the peremptory bark of his hooter behind them might look aghast as he rushed by them before they were well out of his way ; pedestrians might send an unheard imprecation after him as they stepped on one side, with barely a second of time or an inch of space, to escape ; rustics lounging at the village cross-roads might open their eyes in wonderment at the expectation of a glorious smash because *they* could see the parson cycling towards the point of contact up the side road while this mad motorist on the main road could not ; but the fact remained that Julian Bruce Stanniland never did graze the axle of the cartwheel with his off wing, never did send the pedestrian hurtling into the ditch, and always pulled up to dead slow just before he reached the dangerous corner. Top gear and high speed if you like—but he took no risks.

The long ascent had continued for considerably over a mile. He was gradually mounting to the top of the great rolling downland till it seemed, as he gained the flat bit of road on the summit, that he was coming to the edge of things. At present the view was limited, a slight cutting in the road hid the expanse on either side, while in front were only the white clouds scudding athwart the clear sky. Suddenly, however, as the road took a downward turn and the cutting in the bare downs ended, there came the revelation.

" By Jove ! " exclaimed Stanniland, and, as he spoke, declutched and rammed on the brake. The next moment he had jumped out of the car and was mounting the down on the side of the road, the better to see the view. Then he sat down, took off his hat, produced a cigarette case from his pocket, and began to smoke. Julian Bruce Stanniland was as still and quiet as the car in the road beneath him. Things, for the moment, had come to a full stop.

What he saw from the downland height was enough to make any man who loves nature pause with the suddenness with which the view came into his vision. Beneath him, under the great downs, was a broad expanse of low-lying country, bordered in the far distance by a silver streak of sea, while the sun sparkled on estuaries running inland. In the wide sweep were fair green pasture lands, pale yellow stubble fields that the reaped harvest had left, some of them already marked by square brown patches of fresh earth turned up by early autumn ploughing, clumps of trees with here and there a well-wooded space.

Some three miles away, in the centre of the plain, the sun caught a tall, tapering spire, glistening white, and pointing through the suggestion of haze that betokened the smoke of a town. One could also make out the towers of half a dozen village churches dotted over the expanse.

On either side were the downs, their slopes, sometimes gentle, sometimes abrupt, edging the plain in one place, throwing out spurs into it in another ; great, rolling downs, broken up with clumps of trees, green with the short, springy turf, except for the brown or pale yellow of their cultivated bases, rolling on in an unbroken line to the dim distances to right and left.

The man who sat on the turf quietly smoking and gazing over the fair scene was one who would have arrested the attention of the student of humanity as strongly as the downland vista would have appealed to the student of nature. He was above middle height, well built and well dressed, about thirty years of age. His forehead was broad—the brow of the scholar ; his chin square and firm, the chin of the successful business man. His eyes, well set on either side of a somewhat prominent nose—a nose which distinctly indicated the faculty of inquiry—were grey-blue and steady. His hair, accurately parted at the side and short, was inclined to be fair, and his little moustache was fairer still, and did not hide the firm lips beneath. His hands were delicately moulded—the hands belonging to one who, in spite of a face which spoke of mastery, was not destitute of some artistic temperament in his composition.

He took the cigarette from his lips and murmured to himself :

" Now—I like this."

And when Julian Bruce Stanniland said, " I like this," he never said it as an idle remark without reason. He said it with a purpose in his mind. The purpose might be a sudden one—it generally was—but it meant that he was going to follow it all the same, till it either succeeded or failed.

Again Julian Bruce Stanniland said, " I like this ! " Then he went on smoking his cigarette. Presently, as he gazed over the expanse below him, his eyes opened a little wider, his lips parted, his cigarette went out as he held it between his fingers, his face shone with a sudden animation.

" By George ! " he ejaculated, " I've got it ! "

Then he sprang to his feet, waved his hand above his head, and cried out loud :

" Jecinora ! Oh, Jecinora ! "

And, again, he cried :

" Jecinora !—Splendid ! "

He sat down again, lighted a fresh cigarette, and resumed his quiet attitude of meditation.

" It'll do," he said, " and so will this," and he nodded towards the plain beneath him. " I like it." Then he threw away his cigarette, got up, carefully brushed off some bits of dry grass that had stuck to his trousers, got into his car, and started down the sloping road to the plain below.

The spire in front of him loomed larger as he ran, at high speed towards it, through a pleasant village nestling at the foot of the downs—along a broad, level road, past the outskirts of the cathedral city, up the quaint old North Street, slowing down as, turning a corner, he caught sight of the " Red Lion," a decent-looking hotel, stopping by the side of the pavement at the entrance.

"What have you got for luncheon?"

The waiter laid a menu in front of him and he quickly chose his dishes, and the waiter knew it was the best choice.

Luncheon over, he said to the waiter, "Tell the landlord I want to speak to him."

"Yes, sir."

A stoutish, good-natured looking man came into the room. Stanniland summed him up at a glance.

"You wanted to see me, sir?"

"Yes. Will you join me in a glass of port?"

"With pleasure."

Stanniland ordered a bottle and waved the landlord into a chair with a commanding gesture.

"Healthy town, this?"

"Oh, very, sir. You see we're only a few miles from the coast and get the sea breezes."

"Good train service to London?"

"Very."

"Quiet, I suppose?"

"Well, sir, of course we're a cathedral town and have the reputation of being a little sleepy, but there's plenty of business doing. Big cattle and corn markets. And loads of tourists all the summer. I mustn't complain."

"Any house for sale here, with immediate possession?"

The landlord looked at him with fresh interest over the top of his glass.

"Houses are scarce, everywhere. What sort of a house?"

"Fair size; garden; quiet situation," replied Stanniland, with the air of a man who knew exactly what he wanted.

The landlord sipped his wine thoughtfully for a few seconds, and then said :

" There *is* a house for sale, I believe, in the Close."

" Ah, Cathedral property ? "

" No, it isn't, sir. Most of the houses there belong to the Dean and Chapter, but this one doesn't happen to do so. But I understand they're contemplating buying it. You see," he went on, expansively, " they're a little clique all to themselves in the Close, and they like to keep the place—er—well, *select !* "

Stanniland grinned.

" Not my sort, eh ? "

" Oh, I don't mean that, sir—only—— "

" Exactly. Tell me about the house."

" It's a goodish size. Nice garden. But in bad repair. It belonged to old Colonel Walton, who died some months ago, and the executors have to sell it. I believe Pegg Brothers, in St. Martin's Street, the house agents, have got the job."

" All right. I shall stay here to-night. Please have my car put into your garage and send the portmanteau in it to my room. You finish the wine. I'm off to see Pegg Brothers."

The office of Pegg Brothers was situated in a quiet by-street in an ancient building of the same. It was furnished with six wooden chairs, a plain oak table, and two very large desks, presumably one for each brother. Open folding doors at the back displayed a long room beyond. This was the " auction mart," where sales were conducted.

At one of the desks was seated a tall, thin man, with long, cadaverous face, and heavy walrus moustache. This was John Pegg, the senior partner, commonly known in Frattenbury as " Priceless Pegg," the reason being that valuations for probate or property were invariably conducted by his brother, while he consistently refused to appraise the price of any article, from a " commodious mansion " down to a second-hand bedstead. In the " auction mart " beyond his brother, William Pegg, was pasting " lot " numbers on to an array of furniture that had come in for sale. William Pegg, who performed the office of auctioneer, while John kept the accounts, was shorter than his brother; quite a fat little man. Also, his face was clean shaven. Likewise the said face was of a ruddy complexion, but the redness was uneven, both in shade and surface, giving him a strange, mottled appearance which some local wag having once likened to pickled cabbage, had earned him thenceforth the nickname of " Pickled Pegg."

" Good afternoon, sir."

Priceless Pegg spoke in a deep, sepulchral tone of voice, as he looked up inquiringly at the stranger.

" You are Pegg Brothers ? "

" I am one of them," and, with a jerk of his thumb behind him he indicated his partner in the room beyond.

" I understand you have a house for sale, in the Close ? "

" That is so."

" I should like to go over it. Have you the key ? "

In reply, John Pegg turned round and ejaculated:

" William, you're wanted."

His brother came forward, sucking a pencil, a bland look on his mottled countenance.

" This gentleman," indicated John, " wants to look over the late Colonel Walton's house. Have you got he key ? "

"Oh," replied William, speaking in a high tenor voice, and without removing the pencil from his lips, "Yes, I see. Colonel Walton's house. Exactly. But we haven't got the key, John. The Dean asked for it this morning. Oh, yes!"

"Where does the Dean live?" asked Stanniland. "In the Close, I suppose?"

"Yes, exactly. Next door to the house in question. He——"

"All right," interrupted Stanniland, "perhaps you will kindly write him a line asking him to let me have the key. There's my card," and he laid it on Priceless Pegg's desk.

The latter took it up and scanned it. Then he said:

"If you want to see the house, sir, I'll go round to the Close with you, and——"

"Not at all. I prefer looking over it by myself. I won't trouble you."

John Pegg wrote a few words on a sheet of the firm's official paper, put it in an envelope, and handed it over to Stanniland.

"The house is advertised for sale by auction next Wednesday," he announced, in a mournful voice.

"Unless you sell it first by private treaty?" said Stanniland.

"Oh, yes. Quite so," replied Pickled Pegg, "but that is in the hands of the executors. We act for them. You see——"

But Julian Bruce Stanniland had turned on his heel and was already out of the office. Quickly, with decided steps, he made his way to the Close, entering those quiet and sacred precincts through an old gateway in the South Street. And again he said, as he looked around him:

" I like this."

Anyone with an eye for the picturesque would have liked it. At the farther end of the little street he had entered stood an ancient, massive gateway, the entrance to the Episcopal Palace. Immediately on his right was a broad, stone-paved path, on one side of which was a row of beautiful old stone houses, half covered by Virginia creeper, and with neat little gardens in front. As he walked along the nearly deserted street he admired fine old houses, standing back, for the most part, from the road. Farther on, was a narrow lane on the right, at the end of which one could see the opening into the cloisters; while, above all, towered the massive grey pile of the Cathedral, surmounted by its tapering spire.

It was on the gate of one of these old houses, on the south side of the street, that he saw a board advertising its sale, under the heading of " Peg Brothers." He paused for a moment to look at it, and then asked a boy who was passing where the Dean lived.

The boy pointed to the next-door house, a big, square building standing well back in its own grounds.

" There, sir."

Stanniland walked up the carriage drive and rang the bell. The door was opened by a perfect representative of Cathedral dignity, a portly, grey-haired butler, with just the suspicion of whiskers, an exceedingly grave and decorous-looking individual, meet, in every respect, to be the bodyguard of a dean. Indeed, he was a sort of perennial heirloom that went with the Deanery, having served under no less than three masters who were entitled to the appellation of " Very Reverend." He reflected the title. He looked " very reverend " himself.

Stanniland produced the note from Pegg Brothers and intimated that he would wait for an answer. The butler, with great dignity, suggested that he should take a seat in the hall, and disappeared through a door, first placing the note on a silver salver. In a moment or two the Dean himself came into the hall, holding the note in his hand.

The Dean of Frattenbury was a tall, thin man, slightly stooping at the shoulders. His dark hair was slightly touched with grey, his forehead wrinkled, his eyes luminous, but with rather a dreamy expression. His face was relieved from austerity by the slight upward curve at the corners of his mouth. Stanniland looked at him keenly as he walked, slowly, across the hall, and mentally summed him up.

" *You're* not a man of the world, my friend."

Stanniland was right. The Very Reverend Ernest Lake, D.D., the new Dean of Frattenbury, had mixed but little with men and affairs of the world. He was pre-eminently a student. For ten years previous to his present promotion he had been Vicar of a remote country parish, and regularly every two years of the ten had produced a book, until he had made a name for himself as one of the greatest authorities on Liturgiology in the Church of England. Two of his books, *English Mediæval Uses* and *A Study of Some Minor Eastern Liturgies* were recognized standard works.

So they had dug him out of his rusticity. There had been a little conversation between the Member of his constituency—a keen Churchman—and the Prime Minister. The latter had invited his Bishop to lunch with him at the Athenæum, and following a word or two about *English Mediæval Uses*—of which he knew nothing and cared less—had, adroitly, led the Prelate to give information about the author: "A scholar, a gentleman, quite a good family, the Hampshire Lakes. Amiable, no—er—no very decided leanings. A quiet, all-round man, so to speak. Capable—oh, certainly."

Then the Prime Minister had lighted a cigar and suggested Frattenbury.

"I think so," said the Bishop, "not quite the man for a northern deanery—not, er, you see, of a pronounced business tendency. But for Frattenbury—a southern sphere—oh, yes. I think so, certainly."

Probably no one was more surprised than Dr. Lake himself when the offer was made. He accepted it, after a little hesitation. He had always understood that a deanery was a quiet harbour for men of his calibre, and, with the humility which was natural to him, when he compared himself with the rising generation of clergy, he felt that he was not quite so successful in the daily round of parochial work as he was in the seclusion of his study. So, at the age of fifty-three, he had become Dean of Frattenbury, and the butler, who had been recommended to him by his retiring predecessor, found him quite amenable to the very respectful coaching which a long experience prompted him to give from time to time.

"Mr. Stanniland?" asked the Dean, arching his eyebrows in question.

"Yes."

"Oh, I see. You want to borrow the key of the house next door?"

"If you will kindly let me have it."

"Certainly. Only—could I have it back in half an hour's time?"

"In ten minutes," replied Stanniland.

"Oh, I'm not in such a hurry as that," said the

Dean, " only, as a matter of fact, we have a meeting of the Chapter this afternoon and we are going to view the house. You see, it happens to be the only house in the Close that is not our property and we think the present moment is a good opportunity for purchasing it—before it is offered for sale by auction, if possible."

Stanniland smiled. Within himself he said :

" Oh, *not* a man of business ! You're giving the show away, my friend ! Badly ! "

Then a sudden thought seemed to strike the Dean :

" Were *you* thinking of buying it ? " he asked, bluntly.

" Oh, I just want to look over it. I'm passing through the town, and—— "

" I see. Well," and he gave a little laugh : " I don't think there's any chance for outsiders if *we* decide. Yes, here's the key."

Top gear and high speed ! That was the manner in which Julian Bruce Stanniland went over that house. Rapidly he passed from room to room, upstairs, down again, taking it all in with quick, searching glance. Then out into the garden at the back of the house, a pleasant, old-world garden, bordering that of the Deanery, from which it was separated by a wall.

At the bottom of the garden was a surprise—at least to a stranger. The lawn sloped upwards to a broad terrace, which was, in fact, part of the old mediæval wall of the city. This was bordered by a parapet, over which one looked a good twenty feet below. Beyond, were open, pleasant meadows ; a wide, quite pastoral view. Stanniland paused for a moment on the terrace to light a cigarette, and said, more emphatically even than before :

"I like this!"

It was exactly nine and a half minutes after he had received it that he returned the key into the hands of the Dean's butler, and immediately he returned to Pegg Brothers' office.

"I'll buy that house," he announced, without further introduction. "What's the price?"

John Pegg stared at him with rounded eyes.

"William," he said at length, turning towards his brother, who was still at his labelling job in the room behind, "Mr. Stanniland says he wants to buy the late Colonel Walton's house. Are we authorized to sell by private treaty?"

"Oh," said William, coming forward, "you want to buy it? Yes, exactly. Very quick in making up your mind, sir! But, of course, it's a question for the executors to decide. We are not authorized to name any price, you see, and——"

"Who are the executors?"

"Sefton and Prior—offices in the Pallant."

"Can you take me there?"

"Oh, certainly, Mr. Stanniland," and he reached his hat down from a peg.

In five minutes' time Stanniland was explaining the situation to Mr. Melton, a precise little lawyer, one of those precise little men who make it a habit never to be surprised at anything. When he had heard Stanniland he said:

"Well—er—of course we might be prepared to sell by private treaty if——"

"I understand you *are* prepared," interrupted Stanniland. "The Dean tells me the Chapter i thinking of making you an offer. I dare say you've already named the price to them."

"Oh—er—tentatively, perhaps. But, really——"

"Quite so. I don't expect you to tell me what it is, unless you choose."

The lawyer thought for a moment.

"Oh, well," he said, "of course, as far as we're concerned it's a matter of business. Candidly, the Chapter, if they decide to buy, will give us two thousand seven hundred for it."

"Very well. I'll give you three thousand. It wouldn't fetch that at an auction.

The lawyer looked interrogatively at Pickled Pegg. The latter pursed up his mouth and shook his head.

"He's right, Mr. Sefton," he said.

"But—er—we don't know you," said the lawyer. "Of course, you can give us references?"

"Certainly. I bank at Lloyds, Fleet Street Branch. I see they have a branch here. Get them to telephone, if you like. That's my offer, sir. Take it or leave it."

As a matter of fact, at the precise moment when the Chapter began the discussion which was to settle the question of the purchase of that house, Julian Bruce Stanniland was writing a cheque for the deposit money. And when the Dean returned to the Deanery, satisfied, by a unanimous vote, that everything was settled, he saw the stranger who had called upon him earlier in the afternoon entering the gate of the house next door, accompanied by a local builder. Top gear and high speed!

"Ah, well," said the Dean, as he went in to his leisurely bachelor tea, "that young man has come a day after the fair. So much the better. He didn't look *quite* the sort of person for the close of a cathedral."

CHAPTER II

THE Dean of Frattenbury, blissfully unconscious that it was he and his Chapter who were a " day after the fair," sat down to his bachelor tea in his commodious study, and began to open the correspondence which the afternoon post had brought him.

Presently he frowned a little as he read :

MY DEAR UNCLE,

Will you, please, be very nice and put me up for a little while ? I'm on a loose end. The old woman I'm with is going abroad for six months—selling her car, so I'm out of a job once more. I suppose your Bishop doesn't want a chauffeur, does he ? Anyhow I know you'll be a dear old nunky and let me come and cheer you up while I look around for another berth. May I go to you on Tuesday ?

Best love,

Your affectionate niece,

PEGGY.

The Dean poured himself out a fresh cup of tea and gave a little sigh. It was not that he disliked this niece of his. He did not. But, what he always felt with regard to her was that a little of her went a long way. She was the antithesis of an orderly bachelor like himself. He was punctuality personified. Peggy never had any regard for the time of day. He was meticulously tidy. Peggy left a trail of untidiness behind her wherever she went. He was regular in his habits, and as quiet as regular. Peggy had no habits at all; one never knew what she would be up to next, except that whatever she *was* up to was pretty sure to be conducted in a boisterously erratic manner.

But, in a warm corner of his heart, he was sorry for Peggy. She was the only child of an unhappy marriage. The Dean's only brother, Edward Lake, had been the ne'er do well of the family. Years ago he had made a hasty marriage, and his wife had repented of it at leisure. Then, when Peggy was about two years old, a separation had taken place, and Edward Lake had taken himself off—on a chequered career. From time to time he had turned up at his brother's quiet country vicarage, generally with a story of how he had narrowly escaped making a fortune owing to the perversity of persons and circumstances, and begging a temporary loan to enable him to fare forth into the world again where another fortune was awaiting him—provided he could put up fifty pounds.

The Dean had never taken his brother's part in the question of the marriage. On the contrary, he had been a consistent friend to his sister-in-law until her death, two years previous. He had paid for Peggy's education and tried to do his best for her when she had been left an orphan. But it was not easy to do one's best for Peggy. In some respects she had inherited her father's wayward character. A war job as a flapper shortly before the signing of the Armistice had started her in a career which had been varied rather than brilliant. Office work, typewriting, a dash of incipient journalism, finally a course of motor-driving, which had resulted in the post she was just giving up.

The Dean rang the bell and the butler came to take away the tea-things.

"Oh, Peters, will you tell Mrs. Blake that I am expecting Miss Peggy on Tuesday. Ask her to get everything ready."

"Very good, sir. H'm, Mr. Pegg, of Pegg Brothers, wishes to see you if you are not engaged, sir."

The butler was much too solemn to be aware that he had almost perpetrated a pun.

"I'll see him here," replied the Dean.

"Peggy—Pegg Brothers," he murmured to himself with a slight smile as Peters left the room carrying the tea-tray. "Well, that's quite opportune. Ah, good afternoon, Mr. Pegg."

It was Priceless Pegg who entered, with his usual look of deep dejection on his face.

"It's already sold, sir."

"Sold!" ejaculated the Dean, turning quickly in his chair. "To whom?"

"The gentleman we sent to you for the key—Mr. Stanniland."

"Why," exclaimed the Dean, "he didn't see it for ten minutes. Do you mean to tell me——"

"A very sudden gentleman, sir. I've never seen a house sell so quickly in all my experience. Mr. Stanniland only arrived in Frattenbury at one o'clock or so. By half-past three he had bought the house and paid a deposit. Oh, very quick, sir!"

"But the executors? They promised us——"

John Pegg cleared his throat and interrupted:

"Not exactly a *promise*, sir. Mr. Stanniland made a very handsome offer, more than you were prepared to give and more than the house was likely to realize by auction. Sefton and Prior naturally wished to do their best for the late Colonel Walton's legatees, so they accepted his offer."

"They might have consulted us first," said the Dean, testily.

"It was take it or leave it, sir. That seems to be Mr. Stanniland's way of doing business."

"Who is this Mr. Stanniland? Do you know anything about him?"

Priceless Pegg produced his pocket-book, extracted a card from it, and handed it to the Dean. The latter read:

MR. JULIAN BRUCE STANNILAND, F.C.S.

Traveller's Club.

"What does F.C.S. stand for?" he asked the Dean.

"Eh—oh, I think Fellow of the Chemical Society."

"A chemist!" said Pegg. "He looked much more like a gentleman."

"I hope he is one," retorted the Dean, "if he's going to live next door."

"Will he open a shop?" asked John Pegg, sombrely. The very idea of a shop in the sacred precincts of the Close was an outrage on any respectable citizen's feelings. And John Pegg was eminently respectable.

The Dean laughed.

"I hope not," he answered. "There are chemists *and* chemists, you know, Mr. Pegg. They don't all stand behind counters and sell drugs.

"Well," said Pegg, "I am sorry you haven't secured the house, sir. But I trust you will understand that it was not our fault."

"Oh, I quite see that. Here's the key, Mr. Pegg. Good afternoon."

The Dean knitted his brows as he sat down at his writing-table. He was annoyed. Although he had only been a short time in Frattenbury he was beginning to catch the infection of the Close—exclusiveness. Everything had been so nicely arranged, too. There was a retired Colonial Bishop who would have taken the house and joined the little Cathedral community—an adjunct to their society and a help to the Bishop when that functionary was pressed with episcopal work. It was all rather irritating.

He wrote to his niece:

MY DEAR PEGGY,

I shall be pleased to put you up, as you suggest, though I fear you will find it a little dull here. I am sorry to hear of the termination of your engagement; and hope you may soon find something suitable. I shall be greatly obliged if you will kindly let me know what time to expect you on Tuesday.

Your affectionate uncle,

ERNEST LAKE.

And then the butler threw open the door and announced:

"The Bishop."

"I hope I'm not disturbing you, Mr. Dean?"

"By no means. Do sit down."

The Bishop of Frattenbury, a well-built man, showing the full breadth of a glossy apron, a little stern in his sharply cut features, and with a penetrating look in his dark eyes, sat down and produced a cigar-case.

"You don't mind my smoking?"

"Of course not," replied the Dean, reaching for an old briar pipe which lay on the table.

"Won't you have a cigar?"

" No, thanks. I prefer my pipe."

" Ah ! " And he lighted his cigar with a little sigh of satisfaction. Two things were well known with regard to the Bishop of Frattenbury—he was a rigid teetotaler and the most arrant cigar smoker on the Bench.

" I met Burford as I was coming along," he went on, referring to the Canon in Residence. " He tells me you settled that matter of Colonel Walton's house this afternoon. I'm very glad."

" But, unfortunately, we're forestalled," replied the Dean ; and proceeded to explain.

" It's most annoying," said the Bishop, " the house ought to belong to the Cathedral. Dear me ! What an extraordinarily hasty individual the purchaser must be. I hope he may turn out to be an agreeable neighbour nevertheless. Do you know anything about him ? "

" Nothing."

" H'm ! Well, what I really came to see you about was the matter of the Cathedral restoration. I hear you have received the architect's new report—and that it's serious."

" It is—very serious. Exactly what we feared. The foundations of the south-west tower are in a very bad condition, which extends thirty yards or so along the south wall. It means underpinning."

" And that is an expensive matter ? "

" Very expensive."

" Meaning ? "

" He can't give us precise figures yet, but his rough estimate is that it will cost quite ten thousand pounds."

The Bishop took his cigar from his month, blew a

cloud of smoke, pursed up his lips, shook his head, and said :

" You will have to issue a fresh appeal."

" I suppose so. But it will not be easy. Of course, I'm quite a newcomer and have not yet grasped all the facts. But I understand we have pretty well drained the diocese of subscriptions for the work that has been done up to date."

The Bishop nodded his head thoughtfully.

" That is true. Most of our leading Churchpeople have given liberally. I'm afraid you have a hard task before you. I'm sorry, Mr. Dean. I wish I could help you personally, but the utmost I can contribute just now is another fifty pounds. And I can't spare that easily."

" It is very good of you," murmured the Dean, who understood the fallacy of the " fatal opulence " of prelates. " Well, we shall do our best, I hope. By the way, I am thinking of taking a short holiday next month. I haven't had one this year. That ought to freshen me up for the task."

" Where are you going ? " asked the Bishop.

" For a Mediterranean cruise. The boat sails from Folkestone and touches at various places. Ah——" and he stopped short.

" Yes ? "

" I've just remembered that a niece of mine has asked me to put her up—she has no home—and I don't know how long she may want to stay."

" How long are you going to be away ? "

" About a month."

" My dear fellow, don't let that hinder you. If necessary I'm sure my wife would take in your niece while you are away. We should be delighted."

" It's very kind of you—— "

" Not at all. Let me know, will you ? I must get back now."

The Dean went to the door with his visitor and then returned to his study. Seating himself at his desk he began to study the report of the architect. And the more he studied it the more he frowned.

But his equanimity was still further to be disturbed that night. He had finished his solitary dinner and was enjoying an hour of relaxation over a book, when the butler announced :

" Superintendent Walters, sir."

The Dean looked up with surprise as an alert, keen-eyed man, in police uniform came in.

" Yes ? " he asked.

" I'm very sorry to disturb you, sir, but if you can give me a few minutes I shall be grateful."

" Oh, certainly. Sit down, won't you, Superintendent ? "

" Thank you, sir."

He took the proffered chair, placed his uniform cap on the floor, and with slow, deliberate movement drew a notebook from his pocket. Then he fixed the Dean with his keen eyes. Nevertheless, they were kindly eyes, and the man's whole manner was very quiet and restrained. He spoke in a musical, educated voice, with a slight hesitation, as of reluctance.

" It's a disagreeable matter which I have to put before you," he began, " and I hope you will excuse me. Also, I hope I may be mistaken. But I thought I had better come to you at once. Please let me say, to begin with, that at this particular stage, I am speaking in confidence."

" What is it ? " asked the Dean.

The Superintendent consulted his notebook for a moment, and then said :

" Have you ever heard of Melford & Co., sir ? "

" Melford & Co ? " repeated the Dean, in semi-bewilderment. " No, certainly not."

" There have been two or three paragraphs about them in the daily press. I thought you might be aware—— "

" No. I have noticed nothing. Why do you ask ? Who are Melford & Co ? "

" That is a question we should like to be able to answer accurately. At all events we know of Melford —his real name is Corney—by more than one alias, but we are not certain of all who are comprised under 'Melford & Co.' To be brief, sir, Melford & Co. represent a long firm."

" A long firm ? "

The policeman smiled.

" Swindlers, sir, in plain language. They are wanted just now, badly, for a case of bogus company promotion."

" But what has that to do with me, Superintendent ? "

The Superintendent took a type-written paper from his pocket-book.

" Well, sir," he went on, " we have a phrase in our profession, 'from information received,' and that phrase generally means that we are not at liberty to disclose the source of our information. Let me put it to you, then, that 'from information received' Scotland Yard has reason to believe that one of the individuals comprised under 'Melford & Co.' is a certain Edward Lake—— "

The Dean gave a sudden start.

"Oh!" he exclaimed.

"Perhaps I had better read you the description of him, circulated privately."

And, unfolding the paper, he began to read to the astounded dignitary.

"Edward Lake. Height about five feet ten inches, dark hair, tinged with grey, clean-shaven face, brown eyes, heavy eyebrows, sallow complexion, nose slightly aquiline. When last seen was wearing a black morning coat and vest with dark trousers. A little rounded in the shoulders and stoops. Reported to be related to the Very Reverend Ernest Lake, Dean of Frattenbury, whom he is said to resemble slightly."

"Slightly!" repeated the Superintendent mentally as he looked up at the Dean, who had risen from his chair and was standing before him. "It might almost be a description of the Dean himself."

The latter, much perturbed, moved a little across the room, and finally came to an anchor with his back to the fireplace, facing the Superintendent.

"This is terrible news—terrible!" he said. "I—I scarcely know what to say. Are you *sure* this is true?"

"I'm afraid so, sir," replied the Superintendent, sympathetically, "the description has been circulated because the man is wanted. I'm more sorry than I can say to have to bring the matter before you, but it is my duty to ask if you know him?"

"I realize that you could not have acted otherwise, Superintendent. Yes—" he went on, with a sigh, "I am afraid I do know him—Edward Lake is my brother."

There was a strained silence for a few moments. Superintendent Walters was genuinely sorry and expressed it by his manner and looks. Then he said:

"Can you give me any information about him? I won't ask you, if you had rather not reply. You are not obliged to. And anything you say I shall look upon as confidential unless I find it my duty to report it to my superiors, in which case I should let you know. I assure you, sir, I appreciate your position."

"I know you do," replied the Dean, throwing himself into a chair again, "and I am grateful to you. I will be quite frank with you. My unfortunate brother has been a great trouble to me for many years, though I have never associated him in any way with crime, nor do I, even now, believe that he is a criminal. He is foolish, I admit, but I have never known him transgress the law. He is one of those sanguine men, easily led, who imagine that they are going to make money quite easily—and never do make it. On the contrary, to speak quite plainly, he has periodically approached me for financial assistance. It was only six or seven weeks ago that he came to me for this purpose."

"And you gave him money?"

"I did. It was foolish of me, perhaps, but after all, he is my own kith and kin, in fact, my only brother. He promised, as usual, to pay me back in a short time. He had, so he said, an exceptional opportunity, a 'good thing,' as he called it. I have heard him speak so often of his 'good things' that it did not impress me, and I did not ask him for the details. I can only imagine that he has been led into some foolish enterprise, blindly; that advantage has been taken of his weakness and impulsive temperament. Whatever he has done, Superintendent, he has—to use a trite phrase—been more sinned against than sinning. I am convinced of this."

The Superintendent nodded.

"I can quite believe what you say, sir," he said, kindly. "We often come across such instances. The unfortunate fact remains, however, that there is a warrant out for his arrest. Also the fact that he cannot be found, which admits of a reasonable construction."

"You mean that he has a guilty conscience and is hiding. Possibly. But a guilty conscience sometimes arises from fear and not from actual wrong done. And I refuse—absolutely—to believe that he is a criminal. Tell me, Superintendent, what do you know of the whole matter?"

"Very little—so far. The London police have it in hand, and we have only received warnings in case we come across certain individuals. I gather, however that action was taken on certain information concerning Melford & Co., and that their office—a couple of small rooms in the City—was raided. But the birds had flown, and there was only a typewriter —a mere girl—who knew nothing. From papers discovered, however, certain names were found, names of individuals who appeared to share in the complicity, among them your brother's. Warrants have been issued for the arrest of them all, but, so far, none have been taken. I told you that the only man we really *know* is Corney, and he is a very shady lot."

The Dean thought for a moment or two. Then he said:

"Are these names public property?"

"Not at present. They are only known to the police."

"I see. And in the event of an arrest?"

The Superintendent shrugged his shoulders.

"I don't think it would be possible to conceal the *name* of your brother, though it might not necessarily follow that his actual relationship with yourself need leak out."

"You mean?"

"Unless he gave it away himself. We police have no wish to drag family scandals into daylight where it is not necessary."

The Dean bowed his head slightly.

"Thank you," he said, "I fully appreciate your consideration. Though I still have faith that my brother could clear himself of any criminal charge. By the way, I suppose you know his last address?"

The other referred to his notebook.

"Yes—we do. He was residing in a boarding establishment, 19 Wingrave Road, Hampstead."

The Dean nodded.

"Quite so. I believe he had lived there nearly a year. As I say, I last saw him some six weeks ago. We very rarely met."

"Well, sir," said the Superintendent, picking up his cap and getting up from his chair, "I can only say once more how much I regret having to come to you."

"You have done quite rightly." He moved across the room and prepared to put his finger on the button of the electric bell. "You will let me know if there are developments?"

"Certainly—at once."

The Superintendent had his hand on the door handle. The Dean was just about to ring the bell when he turned round suddenly:

"Superintendent!"

"Yes, sir?"

"What am I to do if my brother should come here?"

The policeman paused for a second before he replied:

"Officially, sir, it is my plain duty to answer that question as a representative of the law. You ought to communicate with us at once. Otherwise you would be compounding a felony."

A vestige of a smile hovered about the Dean's lips as he said:

"What would *you* do under the circumstances if you believed your brother was more fool than knave and he came to you?"

For several seconds the two men stood, rigid, looking at one another. Then the Superintendent said, abruptly:

"Good night, sir!"

And opened the door. The Dean rang the bell for Peters to show him out and remained, standing, for upwards of a minute, his brows knit as one in deep thought and perplexity.

CHAPTER III

JULIAN BRUCE STANNILAND showed himself to be a man of command as well as a man of action. He hustled the local builder, and, in a very short space of time the house next to the Deanery was fit for occupation—painted, papered—in fact, to use the builder's terms, "decorated throughout." Nor was the owner long before he took up his abode. Three weeks after his hasty purchase he was there.

Inside the house was arranged to suit his peculiar proclivities. The large drawing-room, reminiscent of stately gatherings of the denizens of the Close in the time of the late Colonel Walton and his wife, was turned into an apartment of a very different aspect—in fact, a chemical laboratory. Retorts, racks of test tubes, delicate instruments, rows of bottles, and jars on shelves, neatly arranged and labelled, were there in profusion.

The dining-room he had turned into a study—a study, however, which much more resembled a business man's office than an abode of literature. It was handsomely furnished with the latest appliances. A large table in the centre, a roll-top desk stretched nearly half across one side of the room, flanked by a small table with a typewriter on it, cabinets containing innumerable drawers labelled A to Z, cabinets for index cards, a couple of luxurious leather covered arm-chairs and three or four equally expensive ordinary ones—an up-to-date business room that implied confidence and security.

A small occasional apartment had been turned into his dining-room. This, too, was well furnished, and in the best taste.

A visitor, going over the house, might have smiled at something that appeared in every room, hanging from a nail in the wall. In laboratory, study, dining-room, in the hall, at the head of Stanniland's bed, over the bath, even in the little summer house at the bottom of the garden and in the garage might be seen a small blank notebook, with a pencil attached to it by a bit of string. Not a common notebook, be it remembered, but bound in a blue cloth cover, and on the cover in large letters of gold,

THOUGHTS AND FLASHES
OF JULIAN BRUCE STANNILAND

Evidently Julian Bruce Stanniland placed a value on his " thoughts and flashes," and made provision to record them whenever and wherever they occurred to him.

He was seated at his breakfast table wearing a Japanese kimono of extremely gaudy colour, the morning paper propped up against the milk-jug and opened at the advertisement page. And the particular column of advertisements that appeared to engage his attention was headed

TYPISTS.

He glanced down the list in a desultory manner, eating his egg and sipping his coffee. Suddenly he exclaimed softly, " Hullo ! "

On the top of the column headed " Miscellaneous," he read the following :

Young lady wants post as typist or secretary or chauffeur. Some experience in journalism. Will not live in. Good salary essential. Box No. 6893.

He gave a little audible chuckle.

" Daughter of the Admirable Crichton, must be ! " he said to himself. " Claims to be able to undertake four different parts. Cheek ! Won't live in, eh ! Independence. Good salary ! Sense of personal value. Cheek — Independence — Personal value ! Three jolly good things to have in this world. I like it ! "

He read the advertisement again.

" May be a wash-out," he went on, but anyhow, I'll look at her. Let's see. To-day's Tuesday. I shall be in London on Thursday. That'll do."

He rang the bell which stood on the table. A boy, in a page's livery, came in.

" Bring me a telegram form. Third drawer on right, top row, desk in office. Hurry ! "

In two minutes the boy was back.

" Wait ! "

He wrote on the form :

Box 6893, *Morning Express*, London. Call at 49 Gordon House, 17*a* Bishopsgate Street Within, Thursday at 12.30. Bruce & Co.

" Take this at once to the post office and send it off. Sharp ! "

Then he cracked his second egg and turned the paper over, propping it up once more. Again it was an advertisement page that faced him, this time a page with some pictured advertisements.

Presently he jumped up from his chair and quickly crossed the room to the place where the notebook hung on the wall. The first of Julian Bruce Stanniland's " Thoughts and Flashes " in his new house was to be recorded. And this is what he wrote :

Picture of man pointing, earnest expression on face. Underneath—" It's your LIVER I'm thinking about."

He stood, regarding it for a moment or two, and then struck out the word " thinking " and substituted " talking "—

It's your LIVER I'm talking about.

That seemed to satisfy him, and he returned to the table and finished his breakfast.

When he came out of the room he paused beside the notebook hanging in the hall and, heading it " Good formula for a cough lozenge," jotted down what looked very much like a doctor's prescription, written as it was in abbreviated Latin with the curious symbols indicative of quantities so dear to the medical profession. Then, still arrayed in his kimono, he lighted his pipe and strolled out into the garden at the back of the house, stood for a minute or two on the terrace at the bottom of the garden gazing over the pleasant meadows and open expanse to the south of Frattenbury, entered the little summer house at the end of the terrace and reached for the particular notebook therein, in the which he made the record :

Suggested name for cough lozenges . . . Voicets—Voikets—Voikats——

These three tentative names, however, he suddenly struck out, and finally inserted :

Voikals.

"Good!" he said. "That would do if I ever brought 'em out."

Then he walked slowly back to the house across the lawn, quite unaware that he was being regarded with some interest by a girl who was looking out of a window in the upper story of the Deanery next door.

Five minutes afterwards the girl in question was seated opposite her uncle at the breakfast table. Breakfast at the Deanery was at a quarter to nine—to the minute—three-quarters of an hour later than Stanniland had fixed the time of his first meal. The Dean usually took, or attended, the eight o'clock daily service in the Cathedral. Hence the hour of breakfast—immediately he returned.

Peggy Lake was a bright, pretty, capable-looking young woman, quite up to date as regarded her appearance. Her bobbed auburn hair suited her. She had inherited this feature from her mother, but her luminous brown eyes, every now and then a-twinkling, were what her uncle's might have been at her age, while the slight upward curve of the corners of her mouth again betokened the relationship. Her chin, however, was firmer and slightly more pointed than his, and an observer might have learned from it that there was a certain amount of determination in Peggy's character which, perhaps, helped to balance a disposition that was at times inclined to be erratic.

"Uncle, do tell me," she said as she poured out his coffee, "who is the Japanese nobleman next door?"

"Japanese nobleman?"

"He looks like one, anyhow. He was strolling

about in his garden arrayed in most gorgeous apparel when I was dressing."

"Oh, that must be Mr. Stanniland. So he's taken up his abode, eh? A most peculiar individual!"

And he told her about the buying of the house.

"Who is he, uncle?"

"I really don't know. I've seen his visiting card, but except that he's a member of the Traveller's Club and, apparently, a Fellow of the Chemical Society—and that he seems to have money—I know nothing about him. In fact, I was wondering whether I ought to call on him or not. I've met him for a few minutes—and we shall have to be neighbours."

"Oh, do call and find out what he's like in his house. He looked so funny just now with a pair of plus fours under a Japanese kimono. I feel quite interested in him."

The Dean gave a short laugh.

"I ought to feel angry with him," he said, "buying that house over our heads in such a hurry. Anyhow, I hope he may turn out to be a decent neighbour. And I suppose I'd better call. But I shall have to put it off till I get back from my holiday—I have no time before I start. That reminds me. What are your plans, Peggy? I'm sorry to put you out, but I'd made all my arrangements before you wrote to me. Are you going to accept the Bishop's offer?"

She made a little grimace.

"Half a minute. This letter will decide. It's very kind of the Bishop—and his wife. But I shouldn't get on with her. I'd shock her, uncle. Anyhow—oh, it's all right. Maisie Jephson writes to say she'll be delighted to put me up. That's settled. I'll write and tell her I'll go to her on Saturday. You leave on Monday?"

"Yes. But what are you going to do ultimately?"

She shrugged her shoulders.

"Don't know. But something is sure to turn up. I'm not worrying."

"You know, Peggy," he went on kindly, "you're welcome to come back here when I return. There will always be a home for you at the Deanery. I want you to know that."

"It's most awfully good of you, uncle—simply topping. And I *do* appreciate it. But, even if I'm your niece, I hate the idea of sponging on you. I've managed to earn my own living so far, and I mean to stick to it."

"A pity you gave up what appears to me to have been a good post," remarked her uncle, dryly.

"Oh, but I just had to. I couldn't stick it any longer. It was all *right*, you know, and I rather liked the work. But the old woman was a holy terror—and I suppose I let her know I thought so. Anyhow, I've made up my mind about one thing. Whatever post I get, I won't live in the house with anyone. It was that which put the lid on."

"Put the lid on?" repeated the Dean, arching his eyebrows.

"Caused me to hand in my resignation," she replied demurely. "You're not up to date, uncle! No, it was all very well running her about in the car, but in the house! Never again!"

The Dean finished his coffee, passed his cup for more, and said, the vestige of a rebuke in his voice:

"I suppose I'm old-fashioned, Peggy, and also that I've lived a retired life for many years, and I don't know that I want to be what you call ' up to date.' But it does seem to me that it would be more desirable if you could bring yourself to adopt some occupation that is more—well——"

" Ladylike ! " she broke in, elbows on table, chin in hands, smiling across the table at him. " *Do* say it, uncle dear. I know you mean it."

" Very well then," he replied. " I do mean it. I don't consider driving cars, or journalism——"

" *Christian* occupation ? " she interrupted.

" That is beside the remark. You know what I mean very well, Peggy."

" Now, what *would* you like me to be ? "

" Well, a post in a school, or——"

" A governess ? Thank you ! Besides, I'm not clever enough. I couldn't teach. Oh, uncle dear, you don't understand. Didn't you, when you were young, just long for adventure ? "

" Adventure ? " he repeated. " Certainly I had ambitions, I suppose. But I can't say I remember looking upon life just as an adventure."

" Oh, but it *is* an adventure, uncle—or ought to be. Now, just try to recollect. What did you do when you were young ? "

The Dean had finished his breakfast and was lighting his morning pipe. His face grew reminiscent as he answered.

" Well, my parents were not well off. My father was a country clergyman, as you know. My chief ambition when a boy was to go to a University, so I set myself seriously to win a scholarship—and succeeded. I went to Oxford. Then——"

" Tell me what you did at Oxford."

" I read theology and history."

She gave a little rippling laugh.

" I don't mean that. What did you *do?* You didn't spend all your time over your books, did you ? "

" Of course not. I rowed third in my college eight, and——"

" Yes, I *know*. But didn't you have any adventures ? "

He thought for a moment.

" Not that I remember. Oh, yes, I was in a railway accident once, but escaped unhurt."

She gave a little sigh of impatience.

" Go on," she said. " What did you do when you left college ? "

" I won a travelling scholarship and went abroad for a year. Part of the time I was at Heidelberg."

" Did you fight in a duel ? "

" My dear Peggy ! No, I read theology chiefly—and German, of course. Then on my return to England I was ordained to my first curacy. Since then my life has been, I suppose, a very quiet one. I have always been a student and, as you know, have used my pen a little."

" I don't suppose you have had a real adventure in all your life," she replied, with all the wonder of youth for what youth looks upon as a humdrum existence.

" Well," he said with a smile, " perhaps not. But I've got along very well without. I'm quite contented."

" Wouldn't you like to have one, uncle ? "

Again he smiled.

" Not at all," he answered. " At my age one has got into a groove. And I like the groove. But we have been wandering from the point. We were talking about yourself."

"I've put another advertisement in the *Morning Express*," replied Peggy, "and I'm going to spend the morning in answering advertisements. So far I haven't had any luck, but something will turn up. Cheerio, uncle! Don't you worry about me."

"Well, I hope you will succeed in finding something congenial. Meanwhile I take it you will stay with your friend, and on my return, as I say, if you still have nothing to do you are very welcome to come here. I must go now."

She sat looking at him as he went out of the room.

"Good old boy!" she soliloquized. "He's as stiff and starch as they make 'em, but he can't help that. And all the time he's rather a dear. And he's been awfully kind to me."

Meanwhile the Dean retired to his study, wrote sundry letters, and then went out to post them, having two or three things to do in the town. He was passing the police station just as Superintendent Walters was coming out. Since the night that the latter had called upon him, he had neither seen nor heard from him. The opportunity aroused his curiosity.

"Ah, good morning, Superintendent. Er—is there any news?"

The policeman hesitated, and then said:

"Would you mind coming into my office for a minute, sir?"

Inside, he said:

"There isn't very much to tell you, sir, but I may say, in confidence, that the London police have succeeded in tracing two of the gang."

The "gang!" The word jarred on the Dean most unpleasantly.

"My brother——?" he began.

"No, sir. So far we cannot locate either Corney or La—— your brother. The two that I've mentioned are part of the 'Co.' But they are quite minor offenders."

"Are they arrested?"

"No. As I say, I am speaking in confidence. They are under observation, and we know where to put our hands on them if we want them. But we don't want them yet—not till we find Corney and your brother. They are only subordinates, and any charge against them—apart from the principals—might fall through."

"And you have no idea where the others are?"

"None, except that it is improbable that they have left the country. Of course the ports have been watched."

"Well," replied the Dean, "I cannot refrain from saying that I hope my brother may still elude you—until he can clear himself of the charge, which I am sure he will be able to do eventually."

The Superintendent shrugged his shoulders.

"I quite understand your feelings in the matter, sir."

"It is not only myself, Superintendent. My brother has a daughter. I am sorry to say he has neglected her badly, and there is no excuse for him. But, all the same, he is her father. I don't mind so much as far as I am concerned, but It would be a grievous thing for a young girl beginning life to suffer from a slur on her relationship."

"I see what you mean, sir. And I wish I could help you."

The Dean came out of the police station sorely distressed. The thing had been weighing on his mind ever since the Superintendent had broken the news to him that night. He had not said a word about it to Peggy, and he did not intend to do so, but the fear at the back of his mind was that his brother might be taken during the time he was away, and that unfortunate disclosures might take place in his absence. He began to wonder whet er he ought to go on his holiday at all under the circumstances. He had already booked his passage and he knew he wanted a change badly.

CHAPTER IV

GORDON HOUSE was a large block of offices. Peggy consulted the names of firms at the main basement entrance, and found that Number 49 was on the third floor. Up she went in the lift and tapped at the door.

" Come in."

She entered a small office in which a man sat writing at a desk, and a girl was clicking a typewriter.

" I've called to see Bruce & Co."

" Have you an appointment ? " asked the man.

" Yes, they wired to me to call—in answer to an advertisement."

" What name, please ? "

" Miss Lake."

He disappeared for a moment into an inner office, and then :

" Will you come this way, please ? "

The individual seated behind a table in the inner office looked up quickly as she entered, with a penetrating gaze. She recognized him at once—the gentleman in the gaudy kimono lounging in the garden next to the Deanery. Just now, however, he was the keen, typical business man. At once the solution of a little problem which had been puzzling her flashed across her mind. The telegram, forwarded from the newspaper office, had been sent from Frattenbury. Now she understood, and an involuntary little smile broke over her face.

But Julian Bruce Stanniland did not return the smile. His attitude was a strictly business one.

" Good morning, Miss Lake. Take a seat."

The chair—the only one for visitors—was in the full light.

" Good morning, Mr.—— ? "

" I am Bruce & Co.," he retorted, with an air of proprietorship which embraced all the " Co." there might have been.

" Now," he went on, taking the advertisement which he had cut from the paper, from the table and, glancing at it, " You claim to be a young lady of parts, I see. Secretary, typist, chauffeur, journalist. Which is it you really want ? "

She met his gaze frankly.

" Which is it you offer ? " she asked in return.

" I don't offer anything, so far," he retorted. " I want to know something about you first. For example, what experience have you had in journalism ? "

" For three months I wrote short articles for the *Midget*. And I've had some stories accepted."

" Ever done anything in writing advertisements ? "

" No."

" Think you could ? "

" I could try."

" That remains to be seen. Now, as to typewriting. How many words per minute ? "

She told him.

" Understand business correspondence ? "

" I was six or seven months in an office."

" Why did you leave ? "

" Another opportunity came along."

" Was it better pay ? "

She laughed outright, and met him on his own ground.

" You don't suppose I should have taken it if it hadn't been," she retorted.

" Good ! " he ejaculated. " Now, what was your last place ? "

" I was chauffeur—to a lady."

" May I ask why you gave that up ? "

" I had to live in the house with her, and I hated it."

For the first time he smiled—only slightly.

" So should I," he replied. " Sure it was not because the work was too hard ? "

" Of course not," she said a little indignantly.

" Don't mind cleaning a car as well as driving it ? "

" Certainly not."

" Understand the mechanism ? "

" Oh, I think so. Fairly well."

" More than I always do," he said. " Can you give references ? "

" My uncle is a clergyman, and——"

" I don't care whether he's a clergyman or a navvy. I'm talking business, not relationships, Miss Lake. I want references from those by whom you've been employed. Now then ? "

For just a moment she was about to retort somewhat hotly. He was positively rude. And yet there was something about the man that she could not help liking. Perhaps it was that every woman really appreciates being dominated by the other sex, even if she will not admit it. So she restrained herself.

" Yes. I can give you two or three names. Also I have brought with me a couple of testimonials."

Presently he said :

" Now then, Miss Lake, you've answered a whole string of questions frankly. Is there anything you would like to ask me before we go any further ? "

" Rather ! A whole heap of things."

He glanced at the clock which stood on the table. Then he looked at her again.

" Fire away, then. Only keep to the point. I can only give you a short time."

" What's your business, then ? "

He laughed.

" Good ! All sorts of things, Miss Lake. I'm a chemist, to begin with. And a company promoter. I invent things from my chemical knowledge and put them on the market with my business knowledge."

" That sounds interesting."

" It is. Go on, please."

" And there isn't really a Bruce & Co. ? "

" I told you. I am the firm."

" Co. as well ? "

" Co. as well."

" Then if you engaged me, you'd be my sole employer ? "

" Quite right."..

" Are you going to engage me, Mr.—Mr. Bruce & Co ? "

" You think you would be willing to work under me ? "

She looked at him quizzically.

" I think you'd be fair and just, and I also think you'd be particular—and a bit difficult to please sometimes."

"Quite a good deduction," he replied, cheerfully.

"Then will you please tell me what you would want me to do?"

"You can do so many things—apparently," he replied, with a slight touch of sarcasm.

"And which particular accomplishment would you choose out of the bunch?" she asked, not a bit abashed.

"All of them. That's why I answered your advertisement."

"All of them?"

"Yes. Let me explain. It isn't so extraordinary as it sounds. I want a sort of all-round person, who can act as my secretary when necessary, typewrite business letters and other documents, and, at the same time, put some of my ideas into writing for the press. Advertisements, and so on. I'm no good at writing. Then it would be handy to have you drive my car on occasions—to fetch people to see me, and so on."

"I should act as your secretary and save you the expense of a chauffeur?"

"Exactly."

"Then I should want a good salary."

"Naturally. That's what you say in your advertisement."

"What hours should I work?"

He answered promptly.

"Nine to one, and two to five. Half-day off on Saturday."

"But suppose you wanted me to take the car out after five?"

"Overtime."

"What do you offer?"

"Four pounds a week."

Her eyes sparkled a little. She had never earned so much in her life. And, somehow, she felt that he knew it.

"If you think I should do——" she began.

"Look here, Miss Lake," he interrupted. "It's only fair to tell you that it is not an easy post—or would not be always. There are times when my particular work goes along smoothly and methodically. And there are times when I should expect you to work like the very devil—when I'm up against a big proposition. And to make up for this there are times when I get lazy fits—don't want to work and *don't* work. And there wouldn't be much for you to do then except carry on. Now then, what do you think of it?"

"I think it sounds like an adventure," she replied.

"Good! My work is a series of adventures. Sometimes they come off, and sometimes they don't."

"Should I have to work in the office here?"

"No. I live in the country."

"I see. You'd want me at Frattenbury."

It was his turn to look surprised.

"How do you know that?"

"First because your telegram was sent off from Frattenbury, and secondly because I saw you in your garden there on Tuesday. I thought you were the Japanese Ambassador on a visit."

"The dickens!" he exclaimed, with a laugh. "Where were you, then?"

"In my uncle's house next door."

"Your uncle?"

"You wouldn't let me finish when I began telling you he was a clergyman. He's the Dean of Frattenbury, you know."

" Good Lord ! He's the old chap I upset because I bought that house before he could get a look in." He had dropped his business manner and was becoming colloquial. " What would he say to your becoming my secretary ? "

" It's nothing to do with him, Mr. Stanniland. That's your real name, isn't it ? " He nodded. " I'm quite on my own."

" You live there ? "

" No, I don't. I'm only on a visit. If you give me the berth, I shall take digs in Frattenbury."

" By George ! If I'd known it I needn't have bothered you by asking you to come up here. I could have seen you at Frattenbury."

" Over the garden wall," she retored demurely. " Well," she went on, " am I to have the berth ? "

His business manner came upon him again in a moment.

" I must communicate with your references first, Miss Lake."

" I should like to know soon. Uncle starts for his holiday on Monday, and I have to clear out. I was going to stay with a friend at Bournemouth on Saturday, but you see, if I knew you would engage me, it wouldn't be worth while going. I should get rooms in Frattenbury instead."

" All right," he replied, and reached for telegram forms. " Those references, please."

He selected two out of the four she gave him and hastily wrote on each form :

Re Miss Lake, late in your employ. Is she honest, willing, painstaking ? Wire reply.

" That'll do," he said, getting up. " Good morning, Miss Lake. You shall hear from me immediately. Here, Jarvis," he went on as he opened the door for her, " send these off. Reply paid."

Peggy marched out of the office, partly elated at the prospect, partly—as she thought of the interview—a little rebellious in regard to the curt methods of Stanniland, though, at the same time, she could not help admitting that he was justified, after all, in treating the affair from a purely business point of view. Also, she felt on her mettle. She called to mind that little sarcasm of his, " You can do so many things—apparently." Well, why not! Could she not show him that she had not underrated her capabilities ? "

And, as she ate her light luncheon, she felt she would be horribly disappointed if he did not offer her the post. And, if he did, she would show him that she was quite equal to facing his eccentricities and curtness, even if it meant, to use his own expression, working at times like the very devil. She could be a devil, too, if she chose, and she knew it.

Naturally, after luncheon, she did what any woman does when she goes to London on business—found her way to Oxford Street, secured what she considered a few bargains with great satisfaction, after the slow, deliberate manner of her sex when shopping, caught a late afternoon train back to Frattenbury, and arrived in time for dinner.

Her uncle, however, was dining out, and did not return till ten o'clock, when she joined him as he smoked his pipe in his study, perhaps upsetting his rather old-fashioned notions by producing her cigarette-case. She was just about to tell him the results of her journey to London—of course he knew she had gone up about the advertisement—when the front-door bell rang and a minute later Peters came into the room, carrying on a salver a note, which he handed to her. It was addressed :

MISS LAKE,
THE DEANERY,
FRATTENBURY,

and in one corner were the words " By hand." Julian Bruce Stanniland had brought it down by the last train and delivered it himself. She tore it open. It was typewritten, and ran thus :

From BRUCE & Co.,
49 Gordon House,
1 ENC. 17*a* Bishopsgate Street Within, E.C.

MISS LAKE,
The Deanery,
Frattenbury.

DEAR MADAM,—Referring to your application of this morning, we beg to inform you that your references are satisfactory. Kindly commence work at 9 a.m. on Monday morning next at Sapor House, The Close, Frattenbury, as per verbal agreement. Enclosed please find cheque representing travelling expenses to this office, a receipt for which will oblige.

Yours faithfully,
p.p. BRUCE & Co.,
J. B. S.

" Cheers ! " she cried. " I've got it. What do you think of this, uncle ? "

And she passed the letter over to him.

He adjusted his pince-nez and read it carefully.

" ' Bruce & Co.—Sapor House ! ' Why, that's the hideous name that fellow next door has put on a brass plate on his gate. 'Sapor House,' indeed! And it has always been known as 'The Chantrey'! Preposterous! What does it mean?"

"It means I've got a berth, uncle—next door! I was just going to tell you all about it. You see, Bruce & Co. are—or rather *is*—Mr. Stanniland. It's his London office where I went to-day."

"But what in the world——"

"Oh, please let me explain. He's an extraordinary man—a regular demon. I mean, you know, he's all sorts of things. He invents and gets up companies to sell things—at least I suppose so. I saw him to-day, and it's all right. I'm to have four pounds a week. Isn't it just topping!"

The Dean looked at her, a grim little smile twitching at the corners of his mouth.

"You are not precisely lucid," he replied. "Try and explain matters a little more clearly, and then I'll tell you whether I think it is—er—*topping* or not."

By degrees he got it out of her.

"But what sort of work does he want you to do?" he asked.

"Drive his car, write his letters, do articles for the papers—and generally make myself useful."

"You *will*," he retorted, grimly, "if you do all that. "But what do you know about him?"

"He's Bruce & Co, and——"

"Yes, yes, I know. But *personally*, I mean."

"Oh, he's fairly good looking—awfully stern and business like. And looks clever, besides——"

"My dear Peggy! I mean, what do you know about his character—his standing, so to speak? Did he give you any references?"

"N-no. I didn't ask him."

"Quite so. And you are willing to engage yourself to a man about whom you know positively nothing."

"Oh, you don't understand, dear. I'm quite capable of taking care of myself."

"I've no doubt you are—not the slightest. But you ought to know more about him. Besides——"

"Besides what?"

"Well—er—to put it plainly, here is an individual who suddenly appears here in the Close. We all know knothing about him except that he stole a march on us—we *ought* to have had that house. I'm not even sure whether people will call on him. Several of them haven't made up their minds yet, and——"

"Oh yes, I know. Canon Burford and the Archdeacon and Sir Hugh Bastonville—your respectable denizens of the Close!"

"Very true. After all, we—er—have our position to maintain"—the Dean, though new to it, was fast falling into the lines in which his life had been cast—"and we have to be—er—careful! And it might be awkward if a niece of mine——"

She had crossed over to where he was sitting, and bent down and kissed him on the forehead.

"Uncle dear," she said, in a wheedling tone, "aren't you all a little bit too respectable? Don't get like the rest of them if you can help it. You're far too nice an old dear! I've got my living to get, and so long as I get it straight and honestly, I don't care a bit what people say. And you don't either, really!"

"Well," he said after a few moments' pause. "At

all events, I shall call on him now before I leave. I owe that to you, Peggy."

"And you'll like him, I'm sure."

"I don't like his taste in naming his house," he retorted, with some asperity.

"'Sapor House'! It isn't exactly pretty. I seem to have seen the name, though. What does it mean?"

"Sapor is a Latin word meaning a relish, and——"

She clapped her hands.

"I know now!" she exclaimed.

"What?"

"We had it for luncheon yesterday—with the cold mutton. 'Sapor relish'! Oh, let me ring the bell, uncle."

Before he could ask why, she had done so. The Dean was in the habit of taking a minute nightcap of whisky and hot water before he retired. Peters evidently imagined his master was ready for it a little earlier than usual, for when he came in he carried a small tray, on which was a decanter, a jug of hot water, and a glass of milk and biscuits for Peggy.

"Oh, Peters," said the girl as he set down the tray on the table. "Is there any Sapor relish in the house?"

Peters stood up, imperturbable, except that his right eyebrow raised itself just a trifle, a manner he had when he was surprised or did not approve of anything.

"Yes, miss."

"Will you bring it, please?"

"Very good, miss."

His eyebrow went up just a shade farther. That was all. In the kitchen, however, he remarked to the cook:

"What do you think Miss Peggy wants now? She's actually going to mix sauce with her milk! Ugh!"

But he was solemnity itself as he brought in the bottle on a salver. Peggy seized it at once.

"Here we are!"

Yes, there we were!

On the bottle a glaring picture of the head and shoulders of a perfectly delighted and satisfied-looking gentleman seated at table, knife and fork in hand, gazing at a heaven-sent waiter presenting him with a bottle of

SAPOR RELISH

Appetizing,
Piquante,
Delicious.

Composed of the purest and most
carefully selected ingredients.

UNIQUE IN FLAVOUR.
Satisfies the most fastidious palates.

For all cold meats and fish.

Excellent for flavouring
SOUPS AND SAVOURIES.

Price two shillings and sixpence.

And, on the bottom of the label:

Prepared solely by Bruce & Co., Gordon House, London, E.C.

Peggy read out this effusion to her uncle, who smiled slightly as he carefully gave himself his modicum of whisky and filled up his tumbler with hot water.

Then she knit her brows and, elbow on knee, rested her chin on her hand and gazed earnestly at the bottle of Sapor relish which she had put back on the table.

Slowly she said :

" I think I could improve it."

" What ? The relish ? "

" No. The label. He asked if I could write advertisements."

" Oh, I was going to say I didn't think you could improve the sauce. In spite of our peculiar neighbour, I will say that it is excellent."

" Yes—it would be," she replied, enigmatically.

CHAPTER V

THE Dean called on Stanniland the next afternoon, and was shown into the room set apart as an office. Here he found Stanniland hard at work at his desk.

"How do you do, Mr.—er—Lake? I don't know if I am addressing you rightly. I'm ignorant of ecclesiastical etiquette."

"I'm generally recognized as 'Mr. Dean,'" replied his visitor, with a smile. "As you are going to be my neighbour I thought I would like the pleasure of your further acquaintance."

"In spite of the fact that I've done you out of this house," retorted Stanniland, bluntly. "That's very good of you."

"Well," said the Dean, taking the chair offered him by Stanniland, "you certainly did take our breath away, so to speak. We are not accustomed, here, to such haste."

"Pity. When you've made up your mind you want to do a thing, it's best to do it at once. I always do."

"Don't you ever regret it?" asked the Dean.

"Sometimes, certainly. But nine times out of ten it pays."

"And once out of ten—one may lose?"

"Quite so. I've done it—badly."

The Dean looked at him a little curiously. In his

somewhat limited knowledge of the world of men he hardly knew how to place Stanniland.

"Lost everything once," went on the latter, "and had to begin over again."

"Indeed! That must have been a very terrible experience, Mr. Stanniland."

"Fairly stiff," replied the other, the lines at the corners of his mouth hardening as if at the recollection of it. "Yes, six years ago I was down and out—in New York—with only a quarter of a dollar in my pocket. Some fix, as they say over there."

"Would it be indiscreet to ask how you—well——"

"How I got on my feet again? Faith!"

"In yourself?"

"And in God. Oh, no, I'm not a religious man, Mr. Dean—not what you'd call one. But I've always had a notion that God helps those who help themselves—and it's come true. I asked Providence to bless that quarter when I changed it for an up-town tram fare to look for a job. I got a job," he added, laconically.

The Dean, unaccustomed as he was to this rough sort of theology in a nutshell, was, nevertheless, a little struck by it—probably mainly by the open simplicity of one the conception of whom in his mind had been that of a sharp-dealing business man of the world. But the question he proceeded to put emanated from the ecclesiasticism in which his life had been cast.

"May I ask, are you a Churchman?"

Julian Bruce Stanniland laughed outright.

"Good Lord!" he replied. "I really don't know. I suppose so. My parents had me christened when I was a kid, I believe. That's all right, isn't it?"

"Well—er——" began the Dean, and might have floundered into a theological dissertation but that Stanniland, who possibly saw what was coming and would not risk it, abruptly changing the subject, broke in:

"I suppose Miss Lake has told you I've engaged her?"

"Yes, she has. To tell you the truth, it is partly on that account that I have called."

"I thought so. No, don't mind my saying it. Quite natural."

"Well," hazarded the Dean, "it is natural, as you say. In a sense, although she is of age, I am her guardian, and I thought it only right that I should satisfy myself—er——"

"As to my respectability. Right! I hope I'm respectable, Mr. Dean. As I told your niece, I'm a chemist and a company promoter—just now. But I act on the square. It doesn't pay me to put goods on the market that are not worth selling. So when I say I'm a company promoter, don't you go away with the notion that I fake the market and play the confidence trick on a gullible public. There *are* shady beggars who do that—as perhaps you know."

The Dean reddened. It was an unconscious home thrust. The thought of his brother rushed into his mind. He remembered what the Superintendent had told him: "Melford & Co." "A case of bogus company promoters."

"Indeed," he replied, "although I know nothing about you, Mr. Stanniland, no such suspicions entered my mind for a moment."

"Right! Well, I can give you references—bankers and solicitors. Will that do, eh?"

He was already scribbling them down on his writing-pad when he suddenly broke off and looked up.

" They'll certify my business integrity," he said, " but if you want to know any more about me, I've got a cousin in the same trade as yourself. Beg pardon. I ought to have said profession, I suppose. I haven't seen him for some years—I've been abroad a good bit—but he knows me, all right. He'll give me a character. Lives at Redminster."

" That's my old diocese," remarked the Dean. " Possibly I may know him."

" Quite likely—he's the Bishop of Redminster."

And as he bent over his writing-pad once more the ghost of a smile lighted up his face. Inwardly he was saying, " *That* fetched the blighter ! "

In a measure it had. The Dean was no snob—far from it—but a man who claimed relationship with the Bishop of Redminster certainly to him showed up in a fresh light. Apart from his episcopal position, the prelate in question came of an eminently good family—which he hoped stretched to cousinship. So, after a few more remarks on either side he found himself saying :

" I am just going away for my holiday, but when I return I hope you will give me the pleasure of dining with me, Mr. Stanniland. I—er—believe I am right in concluding that there is no one else to whom to extend the invitation. You live alone ? "

" That's so. It's very kind of you, and I'll be pleased to accept."

" I hope," went on the Dean, getting up from his chair, " that if my niece comes to you you'll find her useful."

" So do I," retorted Stanniland. " She won't stay if she isn't."

" He may be blunt," thought the Dean, but his manners are not bad," for Stanniland came to the door to show him out, again thanking him for his call, though the Dean might have observed a mischievous little twinkle in his eyes had he looked at him. He even strolled with his visitor down the garden path in front of the house to the big iron gate opening into the Close. Opposite was the grey old Cathedral, a line of scaffolding against the south wall.

" Patching up the old church, I see," remarked Stanniland, pleasantly,

The Dean's eyebrows arched a little as he replied, with a shade of the dignitary in his voice :

" We are restoring the Cathedral, yes ! "

" Big job ? " asked Stanniland.

" Indeed, yes. Much more than we anticipated. Unfortunately the architect has discovered that the foundations of one of the towers and of the south wall are in a very bad condition. I'm afraid it is going to cost a great deal."

" How much ? " asked Stanniland, now really interested, as he generally was where monetary matters were concerned.

" We do not know yet. We have no detailed estimate. But I fear it will mean at least ten thousand pounds."

" I see. Well, I suppose you've got the money. Plenty of that in a show like this, eh ? "

" Indeed, no," replied the Dean, just a little hotly. " We have no assured funds for such work as this. We have to raise the money by purely voluntary subscriptions. And it is not easy."

Julian Bruce Stanniland laughed lightly. They had just reached the gate. He tapped the new brass plate it bore—a very large brass plate—with the inscription, " Sapor House."

" I'll give you a tip," he said. " I'm just going to sell this—Sapor, you know. It's a kind of sauce. On the market already. Good, sound proposition, too. I ought to know, I invented it. You form yourselves into a syndicate and buy ' Sapor.' It'll pay. You'd get your ten thousand much more easily than begging for it."

The Dean had sense and humour enough to laugh.

" I'm afraid that wouldn't do at all," he replied. " We—the Cathedral Chapter, that is—are not business men, you know, Mr. Stanniland."

" Pity! No, I don't suppose you are! Well, good-bye, Mr. Dean. And good luck. I say, send me a copy of the prospectus when it's ready to put before the public."

" The prospectus?"

" Begging prospectus. Job over yonder," explained Stanniland, nodding familiarly towards the venerable pile.

" Prospectus, indeed!" said the Dean to himself, as he went into his house. A most extraordinary individual!"

" Funny old geyser!" mused Stanniland, as he strolled back to his front door, hands in pockets. " I suppose I'd better send 'em a sub, though, if I'm going to live among 'em. Too thin for a Dean. Deans ought to be fat, and——"

He stopped short in the hall, stood quite rigid for half a minute, and then made a bee line for his nearest " Thoughts and Flashes."

In which he wrote:

Idea for advertisement. Fat Dean—seated at dinner-table—letterpress beneath, "a good LIVER."

He looked at it critically. And then added the words:

Is YOURS good?

After which he worked for two solid hours at his desk and then took out his two-seater and raced round the country in a fifty-mile route. Top gear and high speed!

* * * * *

It was "Pickled Pegg" who recommended Mrs. Finch's rooms to the Dean's niece. She had inquired at the office of Pegg Brothers whether, as house agents, they knew of any respectable lodgings. "Priceless Pegg" as usual summoned his brother for assistance.

"Lodgings? Oh yes. Quite so. Not easy to get in Frattenbury, miss. Did you want them for yourself?"

"Yes."

"Let me see. There's Mrs. Saunders—just outside the North Walls. No, she won't do. Don't let rooms to ladies. Too much trouble!"

"Oh, how horrid!" said Peggy, indignantly.

"Well, she's right, so to speak. A man doesn't hang about all day. Goes to work. Only in for meals and evenings, you see. Not so much looking after."

"Just exacuy my case," said the girl. "I shall be at work all day."

"Oh, I see. Quite so. Yes. Let me think.

How about Mrs. Finch, John? Don't you think she might do?"

"She might," replied his brother gloomily.

"I think you might try her, miss. That is, if you don't mind rooms over a shop."

"Not at all. Where is the shop?"

"In the South Street, about a couple of hundred yards down, on the right-hand side. 'Finch, Confectioner.' You can't miss it. Quite respectable, and very nice rooms upstairs."

Mrs. Finch, a buxom little woman with a rosy face, at first demurred. Peggy, however, took care to state that she should be out most of the day. Then the good woman showed her the rooms. The sitting-room was directly above the shop, and possessed a large bow window commanding a view of the South Street. Peggy expressed her satisfaction and settled the terms.

"I'll move in to-morrow, Mrs. Finch," she said. "My things are close by—at the Deanery. I'll have them sent round some time in the afternoon."

"Are you staying at the Deanery, miss?" asked Mrs. Finch, with a slightly more deferential tone in her voice.

"Yes. The Dean is my uncle."

"Oh, indeed, miss. My husband verges him."

"Verges him?"

"At the Cathedral. He's been connected with it for many years. He was a choir-boy there. Afterwards, when he was quite a young man, he became a verger. Now he is the senior verger, and always attends the Dean. You must have seen him."

"Carrying a silver poker in front of my uncle? Oh, yes, of course I have."

"We usually call it a verge, miss," replied Mrs. Finch, who, like every good Frattenbury citizen in any way connected with the Cathedral, was particular in upholding the dignity of everything belonging to it.

The shop was quite a small one. Peggy, who had entered through it, had noticed a girl behind the counter, and Mrs. Finch had explained to her that her daughter attended to the sale of confectionery while she did the home duties.

"Apart from his professional office at the Cathedral"—and she said the words with unction—"my husband is a baker by trade. We make everything we sell, miss. No, don't go out through the shop, please. This is the way to our private side door. I'll give you a key so that you can let yourself in and out when you please. Good afternoon, miss. Everything shall be ready for you to-morrow."

The Dean expressed himself a little more satisfied to Peggy at tea that day.

"Mr. Stanniland is quite an oddity, I admit," he said, "and I wonder a little whether you will get on with him. But I do not dislike him, and I take him to be a gentleman. He tells me he is a cousin of the Bishop of Redminster."

"That's all right, then," said Peggy, with a laugh, "and I'm sure it has relieved your mind."

Then she told him about the rooms.

"That is quite satisfactory," he said. "Finch is one of those individuals one would term as eminently respectable. Indeed, I have to mind my p's and q's when he's about. He hasn't the slightest sense of humour, but he has a tremendous idea of his own dignity, and I always feel that, at present at all events, he looks upon me as one needing much instruction—

at his hands. Only yesterday I left my college cap on the vestry table and, unthinkingly, was about to go into Choir without it. But Finch had me under his eye. He fetched the cap, and the manner in which he said, 'I think you have forgotten this, sir,' as he presented it to me implied a sorrowful rebuke. If he keeps his household under control as he does me, you may rest assured you'll be well looked after."

"I hope he won't try to take his lodger under his protection and coach me in my duties. I shall turn out a failure."

The Dean laughed. "Well," he said, "I must go to my study. I've a lot of correspondence before I leave. To-morrow I shall have to see to my packing."

"And the house will be shut up while you are away?"

"Yes. My three servants will be on holiday. Peters and Fanny leave to-morrow. Mrs. Blake remains on to see to me over the Sunday, but wants to be off by a very early train on Monday morning. She has a cross-country journey to the west."

"What time do you start, uncle?"

"I want to take an early train, too—half an hour after hers. There is a breakfast car on it, so I shall take advantage of it. I have some matters to see to in London in the morning. The boat leaves Folkestone in the late afternoon."

"You have your tickets?"

"Everything. I've ordered a taxi to be here on Monday morning at half-past six—my train leaves at a quarter to seven."

"How about your luggage?"

"I've only two suit-cases. The taxi-man can see to them. There, I must get my letters done."

The following Sunday afternoon, the Cathedral service being over, the Dean made his way back to the Deanery. Not alone. It was the custom at Frattenbury for dignitaries to robe in their own houses in the Close, and to be escorted to and fro to the Cathedral services by a verger. The Dean paced through the Cloisters wearing surplice, scarlet D.D. hood, scarf and college cap. In front of him, clad in black gown with flowing sleeves, holding his silver verge at a correct angle, walked Finch, the verger—a tall, solemn-looking individual with iron-grey hair and drooping moustache of the same colour, a fixed stare in his steely grey eyes. However much the Dean may have wished to hurry, he was powerless. Very slowly, with eminently dignified bearing, the verger led the procession of one. Outside the cloisters they had to cross the road to the Deanery, exactly opposite. But the verger refused to go straight across. He knew the duty he had fulfilled all those years. The street was dry and clean, but, nevertheless, he turned at right angles, walked twenty or thirty yards along the pavement, and led the way over a paved crossing—probably the only crossing that remained in Frattenbury in these days of tarred roads, and very suggestive that it was only in the Close that such a relic survived. Then he turned again at right angles, conducted the Dean along the pavement—he would see to it that no gaitered legs trod the bare road while under *his* control—and finally led the possessor of those legs to his front door, where he turned, lowered his wand of office, and made a dignified bow to the Dean.

Ordinarily a "good afternoon" on both sides closed the solemnity, but on this occasion Finch hesitated, cleared his throat, and said in a funereal tone of voice, " I trust you will enjoy your holiday, sir."

" Thank you, Finch. I believe you are taking yours, are you not ? "

" I hope to absent myself for a short time, sir. I have usually taken advantage of the Dean being away to fit in my holiday."

Finch never spoke of " going away." He always used the expression " absenting himself," even if he only wanted a day off.

" I should like to say, sir," he went on, " that we consider it an honour to be able to accommodate Miss Lake. Mrs. Finch will do all in her power to make her comfortable."

He spoke as if he were conferring an honour on the Dean's niece.

" I'm sure she will. Good afternoon, Finch."

" Good afternoon, sir."

Finch tucked his verge under his arm and walked slowly back to the Cathedral, while the Dean went to his tea with the comforting feeling that, for a time, his labours were ceasing, and that a well-earned holiday lay before him. And he felt that he was going to appreciate it. He needed it. For the Dean of Frattenbury was a little tired, and had not had a holiday since early in the summer of the previous year.

CHAPTER VI

THAT night the Dean was seated in his study. The hour was late, just on eleven o'clock. Mrs. Blake had brought him his whisky and water long ago, had asked if there was anything more she could do for him, and had said good night. Half an hour ago he had heard her footsteps, in the quiet house, going up the uncarpeted back stairs to her room.

But the Dean's book was an interesting one, his arm-chair was comfortable and his pipe was a solace. Also, he knew that every detail for his departure on the morrow was arranged, for he was meticulously careful. Outside, in the hall, stood one suit-case, packed. It contained his clerical dress-suit—silk breeches and stockings, best " apron " and the coat with braid and buttons on sleeves and front—the ordinary " dignitary's " outfit—silver buckled shoes, collars, and so forth. The remaining space was occupied with a few selected books and three or four writing-pads—for he was a man who did not neglect his literary hobby when on holiday.

But that particular dress-suit was the only portion of the dress peculiar to a dean that he was taking. He liked to be particular, wherever he was, in regard to the Englishman's sacred meal of dinner. Otherwise the clothes he was taking were more in vogue with the modern parson's notion of holiday attire.

He had several suits belonging to those not very far away days when he had not begun to go about in apron and gaiters but wore the ordinary trousers and waistcoat of Western humanity. One of these, of grey flannel, was neatly packed, together with his shirts and underlinen, in another suit-case which stood open by the side of his bed, ready to receive, in the morning, his shaving tackle, brushes, sponge and other small paraphernalia.

Another suit, of dark grey cloth, lay on his bed. In this he was going to travel, wearing, for head-gear, a soft hat of the same colour.

He laid down his book on the table, yawned, relighted his pipe, and gave a glance at the clock on the mantelpiece. It was time for bed—but he would finish the pipe first.

The study was at the back of the house, a French window opening from it on to the garden. Immediately outside was a gravel path. The blind was down, but the electric light was a strong one.

Suddenly he gave a slight start and looked up. A faint sound, as of footsteps outside, had arrested his attention. He listened carefully.

"My fancy," he murmured, as he replaced his pipe in his mouth.

But it was not his fancy. Immediately afterwards there came a gentle tapping on the glass of the window. He sprang up from his chair.

Now there are few men who would not be more or less startled at hearing, late at night in a comparatively lonely house, a sudden tapping on the window. To be startled, however, does not necessarily mean fear, and the Dean, even accustomed to a sheltered life as he had always been, was no coward. Hastily striding across the room he threw up the spring blind with a rattle and, in the darkness outside, illuminated by the study light, dimly saw the form of a man, whose face, however, seemed to be half hidden.

"Who's there? What do you want?" was his natural exclamation.

And the answer came back, in a muffled tone:

"Let me in."

"Who are you?" he asked again.

And a sudden, real fear took possession of him as he thought he interpreted the low spoken answer. He undid the fastenings, threw open the window, and in came a man wearing a long, shabby overcoat with the collar turned up, a muffler wound round the lower part of his face, and a soft hat pulled well over his eyes.

"For Heaven's sake shut the window and pull down the blinds."

The Dean did so, without saying a word. When he turned the man had removed his hat, thrown off the muffler, and his worst fears were realized.

"Edward!" he exclaimed.

"Sorry if I startled you," replied his brother, "but I had to get in quietly. That's why I came to the window. I guessed you were sitting up alone and risked it. I say, before I explain, give me a drink. I want it."

The Dean pointed silently to the table. Edward Lake seized the decanter, poured into his brother's empty glass about six times his brother's portion of whisky, added a little water, and drank it off.

"That's better," he said. "Are you alone in the house, Ernest?" he asked, cautiously.

" There's only my housekeeper—and she is in bed," replied his brother.

Nevertheless he went to the door, locked it, and came back. His brother had unbuttoned his coat and had thrown himself into an easy chair. The Dean looked at him searchingly. Beneath his overcoat he was wearing a very shabby old suit. There was a haunted expression on his face, for he looked what he was—a fugitive.

" Where have you come from ? " asked the Dean.

" From London. I got off the train at Marton " —mentioning a little wayside station a good ten miles from Frattenbury—" and walked the rest. I'm about tired out."

" You look it. And why have you come to me in this way—walking from Marton and entering through the window ? "

The other gave a short laugh.

" If you want the truth—because I didn't care to be seen at a large station like Frattenbury. You see, the police are after me.

If he expected the Dean to be horror-struck and startled he was disappointed. The latter asked, very quietly :

" What for ? What have you done ? "

" I've been a damn fool, Ernest, though I swear I haven't committed any crime. I've got mixed up with a set of swindlers, and——"

" Melford & Co.—alias Corney & Co. Yes, I know," broke in the Dean, in the same quiet voice. The other started.

" How do you know ? " he asked.

" Because the police told me—three weeks ago."

" They told you ? "

" Yes," replied the Dean, speaking very slowly. " They also told me that if you came to me it was my plain duty to communicate with them at once."

" Good God, Ernest. You'd never do that? It's not only me. Think of the disgrace to the family—to *you.*"

" I'm afraid the family—such as is left of it—haven't any very great cause to be proud of you, Edward," said his brother, a little bitterly, " and as to what I intend to do—that remains to be seen, after I've heard your story."

" I declare before God I haven't committed any crime."

" But the police say you have."

" I know, I know," cried the other, " and the worst of it is that, as matters stand, I can't prove I'm innocent. Not without time. If I can only have time—and they don't take me—I shall be able to prove it. That's why I've come to you."

The Dean looked at him fixedly for the space of a minute or so. Then he said:

" You have always been a foolish man, Edward, and foolishness brings its punishment, as well as sin, on self and others. Not that you have not sinned as well. You deserted your wife, you have neglected your daughter—she hardly realizes that she has a father, poor girl; and, over and over again you have come to me for help in mad schemes that have been fruitless. You have wasted your life. But I have always tried to think that, in spite of your miserable foolishness, you have kept yourself free from what the law calls crime."

" I *have*—really I have."

" And so," went on the Dean, coldly, " when the

police brought the matter before me I told them that I still believed you were not, really, a criminal. Before I make any plans I want to believe that still. Tell me the truth, Edward."

"I have. Honestly, I have done nothing wrong."

He met his brother's penetrating gaze unflinchingly.

"Very well," said the Dean, after a slight pause, "I believe you. Now tell me, briefly, how you got into this mess."

As the Dean listened he pieced together in his mind the story. An old story, though, with his somewhat limited knowledge of human nature, he was not altogether aware of this. First the specious lure to get money easily, the bait put forward by an unscrupulous man to obtain tools to set his crafty plans in action. The miserable story of a business fraud, engineered by Corney, while one, at least, of the unsuspecting "Co." he had attracted by his wiles was unaware of the real nature of the "firm." Then the collapse—the mistake on Corney's part, the coup that did not come off, the evidence of fraud, inculpating innocent as well as guilty.

"I've been a fool," he concluded, "but there it is."

"You have been a fool," replied his brother, "and how do you propose to get out of it? What did you mean when you told me a little while ago that you only wanted time?"

"What I said, if I could keep safely out of the way for three or four weeks it would be all right. There are only two men who could clear me. Corney's one of them—and he won't. The other has gone to America on business, and I can't get at him. But I know he'll be back in three weeks' time."

" Do you know where Corney is ? "

The other hesitated for a moment.

" Yes—I do. But I'd rather not tell you, he made me prom——"

" Oh, I certainly don't want to know," broke in the Dean. " It's bad enough to have to know where *you* are. Can't you manage to conceal yourself till the three weeks are up ? "

" You don't know what it is to be hunted, Ernest."

" I certainly don't," replied his brother, with a grim little smile.

" It's awful," went on the other. " Only yesterday I felt I was recognized by a man who had been following me. I managed to give him the slip. But it's got on my nerves. That's why I came to you."

" Oh ! " exclaimed the Dean, " and what do you expect *me* to do ? "

" I thought perhaps you could let me stay here for a few days at least, I wouldn't go out, and——"

" Preposterous ! " snapped the Dean. " In the first place I couldn't. I'm starting on my holiday to-morrow and the house will be locked up. But even if I were here, consider the servants. Do you suppose I could have a man staying in the house without rumours getting about ? Of course not. You must go, Edward. I would honestly help you if I could—but how can I ? "

Edward Lake had refilled his glass, and was sipping his whisky and water.

" Couldn't you help me to get out of the country ? " he asked. " If I could only get abroad for the next three weeks."

" If you mean that you have no money, I will give you some—to get abroad with."

The other shook his head.

"Thanks," he said, "but I daren't risk it. The boats are watched, I know. They have my description."

"Then how can I help you? As a matter of fact I'm going abroad myself to-morrow."

"Couldn't you take me with you—as your valet, or something of that sort?" asked his brother, eagerly.

"Preposterous!" ejaculated the Dean again.

He was about to make a further remark when he suddenly checked himself. Something seemed to have struck him. He sat, gazing fixedly at his brother, mechanically filling and lighting his pipe, but without saying a word. Once or twice his brother spoke, but he took no notice. Slowly he took his pipe from his mouth, his lips compressed themselves, his forehead knitted into a frown. Then he gave a little sigh, and said:

"Edward, I'm going to make you a strange proposition. I know it's wrong of me, in the eyes of the law, but I want to help you, not only for your own sake but because of your daughter. I wouldn't like her to be dragged into a family scandal. Now, will you give me your word of honour that if you can get out of the country for three weeks you can prove your innocence?"

"On my word of honour, yes."

"Very well, then," went on the Dean, with the air of a man who had made up his mind on a difficult course of action. "Now, listen. To-morrow I have arranged to start on a trip to the Mediterranean. The boat, chartered specially for the voyage, leaves Folkestone about five o'clock. She calls at Bordeaux and Lisbon, and then proceeds to the Mediterranean, calling at Valencia, Genoa, Naples, and so on. A round trip which should occupy a month. I have my tickets all ready, including the journey from here to London and thence to Folkestone. I propose to hand those tickets over to you and let you take the trip instead of me."

"My dear chap!" exclaimed his brother. "It's most awfully good of you. But—but——" he went on, "what will you do?"

"I shall go for a quiet holiday elsewhere," replied the Dean, grimly. "It wouldn't do to remain here. I shall have to follow your example and hide myself."

And a queer little smile twitched the corners of his mouth. The Dean was embarking on his first real adventure and, even in that very grave moment, the humour of it somehow struck him.

"You mean," said his brother, with a little gasp of astonishment, "that I am to impersonate you? That I am to pretend to be the Dean of Frattenbury?"

"I don't mean anything of the kind. I shouldn't dream of such a thing," retorted the Dean, with no little asperity, "and unless you give me your promise that you will not pretend to be the Dean of Frattenbury I withdraw my offer."

The other laughed.

"I certainly don't want to pose as a dean," he said. "I couldn't do it. But I really thought at first that you meant it. Go on. Who *am* I to be?"

"Well," said the Dean, "I think you can arrange matters. I have not booked my berth in my capacity as a cathedral dignitary. As a matter of fact I took my tickets personally at Cook's office in Ludgate Circus. Of course, I had to give my name as I paid with a cheque. You'd have to go as Mr. E. Lake—which you are."

"But," hazarded the other, "they saw you were a clergyman, at all events."

"Ah—I suppose they did. I hadn't thought of that."

"I'd rather take the risk under another name. But don't you see if I go as Lake I must keep up the idea of being a clergyman."

The Dean tapped on the arms of his chair with his finger.

"I don't like it," he said. "No—I don't like it."

"But there isn't any other way. Don't be afraid, Ernest. I won't disgrace the cloth. After all, it only means putting on a clerical collar."

"I don't wear them, as a rule, on my holidays. Except in the evening."

"All right, then. So much the better. But I must start with one."

The Dean thought profoundly.

"Very well," he said at last, reluctantly. "I suppose it must be so. Let me see. We'd better plan out something."

"What time were you to start to-morrow? And how about your housekeeper?"

"She leaves at six. The taxi was to take me to the station at half-past."

"Splendid!" He was fast recovering his usual careless, sanguine temperament. "Let *me* go in the taxi then, and——"

"But the driver will think you're me," broke in the Dean, regardless of grammar.

"Quite so. But that will be all right. All the better. It will look as if you've started for your holiday. You can slip out later, I'll leave that to you." He was taking things into his own hands with a vengeance, and his brother, having opened the door, had to follow—however reluctantly. " I shall want some clothes, old chap. A complete rig out."

" Yes, I suppose you will. I can lend you an ordinary dark grey suit. You can buy a second one in London if you want one. And you can have one of my suit-cases—with some shirts and pyjamas, and so on. In fact, I've one packed ready. I dare say I can find another for myself."

" Also—excuse my mentioning it—but I've only a couple of pounds in the world."

The Dean sighed, got up, and unlocked a drawer in his desk.

" I cashed a cheque yesterday, for my holiday," he explained. " I can let you have half of it—fifteen pounds. That ought to be enough, as everything is paid for. I must manage as best I can, I suppose."

" Oh, *you* can write to your bank and get some."

" All very well, but I may not want to," replied the Dean, already foreseeing difficulties arising out of his rash proposition. " Now, it is very late. Listen to me, Edward. My housekeeper must not know you are here."

" Rather not."

" Come upstairs very quietly. You shall have the spare room. I'll bring in the suit-case and the clothes, so that you will be all ready in the morning —also a hat. You had better lock your door. Directly my housekeeper leaves in the morning I'll come to you."

" And we'll make the bed, so as to look as if no

one had slept in it, and hide these clothes of mine," said the other, cheerfully. He was quite recovering his spirits.

"Er—I suppose we must," replied the Dean, with a sigh. He was sinking still more deeply into the mire of deception.

"You must not be seen when the taxi comes," went on his brother. "All I have to do is to slip out of the house. The driver can't have any suspicions. And there are not likely to be many people for so early a train."

"I hope not, indeed."

"Don't you worry, old chap. And what are *you* going to do?"

"I don't know yet," replied the poor Dean, "I must think that out. I suppose I must manage to get away unobserved. Dear me! Dear me! I'm beginning to feel quite like a criminal."

"Now you know what I've been going through," said Edward Lake, almost flippantly. "Good luck, old chap. You'll pull through!"—he was quite reversing the position—"only, for the Lord's sake—or rather, for *my* sake—don't you get discovered before I get a start. Or afterwards, either. There's always the wireless."

They were just about to leave the room when Edward Lake stopped, tapped his brother on the arm, and said:

"I've got it. What's the nearest station in the down line direction?"

"Fernley—about three miles away."

"Is there a back way out of the house?"

"There's the little gate at the bottom of the garden—that leads through a passage in the old city wall."

"What's outside?"

"Open meadows."

"That's it then. You slip out there and walk to Fernley for jumping off. It's quite ecclesiastical. St. Paul escaped by the city wall."

"He hadn't been such a fool as I'm beginning to think I am," retorted the Dean.

"Tut, tut!" said his brother.

CHAPTER VII

"I'M just going, sir. There's nothing more you want?"

"Nothing, thank you, Mrs. Blake," replied the Dean, putting his head out of his bedroom door and speaking to her as she stood half-way down the stairs. "I hope you will enjoy your holiday."

"Thank you, sir, I'm sure. And I hope you will enjoy yours. Good morning, sir."

The Dean made a little grimace as he returned to his job of packing his bag—a fairly small one, as he had to carry it to Fernley.

"Enjoy my holiday, indeed!" he said to himself. Then he heard the front door bang. The coast was clear, and he made his way to his brother's room.

He found that individual seated on his bed, smoking his pipe. He was dressed in the Dean's dark grey suit, which fitted him fairly well though the Dean was the taller man of the two. And he wore one of his brother's clerical collars.

"Well, here we are," he said, cheerfully—he had completely recovered his usual temperament—"let's make the bed, Ernest, and stow my old clothes away. Then it'll be about time for me to be off."

The Dean was wearing his grey flannel suit. A soft, turned-down collar and black tie completed his toilet. The position had become exactly reversed:

the cleric had turned layman and the layman cleric. And while Edward Lake, the man who was responsible for all the trouble, was in the best of good humour, his brother's attitude was furtive and despondent. As they stood on either side of the bed, clumsily folding the sheets and blankets and smoothing them down, the contrast between them was very marked.

At length the bedclothes were re-arranged, after a fashion, and Edward Lake looked at his watch.

"Twenty past. You get back to your room, and don't show yourself, whatever you do. I'm all ready now. I'm everlastingly grateful to you, old chap. I'll never forget your kindness."

"I hope," replied the Dean, as the two men shook hands, "I hope it will be all right and that the next time we meet there will be no need for this terrible deception."

"Don't you worry, old fellow. I shall pull through now. Good-bye. Have a good time!"

"A good time!" "Enjoy your holiday!" The Dean positively shivered as he went back to his bedroom and stood just inside the door, listening.

Edward Lake put on great-coat and hat, looked at himself in the glass carefully, pulled the brim of his hat a little lower over his eyes, adjusted a white silk muffler—part of his brother's outfit, of course—round his neck, refilled and lighted his pipe, and waited.

Suddenly the sound of the front-door bell rang violently through the house. Edward Lake had just laid down his pipe on the table to re-adjust the muffler, standing before the glass to do so. He started, forgot to take up his pipe, seized the suit-case, ran down the stairs, and opened the door.

"Good morning, sir. A nice morning," said the taxi-driver.

"Very. Oh—I've forgotten my pipe. You might take this."

Handing the man the suit-case he dashed upstairs again. The taxi-driver, after the manner of one accustomed to take folks to the station with their luggage, glanced into the hall, saw the other suit-case standing there close beside the open door, picked it up, and took both down to his car, depositing them beside his seat in front.

Now this second suit-case, in which were packed the Dean's evening clothes, his books and papers, was a new one. He had bought it on coming to Frattenbury. It was of brown leather and on it was painted, in small black capitals,

THE DEAN OF FRATTENBURY.

One has only to attend Convocation to see many such cases, arranged in the big cloak-room of the Church House at Westminster, many of them bearing the names of leading dignitaries of the Church: "The Bishop of Redminster," "The Archdeacon of Derringford," "Canon Studley-Harper," and so forth. Among clerical outfitters they are often designated "robe-cases," and are used as such as well as for ordinary purposes.

Down came Edward Lake again, stuffing his pipe into his pocket, shut the front door, and hurried to the taxi, never noticing, as he got in, that there were two suit-cases in front.

And, as he did so, the Dean stepped out of his room, hurried across the landing to the front of the house, and, very carefully pulling the drawn blind a little on one side, watched, through the chink, the departure of his troublesome brother.

The taxi turned out of the Close through a fine old gateway into the almost deserted South Street, turned sharply to the right, and made for the station, which was at the end of the street. Just before reaching it, on the left, stood the police station.

The taxi turned into the railway station yard and drew up at the entrance. And, at that precise moment, Superintendent Walters was coming out.

The policeman's trained and keen eyes glanced mechanically at the two suit-cases. On one of them he read the words: " The Dean of Frattenbury." From the luggage he looked at the occupant of the car, who was just getting out, the driver holding the door open. His gaze lingered, not on the passenger's face, but on his legs, and just a slightly puzzled expression flickered in his eyes for a moment. Deans are associated with gaitered legs. And these were clad in ordinary trousers.

Swiftly, however, he remembered that the Dean of Frattenbury was embarking on a holiday. He had very good reason for remembering this for the subject had been uppermost in his mind only five minutes before.

A smile of greeting broke out on his face, he raised his hand to his cap in salute, and, with a cheery " Good morning, sir," passed on.

Edward Lake, a sudden fear striking at his heart, had the sense to return the salute with a wave of the hand and a nod. Then he made his way as quickly as he could through the booking office to the up-platform, having first given the taxi-driver half a crown, a porter following him with the two suit-cases. But he had not yet noticed the duplication of his luggage. He had had a shock at the very beginning of his adventure.

Had he only known it, he had more cause of congratulation for himself than for fear. The smile on the Superintendent's face broadened as he walked across the street and entered the police station.

A slight digression is necessary to explain what had happened. On the previous Saturday there had stepped aboard the *Sunflower*, which was lying in Folkestone harbour in readiness for the cruise, a nondescript-looking individual wearing a very ordinary dark suit and bowler hat, who had asked to see the purser. And the purser had shown him, at his particular request, enforced by an authority which the purser quite understood, a printed list of the passengers who had booked for the cruise together with the numbers of the cabins assigned to them.

The Scotland Yard man, for such he was, had run his finger over the list till it rested on :

Rev. E. Lake. No. 32.

" Hullo," he said, half to himself, " that's queer. Though he's not likely to try to get away under his own name. Still, I'd better make certain."

" Who booked this clerical chap ? " he asked the purser. The latter consulted private memoranda.

" Cook. Head Office. Ludgate Circus."

" Righto," replied the other, entering the information in his notebook. Shortly the telephone was set in action, and not very long after, another nondescript-looking man entered Cook's office and asked for any details they might have anent a person of the name of Lake who had booked for the trip undertaken by the *Sunflower*.

They easily found the information. The tickets had been paid for by a cheque drawn on the Westminster Bank at Frattenbury—which had been duly honoured.

"I remember him quite well," said the clerk who gave the information. "Clerical chap—bishop, or something of that sort, by his togs—gaiters, apron, and a top hat with the ribbon faked into a bunch in front of it."

Such was his ribald way of describing the dignitary's proud badge of office—the rosette.

Then there had come a message to Superintendent Walters asking for more information. Whether any cleric of the name of Lake, who banked at Frattenbury, was living in the neighbourhood, and whether the same cleric was about to take a holiday on the *Sunflower*.

Superintendent Walters had quiet methods of getting information. Finch, the Dean's verger, did not know when he mentioned in a friendly conversation with Police-sergeant Stanton on Sunday evening that the Dean was starting for a trip round the Mediterranean the next morning—he had heard all about it, from Peters the butler—that he was being dexterously pumped.

The Superintendent had been called away that night and could not attend to the matter till the next morning. Finding a difficulty of getting on the telephone exchange—the trunk line was held up—he had stepped over to the railway telegraph office, which was open long before that of the post office, and wired to the effect that all was right—

the Dean of Frattenbury—name of Lake—had booked the passage for himself.

"I wonder what he would have said if I'd told him I was just making things easy for him," he said to himself.

And laughed outright. But he would not have laughed had he known that he had just established an alibi by which, if any proof were wanted that the Dean had left Frattenbury on his propcsed holiday, that proof would come from a high police official.

Meanwhile Edward Lake had suddenly discovered the extra suit-case. An ejaculation of surprise rose to his lips as the porter set the luggage down on the platform, but he checked himself in time. His first idea was to put the redundant case in the cloak-room, but then he remembered that he could not post the voucher to his brother and also that the fact of depositing half his luggage at the starting-point of his journey might, in some way, arouse suspicion. Just then, too, the train came in, so he made his way to an empty compartment, tipped the porter who handed in the suit-cases, and took care, in placing them on the rack, that the legend on the brown one was hidden from view. Once out of Frattenbury, he had given his word that he would not attempt to pass as the Dean, and, chiefly for his own sake, he meant to keep it.

It took him some little time to get over the shock of meeting the Superintendent. It had been a nasty jar. For weeks his nerves had been on end, and though his natural exuberance of spirits had returned to him at the Deanery, once out of those quite surroundings and face to face with the adventure, his courage had forsaken him a little. There was still the gauntlet to run before he was safe on board the boat. Had he only known that the Superintendent had unwittingly opened a door through which he could get safely on to the *Sunflower* he would not have been so perturbed. But, of course, this was hidden from him.

At all events he was thankful that hardly anybody had been on the platform. The first step had been accomplished. He pulled himself together, traversed the corridor to the breakfast car, had a good meal, and returned to the compartment to smoke and think things out.

At length he worked out his plan. He would go to Charing Cross and put the two suit-cases in the cloak-room. One of them—the obvious one—he would leave there altogether. He would keep the voucher and, some day or other, when this beastly business was over, it could be recovered. He would take a train to Folkestone in the early afternoon. What should he do meanwhile? He was bound to be careful. Glancing at the daily paper he had brought, he saw there was a cricket match at Lord's. Excellent. It would be too early to get in on arrival, but he could stroll or sit in Regent's Park—and then—a middle-aged clergyman at Lord's among the spectators was above suspicion.

On arrival at the London terminus he proceeded to put this plan into action. At Charing Cross he deposited his luggage in the main-line cloak-room, remembering, however, as soon as he had walked away, that he ought to have asked for separate vouchers instead of the single one he was putting into his pocket-book.

"Never mind," he said to himself, "I can see to it later on—before I start."

He had not shaved that morning, so he went down the steps to the saloon beneath the station, where he was attended to. Coming out, he strolled to the bookstall, for he was in no hurry, and turned over the leaves of a magazine.

It was just then that he received the second shock of that morning. Glancing along the stall he noticed a man, standing at the corner, who was eyeing him intently over the edge of a newspaper, but who at once raised the newspaper and hid his own face. Weeks of caution had made him suspicious of the slightest circumstances. Controlling himself, however, he looked again at the contents of the stall made a purchase, and slowly moved off towards the flight of steps leading down into Villiers Street.

Without turning his head—he had learned that it was unwise to do that—he walked down Villiers Street to the Underground station, took a ticket, and made for the moving staircase. On the stairs, standing a little sideways, he was able to steal a glance above. The man with the newspaper was there!

Still making a great effort to appear unaware that he was being followed, he stepped off the stairs as he came to the bottom, and, without undue hurry, made his way to the platform. He was just in time to enter a train standing there, but, glancing over the iron gate as the conductor closed it, saw the other in the act of boarding the coach next behind him.

At Trafalgar Square, Edward Lake made no movement, but, through the doors dividing the coaches he could see that the other man was there, seated with his face towards him. At Piccadilly Circus the platform 'was full of people. Also, many were alighting. He pushed his way out, thrust himself through the crowd, keeping as close to the train as possible, and saw the other alighting. Still keeping alongside the train he reached an entrance to it just as the last passenger of a little group was getting in. A bell clanged—the conductor was in the act of closing the gate when, with a sudden side movement, Edward Lake slipped in.

Crash !

Too late.

Crash !

The man who followed had rushed for the next opening, but the gate clanged in his face.

" Stand away ! " yelled the conductor, for the man had seized the top of the gate.

And the train moved on.

Edward Lake sank into a seat and wiped the perspiration from his forehead. It had been a close shave, and had shaken him badly. At Oxford Circus he got out, jumped into a taxi.

" Selfridges ! " he cried. The first word that came into his mind. And then cursed himself for not giving a more distant destination.

At Selfridges he entered the big stores, went up a lift, crossed several departments, down to the basement in another lift, right on, and out at the Orchard Street entrance, instantly crossing the road and boarding a bus which stood there, taking the inside seat next the door, from which point of vantage he could observe the road behind him and also anyone who mounted the same bus. At Baker Street he got off, feeling safe at last, walked to Marylebone

Station and had a cup of strong black coffee to settle his nerves. All thought of Lord's had gone out of his mind. What troubled him was facing Charing Cross Station again. What a fool he had been to come back to London at all, once he had got safely out of it. He ought to have got off at a certain intermediate junction between Frattenbury and London, and made his way by cross-country journeying to Folkestone. But it was too late now.

Slowly, as he smoked over his coffee, an idea took possession of him and his eyes began to gleam a little.

" By George ! " he said to himself, " that's worth trying, if I can only bring it off. Poor old Ernest might not like it very much, but, after all, he's got me into this mess ! "

Such was his gratitude !

" Also," he went on to himself, " it would settle matters once and for all. Gad ! I'll have a shot at it."

He finished his coffee, went out of the station, and walked quickly, through Chapel Street, to the Edgware Road, which he crossed, turned along it to the right, and made his way to the terminus from which trains start to Harlesden and Willesden.

Some way down the Harrow Road, on the right-hand side, are half a dozen dingy and unpretentious-looking little quiet streets which rejoice in the name of " Avenues." He got off the car in their vicinity, selected the " Third Avenue," and walked along it till he came to a house with all the blinds down. On the door he knocked softly—and in a peculiar manner. Two knocks, a short interval, and then three more.

There was no answer. He repeated the knocks. Then he stepped back a little from the door and glanced at the bow window close to him. The blind moved—ever so slightly. He waited. A key turned in the lock and the door opened, but whoever opened it kept out of sight behind it.

Edward Lake slipped through. The door closed, and a voice out of the darkness of the little passage exclaimed in greeting :

" What the hell do you want ? "

" It's all right," replied Lake, " I had to come."

He followed the owner of the voice down the passage to a little room at the back—also with the blinds drawn down. Then the mysterious owner spoke again :

" What the devil do you mean, Lake, in coming here in broad daylight ? You know I warned you not to. How do you know you weren't followed ? It's one of their tricks to track me by blasted fools like you. Otherwise you'd have been in quod weeks ago, I reckon."

" I've been awfully careful, Corney."

" I hope you have. And, look here, don't call me by that name, please. Walls have ears. I'm Smith—plain Smith. Understand ? Sit down, damn you ! "

He threw himself into a chair as he spoke. He was a man of between fifty and sixty years of age—fifty-five probably, with iron-grey hair, rather strong features, and sharp, shifty dark eyes. The several weeks' growth of stubbly hair on chin and cheeks made him look even more of a villain than he really was. In height, as he had stood beside Edward Lake, he looked a shade taller.

" Now, tell me why you've come—and then clear out sharp. Fire away."

"I don't think you'll ask me to clear out in such a hurry when I've told you."

The other looked at him intently.

"Got yourself up as a parson, I see," he said. "What's the game?" And he gave a short laugh.

"I've come to drive a bargain with you."

"Oh, have you," replied the other, with a sneer. "What do you want?"

"Proofs that will clear me. You've got them."

"I dare say! But you'd have to offer something you're not likely to possess before you'd get 'em out of me."

"What's your price?"

The other thought for a moment, a scowl on his face. Then he gave another short laugh.

"Get me safe out of this blasted country—that's my price."

"All right," replied Edward Lake. "And I'm prepared to pay it."

CHAPTER VIII

THE Dean, left alone in the house, made his final arrangements for his speedy departure. He was anxious, if he could, to get clear of Frattenbury before anyone he knew was about.

With considerable misgivings, now that he was really face to face with the situation he had brought upon himself, he finished packing his bag. All the time, however, though he might not have known it himself, for he was a modest man at heart, he was possessed of an indomitable pluck. It was his quiet courage which had sustained him in his early career and had gained him his scholarships, the true courage which never falters when a good end has to be reached. It was the same characteristics of perseverance combined with courage which had given him a name as a theological author. The only thing which was really new to him in the adventure he had undertaken, was its strange inconsistency with his regular habits of life. the suddenness of the undertaking and its element of deception.

The latter he much disliked, but he had set his face to see the thing through and see it through he would. Also, the humour of the situation, in a way, appealed to him, and he even smiled at his reflection when he took a last look in the glass. He, like his brother, had put on a dark overcoat, and had turned up the collar. A soft hat lay rolled up in his bag and he was wearing an old tweed cap which he was in the habit of using for the garden or for railway travelling.

Suddenly he bethought himself of the suit-case in the hall.

" I must get my cheque-book out of it," he murmured to himself, " and I think there's room here for a writing-pad and a book or two."

So he went downstairs into the hall, carrying his still open bag with him, and there discovered that the suit-case had vanished."

" Strange," he ejaculated, standing still in perplexity, " Now I'm certain I left it here. Yes, I remember noticing it when I went upstairs last night. What . . . Oh !"

For the truth suddenly flashed upon him.

" Dear, dear ! That's most annoying. The taxi-driver must have taken it. Surely Edward must have seen. . . . No—no—he couldn't have. When he went out he was carrying nothing. Let me see, he'd find it out at the station. But what would he do with it ? Perhaps he left it in the cloak-room. I must see—no —I *can't !* Oh, dear, dear ! He couldn't want it. And it's got my name on it. Most unfortunate. *Most* unfortunate ! "

There was nothing to be done, however. He gave one final look round the hall, took, from force of habit, an umbrella from the rack, made his way to the garden door at the side of the house, went out, locked the door, hesitated, put the key in his pocket, saying, " It's the only thing to be done with it," and walked quickly and furtively down the garden at the back of the house.

There was a narrow, sunk path, cut through the

grassy slope which ascended to the terrace formed by the city wall, cut, in a little tunnel, through the broad wall itself, leading to a small door, a sort of postern, which was hinged in the outer facing of the wall. Through this he passed, down a small flight of steps, to the open meadow beyond, and reached a footpath leading across the meadows, away from the city.

A youth, driving a herd of cows across the meadow, took no notice of the man who walked swiftly along the path. And he was the only person about at that early hour. The Dean, still walking quickly, came to the end of the meadow, crossed the railway line that bordered it by a foot-bridge, passed on along a field path, still leaving Frattenbury behind him, and never stopped till he came to a point some mile and a half away, where the path entered a lane at right angles across it. He sat for a minute on a stile, over which he had to climb to get into the lane, and consulted a small time-table. Then he looked at his watch. It was just over an hour before a down train was due at Fernley. True, Fernley was only three miles from Frattenbury, on a straight road, but he was taking a circuitous route which would eventually come out on that road not very far from his destination, and he knew he had nearly four miles before him.

He got into the lane, turned to the right, and trudged on. Not a soul did he meet. Finding the bag heavy he had slung it over his shoulder on his umbrella, and looked, as he began to feel, anyone rather than the Dean of Frattenbury. He was thinking, as he went, of his resources. He had about twenty pounds odd in his pocket and felt that, if he could obtain economical lodgings somewhere, this sum ought to see him through. He had made arrangements for meeting his brother when the latter returned and was safe. He knew the approximate date when the *Sunflower* was due back at Folkestone, and, on that date, either of them was to repair to a quiet hotel off Russell Square and await the arrival there of the other.

Meanwhile he was going to take his holiday incognito. But he refused, within himself, to practise any deception apart from a very simple incognito, and had made up his mind to call himself " Dr. Lake," which, indeed he was. Whether he was a " D.D.," an " M.D." or a " D.C.L." did not matter and was a question which concerned no one. They might take him for a layman if they chose. He was only afraid of direct questions. But direct questions from strangers—and he devoutly hoped he would only meet with strangers—were rude, and could be evaded with dignity.

As to where he was going he was not quite decided, except that it was to be westward. Only once, and that many years ago, had he been to the West of England, and, so far as he could remember, he knew no one living in that direction.

In due time he circled round to the main road and began to meet people, chiefly farmers and market gardeners on their way to Frattenbury. He reached the little station of Fernley, and asked for a ticket to Southampton, which seemed to him far enough away to mature his plans at leisure, and waited—not very long—for the train. And he was fortunate enough to find an empty compartment.

This was the start made by the Dean of Frattenbury for his holiday, and if any of the denizens of the Close had witnessed it, there would have been food for gossip and the manufacture of rumours for at least a month in that very select enclosure.

As a matter of fact one individual living in the Close *had* seen him go, but had not for a moment imagined that he was the Dean. And that was Julian Bruce Stanniland, who was shaving himself in his bedroom at the dressing-table which stood before the window at the moment that the Dean of Frattenbury came out of his side door and went down his garden. And Stanniland's window commanded a view of that door and garden.

Peggy arrived, punctually to time, and found her new employer in his office, seated at his desk.

" Good morning, Miss Lake," he said, abruptly, " to begin with, I want you to make copies of these letters," and he handed her a batch. " If you don't understand my abbreviations, please ask me."

He wheeled round again and recommenced his own writing. For a time the clicking of Peggy's machine sounded, interspersed with brief intervals of silence. The letters had been scribbled in pencil. Stanniland's handwriting was not very plain and, every now and then she had to ask him to interpret his peculiar abbreviations. But she managed to get through the task fairly well.

" I've finished them."

" Right ! "

But he did not turn round for a minute or two ; he was absorbed in his own work. She sat, looking at the back of his head, a little smile on her pretty face. Suddenly he wheeled round again, and caught her eye. And also found himself forced into a little return smile.

"Let's look."

Rapidly he glanced through them, made one or two slight corrections, added a sentence at the end of a couple of them, and took up, from his desk, another bundle of letters.

"All right," he said. "They'll do. Now here's correspondence to be answered. I've jotted down briefly what I want written to each—it's on the slip pinned to each letter. I want you to type the replies—in business form, of course. Can you?"

"I'll try," she replied. "If I make any mistakes to begin with you must tell me—and I hope I'll do better next time."

"I'll tell you," he retorted sharply. "But you must not make mistakes—*twice!*"

She gave a little shrug which he did not see. He had turned round again. Presently the typewriter resumed its clicking. Then, after a bit, came a pause.

"Mr. Stanniland?"

"Yes?"

"How am I to reply to this letter, please. It hasn't got a slip pinned to it."

"Let's see."

And he held out his hand and took it. Then he laughed.

"Oh, that's a mistake. I must have mixed it up with the rest. No, there isn't any reply to Melford & Co. And there never will be. By the way"—and he looked at her searchingly—"did you notice anything about that letter that is different to the rest?"

"Yes, I did."

"What is it?"

" It is dated over a month ago. The others have Saturday's date."

" Good ! " he exclaimed. " Keep that sort of thing up and you'll do. What was the deduction you drew from it ? "

" That you must have been a little careless, keeping it so long," she replied, demurely.

" Oh, that's what you think, is it ? One to you, Miss Lake. But you're wrong. I was simply re-reading it out of curiosity when you came in. There's something else funny about that letter. Melford & Co. are rascals. They tried to do me down, but I wasn't having any. The police are after the lot of 'em now. . . . Get on ! "

" Get on, indeed ! " she said to herself—but the typewriter clicked all the same. When she finished he went carefully through the replies, and did not hesitate to point out mistakes. Two letters had to be re-written. Then he said :

" I'd better tell you. I usually go to London, to my office there, Mondays and Thursdays. I've stayed at home to-day to put you up to things."

" That's awfully nice of you, Mr. Stanniland."

He paused a moment, looking at her. But her face was perfectly set and grave.

" So you'll be all by yourself those days."

" Quite lonely, in fact," she answered, cheerfully.

" You'll have your work, see ? And you'll always find, to begin with, a batch of letters to be written and another to be answered. Like these. I shall make out the rough notes before I go."

" I hope I shall be able to read them accurately by Thursday. You don't write *very* plainly."

Again he looked at her. Then said, suddenly :

"What do you gather about what you've been through this morning, Miss Lake?"

"I don't understand."

"But you've got to. What am I engaged in doing?"

"Oh, *that!*" she replied, with a laugh, "why, trying to get a bid for Sapor relish, aren't you?"

"Quite right," he said, approvingly.

"And a good bid, too!"

"I won't sell without."

"Of course not. It's ripping good stuff, Mr. Stanniland. Did you *really* invent it?"

He nodded.

"I think it's awfully clever of you. What's it made of?"

That caused him to laugh out loud.

"That's my secret—for sale!" he replied. "But I don't mind telling you I got hold of the leading idea in China. So you've tried it, have you? Not bad, eh?"

"Uncle had some. He thinks it's perfectly topping."

Which was not exactly what the Dean had said, but it sufficed to please the inventor.

"Your uncle has good taste," he said. "I advised him to buy it."

"He *has* bought some."

"No, no. The whole show. Put it on the market and use the profits to patch up the Cathedral."

She laughed. There was a humorous side to this employer of hers, after all.

"Oh, what did he say?"

"Oh, nothing much." He was back again at his business. "But, to get on. By the way, I ought to have asked you. Have you taken rooms here?"

"Yes. Anyway I had to. Uncle left for his holiday to-day, and the Deanery is shut up."

"I know. I saw that stiff old butler of your uncle's lock up the house and slip out the back way early this morning."

Peggy gave a start of genuine surprise:

"What *do* you mean, Mr. Stanniland? Peters left on Saturday. I was there when he went. You couldn't have seen him."

"That's queer," he replied, "it must have been someone else."

"But my uncle only had his housekeeper with him. She was to leave this morning at six o'clock, and the taxi was to come for him at half-past."

"By Jove! I heard it, too. But it was close on seven when this fellow came out of the house—the side door."

"What does it mean?" she asked.

"We'll find out."

And he seized the portable telephone on his desk, looked up and called for a number, and:

"Hullo—hullo! Are you the police station? . . . Right . . . Stanniland, Sapor House, Cathedral Close, speaking—Got that? . . . Right—Are you the Superintendent? . . . Good—Will you come round to me at once, please? Something seems to be wrong next door. . . . What's that? . . . Yes—the Deanery. Thanks."

Within ten minutes Superintendent Walters was shown into the room. Stanniland began explanations at once.

"This is Miss Lake, Superintendent, the Dean's

niece. She tells me her uncle was to leave his house at half-past six this morning, and that no one would be in it after that hour. She, herself, is not living there."

" That's right, sir. And my men have orders to keep an eye on the house."

" I heard the taxi go by, at about half-past six."

" Certainly you would. I happened to be at the station myself and saw the Dean getting out of it. As a matter of fact I spoke to him. What is wrong ? "

" A few minutes before seven—mark the hour, Superintendent —I saw a man come out of the side door at the Deanery, lock it after him, and go down the garden and the little path that looks as if it led to a gate through the wall.

" The Dickens you did, sir ! " Out came his notebook. " Can you describe him ? "

" Rather tall, stooped a little, was wearing an overcoat with the collar turned up and a cloth cap. I couldn't see his face. He carried a small Gladstone bag and an umbrella."

" Oh ! Was he a burglar, do you think ? asked Peggy. " Oughtn't we to see—— "

" You haven't a key of the house, miss ? "

She shook her head.

" Never mind. We can manage to get in, if we want to, I dare say. Tell me, miss. Who was in the house with your uncle last night ? "

" Only the housekeeper. She was to leave at six —before he went."

He was jotting down notes in his book.

" I see. When did the other servants leave ? "

" Peters the butler and Fanny left on Saturday afternoon. I was there."

He looked at her keenly.

" When were *you* last in the house ? "

" Then—Saturday. I had tea with uncle and left soon afterwards."

" Have you seen your uncle since ? "

" Only at a distance—yesterday—in the Cathedral."

" Was he expecting anyone—any visitor ? "

" I'm quite sure he wasn't."

" And from Saturday afternoon till this morning only the housekeeper—her name ? "

" Mrs. Blake "

Only Mrs. Blake was with him ? "

" Yes."

The Superintendent sucked his pencil and pondered in silence. Slowly, very slowly, his lips began to twitch a little. He was almost smiling. Suddenly he asked :

" Mrs. Blake spends most of her time in the kitchen ? "

" Of course," replied Peggy, wondering what he meant.

" I know the Deanery. The kitchen is right at the back. Yes ! Well," and he shut his notebook with a snap and put it in his pocket. " Thank you very much, Mr. Stanniland. I'll set inquiries on foot about this individual at once. Meanwhile, we'll have a look at the house. I'll send round one of my sergeants now. He's a demon at picking locks. You can go over the house with him if you like, miss. I'll tell him to call here first."

" Stanton," he said, to that worthy sergeant on his return to the police station. " I want you to go to the Deanery at once. Call at Mr. Stanniland's—you know ? Right !—first, and you'll find the Dean's niece there. Take her with you. You'll have to pick a lock or force a window, I'll leave it to you. What I want you to notice is whether there are any signs of burglary, though I don't fancy you'll find any "—he gave a little chuckle—" but be particular to observe how many bedrooms were occupied last night. Yes, and don't mention this to Miss Lake. Best keep her out of the bedrooms. Poor girl," he added to himself.

Then he soliloquized :

" Gateway to South Fields—yes—plenty of chances to get away."

And spent the next quarter of an hour at the telephone, with the result that, by the time Sergeant Stanton had returned, there was some little police activity in the district around Frattenbury, one result of which was that constables set forth immediately to make inquiries at railway stations within ten miles of the city, both on the up and down line.

Very soon the sergeant came back and made his report :

" No signs of burglary, sir."

" Ah ! Anything else ? What about the bedrooms ? "

" The Dean's, of course, had been occupied. So had the housekeeper's. And, in one of the spare bedrooms—— "

" Yes ? "

" The bed had been slept in, sir. Someone had tried to make it look as if it hadn't, but it wasn't anyone accustomed to making beds. Also the basin had been used and there was tobacco ash on the carpet and dressing-table."

" Miss Lake didn't notice this ? "

"No sir. I took care she shouldn't."

When the sergeant had gone out Superintendent Walters gave a long, low chuckle.

"That's it!" he ejaculated. "His brother came, and he hid him, and helped him to get away. Clever, Mr. Dean, oh, clever! I'll not let it out—there's no need for that. Hang it! I'd have done the same if it had been my brother. And the Dean knew it. Good old boy! But we'll have to get that brother of his, all the same. And by gad we will—*now!*"

CHAPTER IX

THE man who presented the left luggage voucher at the Charing Cross cloak-room and marched with assurance through the barrier to the departure platform looked, in every respect, a cleric, in spite of his grey suit. The spectacles he was wearing lent dignity to his gravely composed, clean-shaven face. True, it was the first time he had even played this particular rôle, but in a life that would not have borne much investigation, he had been accustomed to play many parts, and had always got those parts with care, not omitting those little details which are really essential.

Thus, the papers he held in his hand included the *Church Times*, a periodical quite new to him. The porter who carried his suit-cases had glanced at the legend imprinted on one of them, and expected a corresponding tip. He got it. Unlike Edward Lake, who had hidden the inscription when he placed the suit-case on the carriage rack, this man deposited it on the seat beside him, apparently carelessly, but, all the same, those words, " The Dean of Frattenbury," were apparent to his three fellow passengers, who were, accordingly, impressed.

They had also been apparent to a man who lounged about at the entrance of the barrier, seemingly waiting for someone. And he was the same man who had observed Edward Lake over the edge of his newspaper a few hours before. This time he made no move, but only smiled. In his pocket-book he had a brief note—issued that very morning—about the Dean of Frattenbury.

On board the *Sunflower* he discovered, with much satisfaction, that he had a cabin to himself. He asked for a list of his fellow passengers, and, in the privacy of his cabin, made a careful study of them. He knew there was a certain amount of risk, and had to be prepared. Someone out of those passengers might know the Dean of Frattenbury. One name he marked: "The Rev. W. E. Crossland." Clerics were to be dealt with cautiously. Best to avoid them if possible.

He knew that, to begin with, there was not very much danger. It takes a little time for passengers to settle themselves to their surroundings before they begin to form acquaintances or to be inquisitive about each other. So he had no scruples about taking his place in the saloon at dinner that evening. The sea was smooth, no one had been attacked with sickness, and they were all there.

He was all there, too. Before he retired to his cabin that night he had pretty well picked them out. Crossland he had soon noticed. Quite a young man, evidently a curate.

In his cabin he mixed himself a stiff whisky and water—he had brought his own bottle—and then proceeded to unpack his luggage. Edward Lake had given him the key of the first suit-case, the other he managed to force open. It was the contents of the latter that made him smile.

"Hullo!" he said. "Here's a lot of queer togs!

The whole caboodle, buckled shoes and all. I shall have to dress up in 'em some time or other and impress the natives. Books, eh? Precious dry stuff, too."

He glanced at the half-dozen or so books the Dean had selected for holiday study, mostly on Liturgiology. One of them was his own book, a new edition of which he was preparing, *A Study of Some Minor Eastern Liturgies.*

Then, as he went on unpacking, something far more interesting caught his eye—the Dean's cheque-book. He took it up, and studied the counterfoils where cheques had been torn off. Then he lighted his pipe and thought. The man was desperately hard up. It was true that he had enough on him for petty expenses during the voyage, till the return of the boat to England. But then, he had no intention of returning to England at all.

That put him in mind of something else. The Dean had provided himself with a passport, which he had given to his brother with the tickets. He looked over it carefully and saw that, though Edward Lake might have passed the description, there were a few little touches needed for himself—and even then it might be a risk. There was the portrait, of course, but like many of the minute photographs taken for passports, it was not a very good one.

He set to work at once. He did not alter himself with make-up; with the blade of his penknife he delicately erased one or two figures on the passport and re-inserted others with his fountain-pen. He managed to manipulate the rather thinly defined eyebrows on the photograph till they resembled his own thick ones, looked in the glass, looked at the photograph, and folded up the passport.

" It'll do, I think."

Once more he caught sight of that cheque-book. And he wanted money badly. Then he hastily went through all the papers, but they were only blank writing-pads and a notebook or two containing jottings on Liturgiology. The Dean's signature was nowhere.

" Never mind," he said. " I've got the cheque-book—and it may be useful."

So he finished his drink and turned in. And slept soundly.

Seated in a deck-chair the next morning he received a slight shock. Even then he had studied details. The *Church Times* lay on his knees, and he was apparently reading " The Ambrosian Rite." A military-looking man, with stubbly moustache, had brought a chair quite close to him. And the Rev. W. E. Crossland was standing near, engaged in doing nothing.

He had laid down his book for a moment when the military man, who he was aware was looking at him with some interest, said :

" Excuse me, you're Lake, aren't you ? I saw your name on the list, and I noticed your bag when it came on board."

He turned.

" Yes, that's right."

" Don't you remember me ? "

He adjusted his spectacles and looked at the other.

" Yes, your face seems familiar ; yet, somehow—— "

" I'm Heath. We were together at Winchester, you know."

" Why, of *course*," and he reached out his hand. " But it must be a long time since we met."

" It is. Three or four years before the war. were staying together at Hazell's place. Bı shouldn't have recognized you, only the ste pointed you out when I asked which was Lake, your bag had given you away."

The other laughed.

" They tell me I've altered a little. I had illness ten years ago."

" Sorry. I say, what's become of Hazell ? "

" I *did* hear," said the other, reflectively, " bı has quite passed out of my mind."

The other bombarded him with questions reminiscences. For a time he cleverly evaded tl then sought defence by drawing the young clergy into the conversation. The latter was delighted. appreciated being spoken to by a dignitary, tried to return the compliment with a wee touc flattery.

" I should like to thank you for one of your b I've read *English Mediæval Uses* with much int I'm rather keen on the subject."

The " Dean " saw a further complication—a means for retreat :

" Have you read my book on "—by an effo memory he got it—" *Minor Eastern Liturgies* ? "

" No, but I hope to do so."

" I'll get it for you."

Hastily he got up and went to his cabin, retuı with the book and receiving effusive thanks Crossland. But he did not stay."

" Cute move that," he chuckled to himsel he went below once more, " proof positive I'm O.K."

General Heath had stared after him as he wer

" Lake *has* altered," he murmured. " Excuse me," he said, suddenly, to the curate, " may I just have a look at that book ? "

" Certainly."

The General opened it at the title-page. It was signed " E. Lake." Had the deceiver only thought to look, he would have discovered what he wanted. The other books had a printed book-plate in them, and were useless for his purpose. But he did not know he had parted from the only signature of the Dean.

" Yes," mused the General, " that's his writing—not so much altered as himself."

Meanwhile the episode had set Corney's mind at work. He had originally determined to remain on the *Sunflower* as long as possible. It was a very safe retreat. But he feared too much of General Heath's companionship. The weather favoured him. The wind had risen a bit and there was motion. He developed sea-sickness badly, and had to remain in his cabin. Yet the steward was surprised at the choice and quantity of his food. He only appeared on deck again when the *Sunflower* was steaming up the brown, muddy waters of the Garonne, just before Bordeaux was reached. He had his suit-cases ready packed, and it was an easy matter to slip ashore as soon as they were moored at the quay. To the steward, who met him coming out of the cabin, he calmly said he was visiting friends, and would rejoin at Marseilles, travelling overland. Might his cabin be reserved, please !

He put up at an hotel. As yet he had no fixed plan. But he wanted money still more badly. He had to pay for his board and lodging now. Once get hold of a decent round sum and he could get along for a bit. But he had to find someone first who had a sum, and then he had to get it from him.

Even churches must be infested with imps of mischief at times, for it was in the Cathedrale Saint André that such an imp brought about the meeting, on the day after he arrived. He had certainly not entered the sacred edifice for a religious purpose. The afternoon was hot, he had strolled about till he was weary, and he went in to rest and cool himself. He sat down in a chair—and fell asleep.

" Monsieur ! "

He started. The beadle, in all the glory of uniform, cocked hat, sword by side, had tapped him on the shoulder.

" Eh ? What is it ? "

" C'est cinque heures, monsieur. Il fait que je ferme l'église, maintenant."

He spoke rapidly, and the other's French was rocky at the best.

" Eh—what ? " he said again.

" He is sorry to interrupt your devotions, sir, but it's tea-time. That's the gist of his remarks so far as I understand him. He politely requests us to go forth into the wicked world again."

Corney looked round. Standing by his side was a tall, thin man, with clean-shaven face, merry grey eyes, humorous-looking mouth, and pointed chin. Corney at once observed that he was very well dressed. Somehow, he looked opulent.

" Oh, I see. Thank you." And he got up from his seat.

The stranger turned to the beadle, bowed politely, shrugged his shoulders very much *à la français*, and said, with great gravity :

"Voilà, mon ami! Il va. N'est-ce pas? Bon! Fermez la porte, donc. Avez, vous vu la montre de mon oncle? Non! C'est t-r-r-rès grande! Bon soir!"

The beadle looked after him with astonishment as he walked down the nave after the other. He overtook him at the door.

"Thus," he said, "are we expelled from this cool paradise. The angel with the sword was relentless. You are a stranger here?"

"I am."

"So am I. And we're both staying at the same hotel, apparently. I saw you at dinner last evening. I remarked just now that it was tea-time, but, being in France, coffee would be preferable. Shall we go and have some?"

Corney stole a glance at the other. And made up his mind.

"I don't mind if I do," he said. "To tell you the truth I was feeling a bit lonesome."

"So was I. Come along."

They reached a café, took seats outside; the stranger ordered coffee, handed his cigar-case to Corney, and lighted one himself. Then he looked at Corney, who was wearing a soft collar and tie.

"You had a dog collar on last night, I noticed. Parson, eh?"

Corney nodded.

"On a holiday?"

"Yes."

The other smiled. There was a wicked twinkle in his eye. Perhaps he thought a parson was fair game.

"So am I. I *had* to take a holiday—no choice. I've just got over a bad breakdown."

"You don't look ill."

" Not that sort of thing. I've been off my head."

" Off your head ? "

The other nodded.

" That's right," he said, quite cheerfully. " Overwork. More stuffed inside my old brain-box than it would hold. So, as I say, I went quite off my head. Had to have keepers—friends were very nice and called 'em attendants. But *I* knew ! "

He took his cigar from his mouth and blew a long cloud of smoke with the air of a man who gives way to pleasant reminiscences. Then he went on :

" I *was* mad—just about. Did the most extraordinary things. And I'm not right yet," he added, complacently, as he leaned back in his chair and replaced his cigar in his mouth."

Corney looked at him, not quite knowing what to say. But feeling that if this strange individual was speaking the truth, it might be worth while making a close acquaintance. Then he said :

" Oh, I hope you're not so bad as that. You are exaggerating, surely.

" Fact ! " said the stranger, pleasantly. " They've let me loose on my own before I was quite fit. I was never certified, you know. I managed to deceive 'em, and they thought I was all right again," he chuckled. " But don't you worry. I haven't any homicidal tendencies, I assure you. And I'm only queer now and then. By the way, here's my card. I'm a stockbroker. Who are you ? "

Corney took the card and read :

MR. W. GUY MARSDEN.

" I'm sorry I haven't mine on me. I'm—I'm the Dean of Frattenbury."

"Good Lord! Where's your apron? I say, what am I to call you? I can't go on saying 'Very Reverend Dean of Frattenbury' whenever I speak to you. What's your name? You've got one, I suppose, even if you've lost your apron."

"My name is Lake."

"Right! Where's that waiter? Garçon! How much? Combien? Quel domage? Bon! Attendez! Voilà!"

Corney's keen eye marked the pocket-book from which Marsden extracted a note. It was stuffed with them—heavily. They strolled back to their hotel. It was Corney who suggested that they should share a table between them. Marsden readily agreed.

"And if I do anything queer you can be my keeper," he said.

Corney, bent on making an impression, unpacked the leather suit-case. He swore under his breath as he struggled into that peculiar short cassock known vulgarly as an apron, and tried to adjust the sash round it. But when he regarded the result in the glass and put on his spectacles, he grinned hugely. For he really looked the part.

Marsden, clad in faultless dress clothes, greeted him at the table:

"Oh, my eye! Gorgeous! Now you really look like a dean. Do you tie your apron on with strings behind? It's a mystery I've always wanted to solve. You're positively overpowering. Make me feel quite sane. And I'm *not!*"

"What shall we do after dinner?" he asked, as the meal went on.

A little smile hovered for a moment on the face of the dignitary. He knew exactly what he would like to do. A music-hall or a casino. But he had to play his rôle.

"What could we do?"

Marsden put his elbows on the table and his chin in his hands, looked across at the other, and said, quite gravely:

"We *could* paint this bally old town red. *I* feel like that. But I don't suppose you'd care for it."

"I don't understand," replied Corney, quite as gravely.

"You wouldn't. We'll go for a stroll, and if *I* try any process of ruby colouring you can come back and read the *Sunday at Home*. I say, where had you thought of going on to from Bordeaux?"

"I really have no fixed plans. What are you going to do?"

"I'm going to Arcachon to-morrow. Come with me."

It was not policy to give in at once, so Corney asked:

"What are the attractions there?"

"Red trousers," replied Marsden, with great solemnity.

"Red trousers?"

"It's quite true. They wear 'em there. I shall get a pair. So shall you. We *must* go to Arcachon and walk about in red trousers. There are also oysters—and a casino. So we will go to Arcachon to-morrow."

"I don't know about the trousers or the casino," said the other, with a laugh, "but if you really don't mind my company I shall be pleased to go with you."

"Delighted. Garçon!"

"Oui, monsieur?"

" A quelle heure va une train à l'Arcachon demain matin ? "

" À dix heures et demi, monsieur."

" Bien ! Y a-t-il des huîtres et des pantalons rouges là, n'est-ce pas ? "

" Mais oui, monsieur," replied the waiter, with a smile. He was getting accustomed to Marsden's vagaries.

" Savez-vous le Monsieur Pierre Gray ? "

The man shook his head.

" Monsieur Pierre Gray est un homme qui a mangé souvent les huîtres, mais il n'a jamais en assez. Si vous voyez Monsieur Gray ici, l'envoyez à l'Arcachon ! "

And the waiter, who had never heard of the *Bab Ballads*, bowed politely, and replied :

" Mais oui, monsieur. Certainement ! "

CHAPTER X

CANON and Mrs. Burford were entertaining friends to tea. The Canon in Residence was a stout, good-humoured looking man, with a round face, pale grey eyes, hair slightly thin at the top, and a rich, rather unctuous voice. Mrs. Burford was thin, and somewhat angular in appearance.

The house appertaining to the Canon in Residence was a very charming one, situated, of course, in the Close, and next door to Sapor House, which stood between it and the Deanery.

Seated in the drawing-room were an assortment of the elect denizens of the Close, with two or three guests who lived in Frattenbury, it is true, but who were not inhabitants of the sacred precincts. The distinction had once been very nicely put by Miss Marshall, sister of a former Archdeacon, who, at that moment was receiving a minute wafer of buttered bread from Canon Burford. Once, when away from home, she had been asked by someone she had met:

" I believe you live in Frattenbury, Miss Marshall ? "

To which she had replied:

" Not exactly *in* Frattenbury. We live in the Close. There is a difference, you know.

Hartley Norgrove, one of the Minor Canons, was there, with his charming wife. The Misses Prudence, Alethea, and Monica Brand, daughters of an erstwhile

Cathedral dignitary, who had lived in the Close since anyone could remember, and who, from the clatter and fuss which they made when hurrying into the Cathedral for service—they always hurried—at the last moment, were known as " Battle, Murder, and Sudden Death," sat in a row on a sofa. They always sat in a row. Unkind persons said they quarrelled about precedence among themselves. Certainly they had had a special conveyance made for them, a sort of low, broad vehicle founded on the dogcart plan, but without a back seat, and when they took their drives abroad behind their slow-trotting nag, they still sat, all three in a row.

" Outsiders " were old Major Wingrave, a widower, in whose company it was considered tactful to keep off the subject of India, for when he began to hold forth on it he never ceased, and Miss Marshall's nephew, Donald Quarrington, a young man preparing for Orders at the Frattenbury Theological College.

" How is the Restoration Fund progressing ? asked Alethea Brand, speaking across the room to Canon Burford.

" Oh, we haven't received many results, so far. But we live in hopes. We are busy just now sending out the new appeal. We drew it up at our last Chapter meeting, just before the Dean left for his holiday."

" Where has the Dean gone ? " asked Miss Marshall.

" Round the Mediterranean," replied Mrs. Burford, as she poured out tea ; " hadn't you heard ? I hope he's getting better weather for his trip than we are. Such a pity that thunderstorm seems to have broken up the fine spell we were enjoying."

" He looked as if he needed a holiday," remarked Mrs. Norgrove.

"He did—badly," said Canon Burford, "he had not had one for a long time, I believe. And he has found it a little onerous getting into the work here."

He said it with all the complacency of one who had had some years' experience of the work, and considered it onerous himself—though now an adept.

"But I don't imagine he *has* gone round the Mediterranean after all," broke in Major Wingrave, who was standing before the fireplace, legs a little apart, stirring his tea.

"Oh, really!" "Why?" "What makes you say so, Major?" came in chorus.

The Major cleared his throat, a usual preliminary to declamation.

"I had a line only this morning from an old friend of mine, a General Heath. He was with me in the North West provinces years ago. Good sort! He wrote from Bordeaux, and mentioned that he had come across the Dean. He's taking the trip himself—Heath is."

"Yes?"

"Met him on the boat—was at Winchester with him, you know. He didn't see much of him, but thought him very much altered. Well, the boat seems to have put into Bordeaux for twenty-four hours, and he says the Dean left it there. Saw him go ashore with his luggage."

"Indeed!" said Canon Burford, "you surprise me, Major. He distinctly told me he was going the round trip."

"Ah! Perhaps the Bay put him off. It can be nasty, if one isn't a good sailor. I remember coming back from India once—autumn of '82——"

The conversation became general again; presently, in a pause, the Canon said to his wife:

"I thought you said Miss Lake was coming?"

Mrs. Burford glanced at the clock on the mantel-piece.

"Yes—she is. But she can't get away till five. She works till then. She'll be here directly."

"Are you speaking of the Dean's niece?" asked Miss Prudence Brand.

"Yes," replied Mrs. Burford.

"Tell me, dear. *Is* it true what we heard the other day? We all refuse to believe it, of course—but *is* it true that the Dean's niece is employed as house-keeper or something by that horrid man who has bought The Chantry and given it such an odious name?"

"Not as his housekeeper," said Canon Burford, with a laugh, "not so bad as that, Miss Brand. But, yes, it's quite true that she is working for him, as his secretary, I believe."

The three Miss Brands simultaneously gave vent to a little exclamation of horror.

"We *couldn't* believe it when we heard it," said Monica, "though we know she is an erratic sort of girl. But she ought to have considered her uncle's position here. Who *is* this awful man, Canon? Everyone in the Close is perfectly disgusted with him for buying the Chantry over the heads of the Dean and Chapter. And quite right?"

"Who is he?" repeated the Canon, with his bland smile. "Well, we hardly know. Though there's a distinct point in his favour. The Dean called upon him before he left and found he was related to the Bishop of Redminster—cousin, I think he said."

"Oh!" said the three Miss Brands and Miss Marshall. "Oh, *really?*"

And one of them added:

"Then I—I suppose you will call, Canon?"

"Oh, I think so. In fact, after what the Dean said, I told him I would. The Dean asked me to see that he had a copy of our 'Appeal.' He asked for one."

"Oh, *did* he?" remarked Prudence Brand. "Well, we must hope——"

"But they say he is a chemist!" interrupted Alethea, "and who ever heard of a chemist living in the Close? I——"

But as she was speaking the door opened and the maid announced:

"Miss Lake."

And Donald Quarrington, who was bored stiff, but had to be present by reason of his aunt and also of the fact that tea with the Canon in Residence was part of the preparation for his career, glanced up at Peggy as she came into the room, and a look of admiration leaped into his eyes as they lingered on her pretty, animated face.

"So sorry, I'm afraid I'm late."

"Come along," said Mrs. Burford, cheerfully, "your tea is all ready. Charles, get Miss Lake something to eat."

But Donald Quarrington had forestalled him. He had jumped to his feet and was handing her bread and butter. And Miss Marshall watched him narrowly. As his aunt, she considered it her duty to keep an eye on him during his sojourn at the Theological College. Though he avoided her as much as possible.

Mrs. Burford introduced Donald, and then said:

"We were just speaking about—Mr. Stanniland; that is his name, isn't it?"

"Yes?" replied Peggy, demurely. "I heard someone mention a chemist as I came in. He *is* a chemist, you know."

Alethea Brand bent her head and coloured. The Canon, smiling pleasantly—he knew well how to smooth matters over, even if he was a little annoyed at Peggy's sarcasm—said:

"Yes, and a very able one, I hear. I'm told he has installed a laboratory for research work next door."

Conversation became general again. Major Wingrave had managed to corner the Minor Canon and was indulging himself—not the Canon—in a long reminiscence of India. The Canon in Residence was explaining to the audience of three on the sofa the work which had to be done to the Cathedral. Presently Mrs. Burford said to Peggy:

"Have you heard from the Dean since he left?"

"No, he hasn't written."

"Oh, then probably you don't know that he seems to have altered his plans."

"Altered his plans, Mrs. Burford, what do you mean?"

"Major Wingrave has just been telling us that he heard to-day from a friend who was on board the same boat as your uncle. He says the Dean got off at Bordeaux."

"Really? I can't understand that at all. He was so much looking forward to the voyage round the Mediterranean."

"Very likely you'll hear from him soon, and he'll explain. Tell me, do you like your new post?"

There was a certain amount of pumping about Mrs. Burford's questions, but Peggy stood the attack quite well. Presently a move was made. The Misses Brand arose simultaneously from the sofa, said good-bye, and departed. Donald Quarrington managed to elude his aunt, come out into the hall when Peggy left, and joined her walking down the drive.

"I say," he ejaculated, "weren't you fed up with all that crowd? I was. Precious slow, eh?"

"*Rather* dull," replied the girl. "Why did you come?"

"Oh, you see, I'm up at the College here, and my aunt—Miss Marshall, you know—lives in the Close I have to do this sort of thing sometimes. Which way are you going?"

"Back to my diggings. I hang out in the South Street."

"But the Dean's your uncle, isn't he? I suppose you live in the stately edifice—pointing to the Deanery—" yonder, when he's at home."

"Indeed I don't. I only come on a short visit to him a few weeks ago."

"Where's your home, then."

She laughed.

"I haven't got one," she replied, "I'm accustomed to being on my own. You see, I'm one of those people who have to earn their living."

"Oh, yes, I remember. One of those old cats sitting on the sofa was talking about you. Seemed to think you were jolly well letting your uncle down by acting as secretary to that awful man next door, as she called him. I say, you got one back nicely on the gossipping crew when you said you'd heard 'em talking about a chemist. I nearly laughed."

"Well, it's no business of theirs," said Peggy.

"Rather not. I say, doesn't the chap they were talking about drive a ripping little two-seater? I saw a fellow coming out of that house in one."

"Yes. I drive it sometimes, Mr. Quarrington. I look after it for him."

"No! I wish you'd take me for a run."

She smiled. He was getting on.

"You must qualify as one of Mr. Stanniland's business friends first. They are the only people I am allowed to drive about, she replied. "Now I must say good-bye, for I live here. Thanks for seeing me home."

"I hope we shall meet again, Miss Lake."

"We very likely may—at another tea fight," she said, opening the door.

"Oh, look here, I didn't mean that—— " he began, but she had passed inside.

* * * * *

"My husband starts on his little annual holiday to-morrow, Miss," announced Mrs. Finch, as she laid the cloth for Peggy's supper. "He's rather late in going this year, because of the Dean."

"Why?"

"Well, you see miss, Finch, he don't like bein' away all the time the Dean's in residence. Especially a new Dean, beggin' your pardon, miss, one as isn't altogether used to the job, so to speak. Finch is very particular, and don't like to leave things to others. He generally takes his little holicay when the Dean's on his."

"And are you going too?"

"Lord bless you, miss, I can't get away. I have

to do the baking when Finch goes. It's very rare as we gets away together."

"Where's he going to?"

"Well, miss, Finch do like variety when he goes away. He don't fancy staying in one place all the time. He likes a little tower, so to speak. He's thinking of taking a steamer from Southampton to Plymouth, and then he don't quite know what he shall do. But he generally tries to visit a cathedral or two if he can."

"I see—he wants to learn something?"

"To *learn* something, miss? Oh no! Finch ain't a man as thinks he can learn anything in that way. But he likes to see how things are done in other places and finds a satisfaction in criticizing them. Supper's ready, miss."

"All right. I'm just going over to the post office first before it closes."

"It'll get cold, miss."

"I'll be back in a minute. That's all right."

The post office was opposite. Coming out of it she met Superintendent Walters going in. He saluted her, but was not going to speak till she stopped him.

"Oh, have you ever found out anything about that man, coming out of my uncle's house that morning?"

He hesitated a little. It was an awkward question.

"Not very much," he replied. "We traced him to Fernley Station, where he took train. Then we lost sight of him."

"Who *was* he, do you think?"

"I can't say. Though we are pretty well sure he was not a burglar. The Dean may be able to explain when he returns."

" Are you still after him."

" Well—er—we like to satisfy ourselves, Miss Lake. But, as I say, we've lost trace of him for the time being. Good evening, miss."

" All the same," he said to himself, with a chuckle as he entered the post office, " I expect we shall be able to lay our hands on him, even if he has given us the slip to begin with. He's gone to the West, I feel certain. It will take a bit of a rise out of the Scotland Yard men if we provincials succeed in locating one of the Melford & Co. lot before they get a line on Corney ! "

CHAPTER XI

THE Superintendent's surmise about the Dean's westward trip was correct, but it was a conclusion to which he had only come after several days had elapsed. As a matter of fact, the Dean, quite innocently, had effectually covered his traces for the time being. Quite as astutely as if he had planned to do so. On his arrival at Southampton he had at once made for a restaurant, to partake of a tardy breakfast. The ticket collector, on being questioned by the police, produced a single ticket from Fernley and, vaguely, recollected the man who had given it up. Whereupon both stations were watched, and Waterloo communicated with in case the quarry was making his way back to London. Also, all outgoing boats and the steamers to Cowes and Ryde.

But it was by none of these routes that he took his journey. On coming out of the restaurant he noticed a large charabanc, with a board on it advertising " Day trip to Bournemouth through the New Forest," taking in passengers. A sudden thought struck him. The day was a fine one, he had never been in the New Forest, and, in his troubled state of mind, a ride through the open country appealed to him more than a stuffy railway compartment. There was a vacant seat and he took it.

And, for the first time in his life, the Dean of

Frattenbury found himself a nonentity among a crowd of trippers.

Also, he began to enjoy it. After all, he was on a holiday, even if the holiday was different to that which he had planned. And he had done no harm. The more he thought it over the more he came to the satisfying conclusion that if he was being the means of clearing his brother from an incriminating charge and escaping from an unpleasant prosecution, the somewhat drastic measures he had taken to do so were justifiable.

The only thing for him to do just now was quietly to keep in retirement for the next few weeks, and that ought to be both easy and innocent. He must try to find some secluded spot where he could spend his holiday in peace. He would purchase writing materials and fill in his spare time with his hobby. It was not so bad, after all.

It was just then that he overheard the conversation of two men who sat next to him on the seat of the charabanc, two decent-looking, middle-aged men who were discussing holiday resorts.

" Yes," remarked one, " what you say is quite right. Charming little places on the coast that were practically unknown only a few years ago, are crowded out now. Bungalows and bathing-huts everywhere."

" Look at the bit we're coming to," replied the other. " Houses practically from Barton to Poole. If you want to get away from trippers just now you must go to some out-of-the-way spot in Cornwall or North Devon. And, even then, you won't escape them."

" Or South Devon, said his friend; " I know one little place there that isn't spoilt yet—though they have begun to build a bit."

"Where's that?"

"East Porthmouth. I was there last year. Good fishing and boating, and you can wear old clothes in peace. Hardly any trippers. And it's a beauty spot."

"Excuse me," broke in the Dean, "but I could not help overhearing you. I am on the look-out for a quiet place for a restful holiday. Where is East Porthmouth?"

"Just opposite Salcombe. Salcombe itself is not bad—too out of the way for cheap trips. But East Porthmouth is really delightful, if you want sea and country and quiet."

"How does one get there?"

"Train to Kingsbridge, via Brent Junction. At Kingsbridge you can take coach to Salcombe and cross the ferry to Porthmouth. Or, if you prefer it, the boat from Kingsbridge to Salcombe touches at Porthmouth before it crosses the estuary."

"Can one get rooms there; I mean is there any difficulty?"

"I should think not, this time of year. The season is practically over. I should think you would easily get rooms. Do you mind quite simple ones?" he added, looking at the Dean a little intently, for, in spite of his rather ordinary, lay appearance, his voice was dignified and his face and bearing that of a distinctly superior person.

"Not at all. In fact, I should prefer them."

"I was quite comfortable last year there. I'll give you the address if you like."

"It's exceedingly kind of you. Thank you very much."

On the evening of the following day the Dean

stepped off the boat that plies between Kingsbridge and Salcombe on to the tiny little landing-place at East Porthmouth, half hidden in the trees, which grow close to the water's edge, and asked his way to the address, which had been given him. He found it, a small cottage on the rising ground opposite the little town of Salcombe.

Fortunately the rooms proved to be vacant. They were very small, plainly furnished, but scrupulously clean. And the price was quite moderate. The landlady told him her husband was a fisherman and suggested fish for supper. As he sat over the meal, looking out of the window at the beautiful harbour and the quaint little town straggling up the opposite hills, a scene that is reminiscent of an Italian setting, he found himself murmuring a verse from a Psalm :

The lines have fallen unto me in pleasant places.

And supper over, he strolled out, lighted his pipe, and felt at rest with himself and his surroundings. Here was an ideal spot where he could remain in seclusion until such time as his brother's innocence was established.

He might not have felt so secure in his retreat, however, had he known that those very busy people whose official uniform is dark blue and who often seem so stolid were, in their patient way, still endeavouring to follow up the track of the man who had given up a ticket from Fernley to Southampton the previous morning. Scotland Yard knows how to bide its time, and Scotland Yard just then, though baffled for the moment, was particularly anxious to achieve the capture of Corney and his subordinates. And it is not wise to imagine that because Scotland

Yard does not always act at the moment that it forgets.

The next morning he crossed by the ferry to Salcombe. He wanted to lay in a stock of writing materials. He was still a little apprehensive lest he should meet anyone he knew, some chance visitor of his acquaintance who might be spending a holiday there. He wore a soft collar and black tie, but then, like many clergy, he generally discarded the clerical collar when on holiday. And, to the landlady, he had given his name as "Dr. Lake," which, of course, was the truth. But, as he made his way along the narrow "Fore Street," the main thoroughfare of Salcombe, he felt that he attracted no particular attention. It was the tail end of the season, and not many people were about. So he made his purchases, including a daily paper.

Waiting for the ferry boat on the little quay, he scanned the paper. His face lightened with interest as he caught sight of the heading:

RESTORATION OF FRATTENBURY CATHEDRAL.

THE NORTH-WEST TOWER IN DANGER.

FRESH APPEAL FROM THE DEAN AND CHAPTER.

It was a sympathetic announcement which followed, a bit of well-worded journalism about "our venerable cathedrals," "historical associations," "an appeal which we trust will meet with a generous response."

And the concluding paragraph was pleasingly flattering:

The Dean of Frattenbury has thrown himself into the task of raising funds with that thoroughness which we should have expected of him by a study of his comprehensive works on Liturgiology. We imagine, from its style, that the wording of the appeal is a product of his facile pen and that it should do much to increase the interest of Church people in the restoration of one of the most beautiful of our English cathedrals.

Just underneath, for the whole column was devoted to "Ecclesiastical Intelligence," was the announcement:

The Dean of Frattenbury is away on holiday. He was among the passengers on the s.s. *Sunflower* which sailed from Folkestone on Monday afternoon for a Mediterranean cruise.

If the first announcement had brought a look of pleasure to the face of the Dean, the second quickly dispelled it. He frowned, and shook his head a little.

"Dear, dear!" he murmured to himself. "This is very annoying. Edward promised me faithfully that he would not attempt to pose as me. I wish he would be more careful. Perhaps, though, I may be blaming him unjustly—someone else may have known I was going, and—really, these newspaper people are too inquisitive! I hope nothing wrong will come o it. Most annoying!"

He looked up from his paper and caught the eye of a man seated beside him who was occupied in a similar manner, but who had just laid down his newspaper to light his pipe, a man wearing white trousers and an old, but well-cut brown sports jacket, throat bare at the neck, for the turned-down collar of his shirt was thrown open; soft, old hat on the back of his head, and a sunburnt, resolute-looking countenance. The glance was one of those quick, mutual ones, which sometimes prelude an acquaintanceship.

Indeed, the stranger, having put his pipe into full blast, said :

" Fresh morning ! "

" Very," replied the Dean.

" Don't like the look of it, though. There's a storm working up, out there."

And he threw out his arm in the direction of the harbour entrance.

Remarks on the weather in general and the local aspect of it in particular, were exchanged, then the ferry boat came in and the two men found themselves the only passengers for the Porthmouth side. Half-way across, the stranger, shading his eyes with his hand, gazed earnestly at a little yawl rigged half-decker yacht which rode at her moorings in the harbour.

" Little beauty ! " he said.

The Dean followed his gaze.

" That boat ? Yes, she looks it. Who does she belong to ? "

" She's mine," said the other, with almost a caress in the tone of his voice.

" Indeed ? "

" Yes. Only bought her this season. She can walk away from most of 'em here."

" I'm told that this is a very good place for yachting ? "

" You can't beat it. I've been down here every summer since the war. It's my hobby, you see. We've got a little shanty up yonder, near the church," and he pointed up the steep hill on the Porthmouth side, " and I don't want any other kind of holiday. Do anything in the same line yourself ? "

"I can't say I do, though I'm exceedingly fond of boating. In my younger days I pulled an oar."

The other looked at him and summed him up, somehow, partially correctly.

"For your college?" he asked.

The Dean nodded.

"Ah! I never was much of a rowing man, but I can handle a tiller, I hope. Here we are."

The ferry boat ran her nose into the little landing-stage and they stepped ashore. Their way, to begin with, lay in the same direction, and they walked together. Then the storm, which had been blowing in from the open sea, suddenly broke and the rain came down in torrents. They were close by the Dean's lodgings. He hesitated a moment. He was not particularly anxious to risk a more intimate acquaintance, but his good nature and instinctive hospitality prevailed.

"These are my rooms," he said, "won't you take shelter till the storm is over?"

"Thanks, I don't mind if I do. It's a slow climb up the hill, and I stand a good chance of a soaking."

So they went into the tiny sitting-room and sat down.

"Nice little place," said the stranger, "and a good view. This your first visit here?

"Yes, I only came last evening."

"I think you'll like it."

The rain still fell heavily. Conversation turned on the day's news. The stranger pointed to his paper.

"I was reading just now about the restoration of Frattenbury Cathedral——"

"Do you know it?" broke in the Dean, hastily.

The other laughed.

" Never been there. Cathedrals are not in my line. I was going to say, though "—the Dean gave a little sigh of relief—" that I see they want ten thousand pounds. And ten thousand pounds would build a couple of dozen good houses for artisans. And the country's crying out for houses. Something wrong, eh ? "

The Dean was a little horror-struck, for he was not accustomed to be spoken to in this way. People do not, in polite society, speak in this way to deans when they know they are deans.

" But," he said, " you wouldn't have the Cathedral —er—fall down, would you ? Surely—— "

" Oh, I don't know," replied the other relighting his pipe. " It wouldn't matter to me if it did. And it wouldn't matter to the twenty-four families in those twenty-four houses I spoke of. Would it now ? "

" But my dear sir," expostulated the Dean, " a cathedral is of national importance."

" So are houses."

" Yes, but there's a difference."

" Quite so. People don't live in cathedrals."

" Of course not. But, by your argument you'd demolish the Tower of London and the British Museum, and use the stones to build a row of houses."

" Good, strong houses, too ! "

The Dean laughed. The humour of the discussion was appealing to him, as well as the good-natured, smiling face of his opponent.

" And you could take all the yachts in Salcombe Harbour and build a wooden house for a British workman. Not so strong, I admit; but when people are crying out for houses, why use timber for pleasure boats ? "

The other broke into a laugh.

" Got me there," he admitted, " but, look here : What's the use of a cathedral, anyhow ? "

" Do you know anything about cathedrals—from the inside ? "

" No, I don't.'

" And do you appreciate spiritual values ? "

The other shrugged his shoulders.

" No ? But, you see, there are people who do," went on the Dean quietly, and they have the idea, fortunately, I think, that there is something in ascribing glory to God by means of a beautiful building and its services."

" The glory of humanity is the glory of God. That's how it appears to me."

" And you will not find very much glory in humanity, I think, unless you keep the glory of God in due perspective as a living entity. And that is what, in a measure, a cathedral serves to do."

The other was silent for a moment. Then he said, with a return to his light laugh, and opening his newspaper :

" I'm a scoffer, I expect, but really, as a man who has knocked about the world, this made me smile. I'm going to drop my attack on sacred edifices and transfer it to Cathedral dignitaries. Look here : ' The Dean of Frattenbury has thrown himself into the task of raising funds with that thoroughness,' and so on. What has he really *done?* Written an appeal, it seems. Probably an hour's work. Now here's a man with very likely a couple of thousand a year—— "

" One moment," interrupted the Dean. " I happen

to know that the Deanery of Frattenbury is worth six hundred, and that it entails keeping up a large house."

"Oh, is that so?" He was wallowing in the ignorance of the average layman concerning clerical matters. "Well, at all events, what does he do to earn that? It's a jolly easy life, I fancy, being a dean."

"Not always, I imagine," replied the Dean, a twinkle in his eye. "There may be times when even a dean may find life—a little awkward."

"Oh, there are always the 'slings and arrows,' in every life, of course. But what I mean is, what on earth does a dean *do*—apart from writing appeals and getting a newspaper puff for doing so. Do you know?"

The Dean was silent for a moment. The corners of his lips were twitching. There was so much he would have liked to say. So much that he dared not say.

"Well," he replied, at length, "to a certain extent I can—er—imagine some of the things that he—er—probably does."

"Yes?"

"You might not understand easily. So often we are inclined to underrate, I suppose, other people's jobs which are not our own jobs. But, for example, this business of Cathedral Resoration, I can imagine,"—and he smiled in spite of himself—"many anxious hours and discussions with the architect, meetings of the Chapter, analysis of expert reports, consideration of tenders; in a way, the supervision of the work itself. In short, my dear sir, an amount of time and trouble that the manager of some business or factory would certainly not give in exchange for six hundred a year with the cost of the upkeep of his house deducted from it. You may not appreciate it, but then, *I* may not appreciate *your* work, whatever it is."

The other laughed once more.

"As a matter of fact," he said, "for the time being I haven't any work. I retired from the Stock Exchange three months ago."

"Ah! Then I *don't* appreciate your present position as—er—one of the unemployed——"

"But without the dole. Don't forget that."

"The dole of a lazy life—having nothing to do—stands a chance of bearing a comparison with the dole you speak of. And as to the Stock Exchange, well, I know nothing whatever about it, but I'm told that more than six hundred may be made in a few hours by opening one's mouth and entering transactions in a notebook. I may be wrong, of course."

"And it's quite as easy to lose that sum in a few hours," replied the other, with a grin.

"Yes?"

"When one takes a nasty risk."

"Ah! Well, I daresay even a dean takes nasty risks sometimes."

"Not often, I should say."

"Let us hope not," replied the other, fervently.

"Hullo!" ejaculated the stranger. "It's clearing up. I'll be off. Thanks for shelter and an argument. I always enjoy an argument. I hope we may meet again. My name's Hinton.

"And mine—Lake."

"All right. Would you like to come for a sail one day?"

The Dean hesitated. He had, in a way, brought

the acquaintanceship on himself by asking Hinton into his rooms. And, the argument ended, he felt he had been skating on thin ice in defending the Dean of Frattenbury! A little further talk on the subject of Cathedral Dignitaries and he might give himself away, which he was anxious not to do at this juncture. Yet he could not very well decline.

"Thank you very much."

"And look here, you're all alone in Porthmouth?"

"Yes."

"You must come up to my place and have a meal. My wife will be delighted to meet you."

"It's very kind of you."

"That's all right. Good morning!"

CHAPTER XII

When Julian Bruce Stanniland had told Peggy that there were times when he expected her to work like the devil, he had not spoken in vain. Not many days after she had taken up her post such a time commenced. And before it was over she had "Sapor Relish" on the brain.

For "Sapor Relish" was in evidence everywhere in Stanniland's establishment. The company had at length been formed and the public were being invited to subscribe.

There had been meetings of directors in London, consultations at Frattenbury, interviews with advertisement agents, the drawing up of circulars and prospectuses, negotiations with underwriters, correspondence here, there, and everywhere by letter, telegraph, and telephone, and all directed by the keen and alert brain of the untiring Stanniland.

For he was untiring. He did not seem to know what fatigue was. Peggy, when she arrived in the morning, would find him at his desk hard at it and, by the amount of correspondence instantly handed over to her, knew that he must have been hard at it for at least a couple of hours. When she departed, late in the evening, for these were days of "overtime," she would leave him at it still—alert and vigorous.

She felt the strain, naturally. But she also felt she was on her mettle. The psychological effect of the man was powerful and an incentive to activity. By an effort of will she conquered her somewhat lax and untidy temperament. She was punctual as the clock, her work became systemized in harmony with the systemizing methods of her employer. Not always easy, for Stanniland, in spite of his orderly methods, struck off at sudden tangents, tangents which, however, invariably converged again to the main line of action.

He would break off abruptly in the midst of dictating a letter to ask her to improve upon an advertisement, check the result, give a nod of approva when it was finished, dispatch it at once to his London office by special messenger. He would tell her to leave on an instant and run the car around on business. Once she drove frantically at his behest the sixty odd miles to the London office and back.

She never resented it. She began to take almost as keen an interest as himself in the placing of " Sapor." Besides, Stanniland was exercising a fascination, as far as she was concerned. She told herself she liked him. He did not hesitate to blame or criticize her work sharply if it was not up to his standard, but, on the other hand, he was equally frank with his praise. He was generous, too. She soon discovered that, with all his keenness for making money, he was no miser. If, in those days of stress, he kept her overtime, he paid her handsomely for it —and told her bluntly she was worth it. One or two local charities applied for donations. She handled the correspondence. It was not thrown in the waste-paper basket. Stanniland found a few minutes to make curt inquiries and, if satisfied, the cheque he sent was a liberal one. A beggar accosted him one day, came up to the door as he was standing there, and she saw him give him a Treasury note.

"I've been down and out myself," he said to her, as if in explanation.

He suggested, in those rushing days, that, to save time, she might lunch with him. She accepted. The meal, if of the "quick" variety of lunch, was always recherché, and he never allowed a word of business to be spoken during its consumption.

"Turn your brain off it, Miss Lake. I'll dock your salary if you mention 'Sapor' in the next half-hour."

At these times his attitude was exemplary and courteous. Instinctively she felt he was, at heart, a man of strict morality and good breeding. He never presumed, but always treated her as an equal, and was interesting. He would talk about his travels abroad, which had been extensive.

"I owe a great deal to knocking about the world. In China, for instance, I discovered the clue to 'Sapor'—eh? Of course. We won't name it. And in India, last year, I got hold of an idea from a native doctor . . . but, no. That's business. You shall hear about it when we've finished the job we've got on hand."

His "Thoughts and Flashes" received many entries in those days. Every morning at ten o'clock the page-boy would bring in the whole collection of them, culled from every portion of the house, and Stanniland would make an analysis of them.

Twice every week he went to his London office—sometimes oftener. And poured out streams of directions thitherward through the telephone when at home. He kept in touch with every detail.

Meanwhile, the laboratory rarely saw him. He explained this one day to Peggy.

" After this job's over I shall get back a bit to chemistry. That's my method. Things begin in the laboratory—that's science. Then they have to be placed—that's business. I'm placing now. Work before pleasure."

" You call chemistry your pleasure ? "

" I love it," he replied.

It was one afternoon about four o'clock, ten days or so after the Dean had left for his holiday. The clicking of Peggy's typewriter had stopped for some minutes, and she sat in her chair waiting for the next order. She looked a little tired, and there were dark rings under her eyes. The last three days had been a terrific strain.

She knew better, from experience, than to interrupt Stanniland at that moment. As he sat, with his back to her, at his desk, his left hand was on the nape of his neck, a sure sign that he was engrossed. Now and again, in the silence, came the scratch of his pen—suddenly a sort of vicious scratch. That meant he was signing his name.

All in a moment he swung round in his chair and faced her, a grim little smile on his face. Then he did what she had never seen him do when he was working in the office, took a case from his pocket, extracted a cigarette from it, and lighted it.

' Done ! " he exclaimed.

" What ? "

"The whole caboodle. Finished at last! Have a cigarette, Miss Lake?"

And he handed her his case.

"Thanks. I was just dying for one. Have you really finished?"

"*We* have finished," he replied, with a kindly smile, "for I've got to thank you a lot. You've worked like a Trojan. Yes, it's all done. The prospectus will be in the hands of the public to-morrow."

"Good luck to 'Sapor!'" she exclaimed.

"I think so. It ought to take on. There's nothing more to do now but to wait for the money to roll in. They'll see to the allotments in London. I've arranged all that. Good prospectus, eh? Ought to fetch 'em. And it's jolly good stuff—'Sapor' is."

"Jolly good stuff!"

He took a copy of the prospectus from the table and studied it. The usual thing—"Capital, £50,000 in 20,000 7 per cent. accumulative preference shares of £1, the whole of which are offered to the public and 30,000 ordinary shares of £1, 20,000 of which are offered to the public. . . ." "Directors"—here followed half a dozen names, ending with "Julian Bruce Stanniland, Esq., Sapor House, Frattenbury, who will join the board after allotment." . . . "The vendor will receive 10,000 ordinary shares in part payment."

He looked over the edge of the prospectus and suddenly said to Peggy.

"I suppose you think I'm making a big lot of money out of 'Sapor,' eh?"

"Well, aren't you? You're selling it for fifty thousand pounds. Of course, I can see there are no end of expenses," she added.

"More than you think," he retorted, grimly. "I'll tell you, if you'd like to know."

"Naturally, I'm interested."

He threw one leg over the other, lighted a fresh cigarette, and said:

"I told you the other day I was down and out. So I was. Six years ago. I came a big cropper down the ladder, but I've been climbing up ever since."

"I think it is just what you would do," she said, with a touch of admiration in her voice. "I can't, somehow, imagine you caving in to bad luck."

"That's so. But it's been a stiff climb. One thing led to another, though, and I went on till 'Sapor' came along. I knew it was a good thing when I invented it. I'd scratched a bit of money together—and it wants money, too, to put a thing on the market and get it known. That's what I've had to do before I could get others to take it up and form a company to sell it. I did it, though—yes. But I've had to get financial help, and a lot of the purchase money will be swallowed up in clearing it off. When all's said and done I shall get about five thousand—*and* the shares. That's all."

"I think it's a horrid shame."

"I don't. I'm quite content. I'm out for a quick profit—and I've got it. I know if I'd waited a year before I sold I might have doubled it. But that didn't suit my book."

"Why not, Mr. Stanniland?"

"Because I only look on 'Sapor' as a stepping-stone to a bigger thing. Mind you," he went on, raising his forefinger in admonition, "I'm telling you all this because if you remain on with me I want you to be interested. People work ten times better if they're interested, and, by George, you'll have to work if you stick it."

The spirit of his own enthusiasm caught hold of Peggy, and she said:

"I'll try to stick it. I should love to help. What is this bigger thing, Mr. Stanniland?"

"Jecinora!" he replied.

"Jecinora?"

He lighted another cigarette, got up, and commenced walking to and fro across the room.

"I want to see on every hoarding—on every railway station—on omnibuses—everywhere—look here, I've got it down in my notes, though I can't draw"—he paused to take a notebook from his desk—"See? That's meant to be the head and shoulders of a man—striking, solemn, compelling look on his face—Jove! We'll have a good artist on the job, too. Pointing straight at you with his finger. And underneath—read it, Miss Lake."

He pushed the notebook into her hands, and she read:

IT'S YOUR LIVER I'M TALKING ABOUT!
TAKE "JECINORA"!

She threw herself back in her chair and gave way to a peal of laughter. He stopped short in his perambulation, and said:

"What are you laughing at?"

"Oh, it's too awfully funny. Priceless!"

"Price two-and-sixpence a bottle, small size. That's what it'll be, young lady! Makes you laugh, does it. Ha! That's what I want to see. D'you think it will attract attention?"

" It ought to. It's perfectly topping. You should put one on your front gate. The Miss Brands would love to see it there."

" Why not ? " he ejaculated. " I'm not ashamed of it. Take down ' Sapor House '—Sapor can go to the devil when I've done with it. ' Jecinora House,' with an enamelled plate over the label—in colours. I've half a mind to do it. By gad, I know what I should like to see, though."

" Oh, do tell me. Is it anything still funnier ? "

" Funnier ? It's business. I should like to see ' Take Jecinora ' in big letters on the scaffolding of the old church over the way. You could pick it out from every train that passes. And they'd write it up in the papers. Jove, I'd give your uncle a hundred quid for his restoration fund if he'd let me put it there. Of course he wouldn't, though," he added regretfully.

Again Peggy roared with laughter.

" I'd love to see it there myself," she said, a wicked twinkle in her eye. " But you haven't told me yet what Jecinora *is*. Won't you ? "

" Comes from Jecur, Latin for liver. Nothing like a Latinized name. I've nearly completed the formula. Next week I shall. Did I tell you I got some notion from a native doctor in India. Had an awful attack of liver trouble and there wasn't a white medico near. But he cured me. And I found out a bit about his treatment. There's a certain herb out there—I've got half a ton of it on it's way here. And I'm going all I know for Jecinora."

" But, Mr. Stanniland, aren't there no end of liver cures as it is ? "

" Don't matter. This ought to lick 'em. It's

good stuff, mind you—like 'Sapor.' I'm not a quack, I *know*."

"But, do you think it will take on as well as 'Sapor'?"

"Better. Good Lord, yes. I'll tell you why. 'Sapor's' for people in good health. A food, so to speak. But there's more to be got out of the public by working on their diseases than on their health. A man with a healthy stomach——"

"Isn't such a paying proposition as one with a diseased liver. Yes, I see!"

"That's right. Look at the big patent medicines? Get your public to analyse their symptoms, real or imaginary, and the bally thing goes down. They know they want it. Can't help it. The very fact of my advertisement Johnny talking about your liver makes you think about your liver. See!"

"I wasn't."

"Wasn't what?"

"Thinking about mine."

"Don't. Still, all the same, if it goes wrong I'll give you Jecinora. It'll cure you."

The girl looked at him steadily, her face becoming serious.

"Do you really believe in it yourself?" she asked.

"I do. Or I wouldn't try to sell it. You don't think I'm out to swindle the public, I hope, Miss Lake?"

"No——" she said, slowly. "I'm sure you're not," and a slight colour mounted to her cheeks. "If I didn't think you were genuine I wouldn't work for you."

He returned her gaze for a moment or two, and then went on:

"I'm going to put everything on Jecinora. I'm done with 'Sapor.' If the shares rise to a premium I sell out and retire from the directorate. That's understood. I shall want all I can get to bring out Jecinora, and when I do, I shall be in a position to command a jolly sight more than I've got for 'Sapor.'"

Peggy was not laughing now. Her face was still grave.

"Isn't it rather a big risk?" she asked.

He thought a moment.

"How shall I put it. Look here, your uncle's a parson, eh? I've not heard him preach, but I suppose he tells folks to have faith, and to take a risk on faith. Well, it's the same here. I've got faith in Jecinora. And I'd plank my bottom dollar on what I believe in."

"I think—you're rather splendid," replied Peggy. But he did not acknowledge the compliment. Instead, he took another paper from his desk.

"Talking about the Dean. Here's *his* prospectus."

"What?"

"Appeal for the Restoration Fund. I asked him to let me have one. I've read it. Not badly put together, on the whole, but I bet I'd have made it a bit more fetching if he'd asked me to draw it up."

"I'm sure you would," she replied, smiling again.

"Ten thousand pounds additional capital, eh? That's the invitation to the subscribing public. Can't underwrite any of *this!* Well, I suppose as I've bought this house and live here I'd better contribute. What do you think?"

"I think it would be awfully decent of you to give something. Uncle was positively desperate about getting the money before he left. You see, Mr. Stanniland, he has only recently come to be Dean here, and it's rough luck on him to have to begin with such a job."

"Er—yes. Where's my cheque-book. Let's see. What shall it be? Shall I make it out for fifty pounds?"

"Oh, that's ripping of you. Why, you have only just come to live here. Uncle ought to be awfully grateful."

"Think so? Well—decent old chap, that uncle of yours—and, you see, he seems to think I owe him something for getting a rise out of him—this house."

"He's a perfect dear," said Peggy. "I don't know how I should have got on without him. Oh, I wish I could afford to send him something myself for this old fund."

Stanniland paused in the act of filling in the cheque, wheeled round in his chair, and asked, abruptly:

"Got any money?"

She laughed.

"I've only about sixty pounds in the world," she said; "it's in a bank, and I don't want to draw on it if I can help it. You may give me the sack," she added, demurely, "and I must have something to fall back upon."

He ignored the insinuation.

"Got a cheque-book?" he asked.

She tapped the little dispatch case which lay on her table.

"I generally carry it in here."

"Good. Now, look here. If I don't make any mistake, 'Sapor' will have a small premium on the ordinary shares pretty soon after allotment. You take my tip, and apply for a couple of hundred."

"But I've only sixty pounds."

"Really, Miss Lake," he replied, dropping into his hard, business manner, "You ought to know by this time that it's only half a crown per share on application and half a crown on allotment and three weeks before the first instalment of five shillings. How much for two hundred—sharp?"

"Twenty-five pounds."

"Write out a cheque for the amount then and fill in this application form. All right. Don't worry. I'll guarantee 'em. Whatever price they stand at this day three weeks I'll buy 'em back at par if they're at a discount. Give you an undertaking. If there's a premium, you sell out and give the profits to the bally old Cathedral, see?"

"It's most awfully good of you, Mr. Stanniland."

"Rubbish! Mind you, I don't think there's going to be a big premium. But if it's only sixpence, that means a fiver. If a shilling, ten pounds. That's right—full name and address."

He added a line in the corner of the application form, and initialled it.

"Preferential treatment," he explained, "if the thing's oversubscribed you'll get your full allotment all the same. You can post it when you go out. Now—this cheque of mine——"

"Mr. Stanniland?"

"What is it?"

"Won't you do the same—in a way?"

"What?"

"You said you were going to sell out your own shares later on."

" Well ? "

" Won't you be a sport and make the amount of your subscription depend on the premium—if there is one ? I don't mean the whole of it. Say threepence a share."

" Work it out," he retorted, grimly, and smiled a little when he saw she was doing it in her head.

" One hundred and sixty-six pounds, three shillings and fourpence."

" Right ! "

He tapped on the table with his fingers for a moment or two. Then said :

" You've got cheek."

" Dear old uncle would be so pleased."

" Would you ? "

" Why, of course I should. I should think it ever so ripping of you."

After a slight pause.

" Look here, Miss Lake. I'll tell you what I'll do. I'll offer a more sporting chance than threepence per share. Whatever the premium is—if there *is* one—when I sell out I'll give two-thirds of it to the Dean's fund—*but*—and he lifted up his hand to stop her thanking him, " there's a condition. If I sell at par, I'll only give a cheque for ten pounds. If at a discount, then a fiver. It shall rest with you. Shall I finish filling in this cheque for fifty pounds and have done with it, or will you take the risk ? "

And she answered, without a moment's hesitation :

" I'll take the risk. You said one ought to have faith."

" Right."

And he tore up the spoilt cheque.

Peggy gathered together her belongings, drew on her gloves, and prepared to go. The clock on the mantelpiece had just struck five, and there was no overtime that day.

" There won't be very much to do to-morrow," he said.

" Then I can overhaul the car."

He made no reply.

" Good-afternoon," she said, standing at the door with her hand on the knob, " and ever so many thanks."

" Oh, that's all right. I hope you're satisfied.

She lingered a moment.

" I think you're a perfect dear ! " she said, throwing it back at him as she closed the door.

Stanniland sat still—looking at the door.

" Good Lord ! " he ejaculated.

And, after the space of a full minute, added :

" Now, I like that girl ! "

CHAPTER XIII

WHILE the genuine Dean of Frattenbury was congratulating himself upon his quiet refuge beside the little harbour of Salcombe, Corney, the bogus dignitary was also residing by a harbour on the west coast of France. But Arcachon, with the exception of being a yachting and fishing centre, bears little resemblance to the beautiful South Devon seaport.

The Bay of Arcachon is a large one, almost enclosed; the shores are low and flat, and pine forests grow down to the very edge of the water, pine woods which are redolent with odour as one walks through them, for the trunks of the trees are constantly being tapped and hanging on them are queer little buckets to catch the fragrant liquor which oozes out.

There are the usual hotels and villas, a squat little pier which serves as a landing-stage for the fishing boats and the small steamers which ply on the bay—and there are red trousers and oysters.

For Marsden was quite right. Not only do many of the fishermen array themselves in nether garments of a dark crimson hue, but even yachtsmen do not disdain, temporarily, to adopt the local fashion. And people cross the bay in steamers for the sole purpose of eating oysters at the restaurants opposite.

Marsden, as good as his word, had purchased unto himself a pair of these conspicuous trousers. He had also done all in his power to induce Corney to do likewise.

"Think how pricelessly unique it would be, my dear chap. You'd positively be the only dean in England who could boast of having worn red bags. You could have 'em made into breeches when you got home; they'd go fine with the silk apron on top. *Rouge et noir.*"

But Corney, laughing with him, had refused to do anything of the kind. He had his rôle to play and his object to attain. And, very cleverly, he acted his part. He saw that it afforded Marsden intense amusement to get a rise out of him, and frequently let him get a rise. But he took very good care never to do anything derogatory to the position he had assumed. Marsden, with all his midsummer madness, was sane enough to have discovered any glaring flaw in the character of a Church dignitary, and Corney was well aware of it.

To himself, Corney chuckled much. The scheme was working admirably. Marsden enjoyed having a butt for his mad wit and, at the same time, was a man who appreciated a good-humoured companion. Friendship increased rapidly, as Corney intended it should do.

So Marsden sported his red trousers and, in other ways, enjoyed himself. He amused himself by firing off his execrable French to sardine fishermen and loiterers on the pier and sea walk, interspersed—when he was at a loss—with gravely delivered sentences from the elementary French course so familiar to schoolboys, announcing that he had read the book of his friend, or asking some astonished individual if there was a flower in the garden of his sister, sometimes, when he was at a loss for a sentence, rapidly conjugating a tense or two of a French verb.

"They say an Englishman is no linguist, my dear Lake. But you see? *I* have no difficulty. I talk to them all in their own language and they smile and are happy. It is good to make other people happy. You preach it; I practise it. Come and have a bock!"

But Corney never had a bock with Marsden. At table he drank wine, sparingly, on other occasions coffee or an innocent "sirop." He was a master of detail.

For this reason he took good care not to accompany Marsden to the Casino or the Salon des Dances. Marsden patronized both every evening. He punted on *rouge et noir* and *petits chèvaux*, seemingly not caring whether he won or lost. He danced with great energy, not particular as to his partners.

Meanwhile Corney's scanty stock of cash was diminishing. They were staying at the Grand Hotel, and the Grand Hotel was not cheap. But he knew, from past experiences in similar games of craft, the wisdom of posing as affluent, and was quite content for the time being. He was worming himself into the confidence of a happy-go-lucky individual who had plenty of money and threw it about a little recklessly—paying more than his own share. Corney saw to *that!*

And he was maturing his plans. He had no wish to maintain at any length the character he had assumed. It was all very well to get out of England as a dean, but he was not going to remain a dean a moment longer than suited him. He was pretty safe in Arcachon, for few English people are to be found there, and he and Marsden were in a large minority. But he wanted to get away as soon as possible, to sink himself into a more obscure personality and, from Marseilles, to escape to South America. For he was acquainted with the Argentine.

He played his cards warily. He began by hinting that the supply of change was running out and that he would soon have to draw a cheque. He steadily refused Marsden's instant offer to lend him a couple of hundred francs till the banks opened on Monday morning.

"Certainly not," he said, with a laugh, "it's not so bad as that."

"All right," said the other, "on Monday I want to draw some money, too. I had a run of bad luck last night. Let us live on credit over the week end and be happy. To-morrow's Sunday. If you're a very good boy you shall read me one of your sermons while I take my afternoon nap."

On Monday morning Corney, his tongue in his cheek, gravely wrote out a cheque payable to himself, signed it "E. Lake," and marched into the bank with it. What happened was precisely what he had anticipated *would* happen. The cashier very properly refused to cash it.

"Pardon, monsieur, mais vous n'avez pas une lettre de crêdit? Non? C'est impossible!"

He returned to the hotel apparently a very perplexed ecclesiastic.

"I don't know what I shall do," he said to Marsden, "the bank won't cash my cheque."

" Why not ? You've a letter of credit or an order, I suppose ? "

" They asked me if I had a letter of credit. What is it ? I don't understand."

Marsden roared with laughter and pointed his finger at him.

" Behold the spotless innocence ot an unsophisticated very reverend dean ! Do you mean to say you came abroad, without making any arrangements to get your cheques cashed ? "

" But I have no difficulty at home."

" Good Lord ! You're the most priceless old bean I've ever met. You're not fit to be trusted on your own. We'll reverse positions. If I'm mad, you're a fool. I'll be keeper. Haven't you ever been abroad before ? "

" Why, yes."

" How have you managed ? "

" I've usually stayed in one place—and written home to my bank for any money I required. That's what I must do now, I suppose."

" Yes—and it'll take a week to get it. And I was just going to propose that we should move on tomorrow. You're the bally limit. Look here. Add this to your collection of hymns."

And he rolled off an impromptu :

There once was an innocent dean,
A perfectly priceless old bean,
When he wanted some cash
He got stewed to a hash—
Oh, wasn't he gorgeously green !

But Corney apparently did not see any joke in it at all. He frowned.

"That's all I can do," he said, gloomily, "I suppose." And got up.

"Where are you going?"

"To get my fountain-pen—it's in my room. I'll write home at once."

"Here. Wait a bit. Perhaps I can help you out. how much do you want?"

This was the psychological moment which Corney had anticipated. He wanted all he could get. But he knew there must be a limit. He also knew, keen judge of human nature that he was, that the naming of too small a sum would lower him in the estimation of this carelessly wealthy man. He had worked out all proportions already in his subtle brain and replied instantly, taking from his pocket, as he did so, the cheque he had not succeeded in cashing, and laying it face upwards on the table.

"I wanted seventy-five pounds—just over seven thousand francs, I think it comes to, according to the exchange. I put it on the cheque in French money. Is that right? It's a lot of money, but I have some purchases to make."

"Oh, you sweet innocent! You write out a cheque for seven thousand two hundred francs and take it to a bank that knows nothing about you, and expect 'em to pay up and look cheerful. Now theh. Cheerio, old dear. What you'd have done without your keeper I don't know. Let's tear this up. There. You write out a cheque for seventy-five quid, payable to me, W. Guy Marsden. I'll cash it for you now, and post it to my banker at home. I'll get some more "rhino" for myself out of the bank here this afternoon.

" Really, it's most exceedingly kind of you——. I hardly like——"

" Bosh ! The recording angel will register W. Guy Marsden as having rendered timely assistance to a distressed dean. That'll put me up a bit on the books up above. Now then, write out the cheque."

Corney had laid his cheque-book on the table. All was " according to plan."

" I'll get my pen."

While he was getting it, Marsden did exactly what Corney had thought there was a chance of his doing. Careless as he was, the bump of caution, about the size of a pin's head in his case, asserted itself.

He took up the cheque-book and examined the counterfoils. And it all looked so perfectly innocent. As it was.

The cheque was drawn and changed hands. " E. Lake " was, of course, no attempt at copying the Dean's signature. It was, really, entirely different from the sign manual of that dignitary.

And the notes changed hands.

After luncheon Marsden wrote to his London banker enclosing Corney's cheque and started off to the local bank, with his letter of credit, to get some more cash for himself. Corney remained in the hotel.

" I think I'll take forty winks," he said.

" Oh, will you ? All right, then. I shall hire a motor-boat and have a run round the bay."

" That'll suit me very well," thought Corney. As soon as the other had gone, instead of taking a nap, he paid his hotel bill up to date, went to his bedroom, and packed one of his two suit-cases— not the one, however, labelled " Dean of Frattenbury." He grinned at the black coat, silk "apron" and stockings, which he had left hanging on a chair after getting out of them the previous evening.

"I've done with you," he said to himself, "never mind. You've served me a good turn."

He was just about to go out, when a thought struck him.

"Just as well to put the fool off the scent while I make a get-away," he said, and wrote the following:

DEAR MARSDEN,

I've changed my mind. I have a fancy for a good walk. Don't wait dinner for me—I shall very likely get it out. If so, see you in the morning.

Yours.,
E. L.

He knew Marsden made a bee-line for the Casino directly after dinner and returned late. This note he laid on Marsden's dressing-table.

Then, carrying his suit-case in his hand, he sneaked downstairs and evaded the hall porter by making his exit out of a French window at the side of the hotel. And so to the station. *En route* to Bordeaux he studied a railway time-table, following out the intricacies of a cross-country journey to Marseilles. Though, at this stage of it, he had only booked to Bordeaux.

Marsden returned to the hotel about half an hour before the time for dinner. In his usual mood of merriment, having thoroughly enjoyed himself by trying to translate into French, for the benefit of his boatman, "The Yarn of the Nancy Bell." The unhappy man had become nearly frantic in trying to understand, and Marsden had never smiled once.

He looked into the lounge to see if his friend were there, and then went upstairs to dress for dinner. As he went along the corridor to his room he tapped on the door of Corney's bedroom. No answer.

"What! Is the blighter still having his forty winks?—I'll——"

He opened the door and looked in. The room was empty. Glancing round it his gaze fell on the Dean's clothes, lying on the chair. Suddenly a wicked look came into his eyes and he grinned in exultation.

"By George," he exclaimed, "I'll astonish the old buffer, what? 'O, wad the gods the giftie gi'e us, to see ourselves as others see us:' And you *shall*, too! Here's a game! I hope there's time before he comes in."

He snatched up coat, apron, silk breeches, sash, buckled shoes, and silk stockings, rushed with them to his own room, locked the door, threw off his clothes, and began getting into the dignitary's garb, grinning at himself in the long glass of the wardrobe as he did so. Presently he was fully arrayed in all the glory of borrowed plumes. He executed a little *pas seul* in front of the glass, throwing up a stockinged leg in fine style, and then turned to the dressing-table to part his hair in the middle and to study facial expression. It was then that he saw the note, and tore it open. A shade of disappointment passed over his face.

"Confound the old bean," he said, "he won't be here to see. No matter. There'll be others. I'll show 'em what a right reverend dean is like when he takes his walks abroad. Now for it!"

His table waiter stifled a laugh when he entered

the dining salon. He stalked gravely, with extremely dignified air, across the room, and took a seat at the little table. By this time the waiter had become a little accustomed to the mad Englishman's vagaries. Besides, he was enjoying the joke.

"Apportez-moi une verre de vermouth!"

"Bien, monsieur."

The pseudo Dean looked round the room with haughty glance. He was pleased to observe that the guests—few as they were—were new ones. Not one of them had seen Corney in his dress clothes.

They appeared to be all French, with one exception. Seated on the opposite side of the room, facing him, was a young man with a decided English type of countenance and bearing. He was, in fact, one of the little group of Englishmen engaged in the wine trade at Bordeaux. But he happened to have another occupation which brought him a little extra remuneration. He was one of that army of unnamed and unknown individuals employed by editors as "our correspondents." That is to say, he contributed short paragraphs likely to interest people at home to a certain London newspaper.

His attention was only really aroused when Marsden ordered a second bottle of champagne, and his eyebrows unconsciously arched themselves as he saw his *vis-à-vis* drain his new-filled glass at a gulp. Also Marsden's assumed dignity was giving way to his usual farcical behaviour. He addressed facetious remarks to the waiter and had held up his glass towards an elderly Frenchman at the next table with:

"À votre santé, monsieur. Aimez-vous l'Entente Cordiale? Je l'aime, tu l'aimes, il l'aime. Bien!"

Presently Marsden, lighting a cigar, strolled into the lounge and ordered coffee and cognac. The young Englishman, still observant, went to the hotel office and consulted the book which lay on the counter, the official register of guests. There it was, for Carney had not done things by halves:

E. Lake, Dean of Frattenbury.

After a bit Marsden got up, took down his light trilby hat from its peg in the hall, placed it at its usual rather sportive angle on his head, and sauntered out into the street. It was a fine evening, and he wore no overcoat. People turned and stared a little at the unusual phenomenon, but Marsden appeared to be sublimely unconscious.

The young Englishman followed him. This was a quarry worth keeping in view. What was the Dean about to do?

What the Dean did was to turn into the Casino, make straight for the roulette room, take a vacant seat at the table, and bring a roll of notes from his pocket. Again people stared. Again he took no notice.

"Faites vos jeux, messieurs et mesdames, Faites vos jeux," said the croupier, in monotonous voice as he set the board spinning.

"Avec plaisir, mon ami," retorted the Dean, "Je fais le jeu sur mon âge!"

And he placed a note on the number thirty-three. He looked fifty-three, if a day. A titter of laughter ran round the room.

Thirty-three won!

The croupier rapidly counted out notes and pushed them to Marsden across the table.

"Merci bien. Quelle âge avez-vous, monsieur?"

The croupier only grunted.

"Il n'a pas une âge!" said Marsden, in his execrable French. "Voyez donc!"

And he placed a note on zero. There was a roar of laughter. Number twenty-four won, and the croupier raked the note into the bank.

"Il mente," remarked Marsden, "il a vingt-quatre ans!"

This set the table in a titter again. The young Englishman, who was only looking on and not playing, remarked to himself:

"They are not *all* gloomy deans in England. That's certain. I must speak to this Johnny, somehow."

The opportunity came later. Marsden, tired of the game, sauntered away, amid the laughter and following glances of the occupants of the roulette table. He made his way to the brilliantly lighted restaurant, and took his seat at a table on the terrace facing the bay. The young Englishman sat down at the same table. Marsden looked up.

"Bon soir," he said, affably. "Avez un avec moi. Nommez votre poison!"

"I beg your pardon!"

"Oh, English are you? I interpret then. I said, have one with me?"

"Thank you!" said the other, with a laugh, "I don't mind if I do. Excuse me"—he was going to the point at once—"but we are staying at the same hotel and I think I saw your name in the register. The Dean of Frattenbury?"

"C'est moi. That's me," replied Marsden, "Don't I look it?"

"Well, yes," said the other, "though you don't, somehow, seem to fit in with your surroundings, sir."

Marsden looked at him quickly, the wicked twinkle in his eyes.

"I always believe in enjoying myself on a holiday, young man. I get enough of the other sort of thing when I'm at home. Now, don't you think I'm really a rather jolly old dean, eh?"

"You certainly are, sir."

"I *am*," replied Marsden, suddenly relapsing into extreme gravity. "And I mean to be while I'm here. Do you dance?"

"Not very much."

Marsden finished his drink and sprang to his feet.

"Come and see *me* dance," he said. "Regular dancing rig, eh?" And he threw out his leg. "*I'll* show 'em!"

He did show them—in the dancing saloon—showed them so enthusiastically that, at length, the director of that rather mixed establishment, politely, but exceedingly firmly, requested him to retire, a request which was only acceded to by a threat to call in a gendarme. By this time the young Englishman had disclaimed any further acquaintance with him, but still watched the proceedings, with an occasional application to his notebook.

Marsden came out of the establishment, cocked his trilby over one eye, managed, after difficulties with the "apron," to stick his hands into the pockets of his silk breeches, and walked back to the hotel, cheerily whistling snatches of the latest music-hall songs.

"I've had the evening of my life," he told himself,

as he walked upstairs. " And, by jove, before I go to bed I'll show myself to that dear old blighter. He'll think it's the ghost of himself ! "

He opened the door of Corney's room, fumbled about for the electric switch, found it, and turned on the light.

The room was empty. He gave a long, low whistle.

" Hullo, hullo ! " he ejaculated, " what's *he* up to, I wonder. Not back to dinner. See me in the morning. Oh, you naughty, *naughty* Dean ! "

And then he went to bed and slept the sleep of the joyous.

CHAPTER XIV

THE Dean of Frattenbury settled down to his quiet holiday at East Porthmouth, and as the uneventful days went by, congratulated himself that all was going well. Being a bachelor, and having lived alone for many years, he had no difficulty in accommodating himself to his solitary life. He bathed in one of the little sandy coves on the Porthmouth side—he was a good swimmer—he wrote a little in his lodgings, he found a library at Salcombe from which he could take out a decent book or two, and he went for long tramps along the cliffs and inland. His anxiety as to his financial resources had ceased. In his very simple rooms and with his very moderate tastes he felt he had ample means to keep him going until he joined his brother, without having to apply to his bank—which he was not anxious to do.

As far as possible he avoided people. Thus, he never made use of the steamer that plied between Salcombe and Kingsbridge, and kept, for the most part, to the Porthmouth side of the harbour.

The only person with whom he struck any acquaintanceship was Hinton. Truth to tell, he rather liked the somewhat outspoken stockbroker. Like so many others of the clerical profession, he had rarely met laymen on equal terms, for the dog collar is generally a barrier which prevents the layman, polite or impolite, from unmasking the entire battery of his thoughts when expressing opinions. The experience, novel as it was, proved not unpleasing to the Dean. Although he had lived and moved in comparatively narrow circles of life, he was, by temperament, more broad-minded than perhaps he was ready to admit. And although he held his own fairly well in arguments which arose, he was learning something about other points of view—very unfamiliar points at times—but still, not without interest.

There was opportunity for these arguments. Hinton was as good as his word, and on several occasions had taken the Dean for a sail, across the bar into the open sea, or exploring the picturesque estuaries that branch out on either side between Salcombe and Kingsbridge.

On one of these expeditions Mrs. Hinton came with her husband. She was still a handsome little woman, and had evidently, in her younger days, been beautiful; rather under middle height, quiet and deliberate in manner and movement, with a pleasant voice rendered none the less pleasant by the tinge of a drawl in it. There was a stiff breeze on that particular day, and if the Dean had been a yachtsman he would have admired the way in which Mrs. Hinton assisted her husband every time he put about.

"Won't you climb the mountain and have a meal with us when we get in?" asked Hinton, as he steered for his moorings.

"Yes, do, Mr. Lake," said Mrs. Hinton, "we shall be so pleased."

He had not told them that he was "Dr." Lake.

"You are very kind," he said, "but I have no evening clothes with me."

And, instantly, he bethought himself of a certain leather suit-case with his name on it, and wondered as to its whereabouts at that precise moment.

Hinton laughed.

"My dear chap," he said, "we're quite informal here. That's all right. It isn't dinner, you know, only a pot-luck supper."

"I'll come with pleasure," replied the Dean.

The Hintons had one or two purchases to make on the Salcombe side, and it was arranged that the Dean should precede them over the ferry, and that they should call for him at his rooms on their way home

When he reached his rooms he overhauled his scanty belongings. His brother had gone off in the dark grey cloth suit, he himself had come in his flannels, but had packed—cramming it as well as he could into his bag—an old black suit that still belonged to him—not a clerical coat, but the ordinary shaped black jacket which so many parsons wear to-day in lieu of the collarless frock-coat. This suit he put on. He had three or four clerical collars with him and habit urged him a little to use one—after all, there was no harm in being taken for an ordinary clergyman—but caution prevailed, and he donned a turn-down collar and black tie.

Now the modern parson is quite loose in his notions of dress, especially when on holiday. But, over and over again, if you are an observant person, you can spot him nevertheless—especially when he speaks. Somehow or other he does not always "carry" lay clothing like a layman. The Dean of

Frattenbury, nevertheless, did not possess that peculiar attribute—the parsonic voice. He abhorred monotoning ordinary conversation. So, in his grey flannels, he passed muster very well. But, somehow, black clothing, *with* a black tie, seemed to bring him back a shade nearer to what he really was. Perhaps because very few laymen dress in complete black morning clothes—except for a funeral.

Perhaps it was this which made Mrs. Hinton, when she and her husband called for him, look at him for a moment or two with a quietly penetrating expression. But, anyhow, she said nothing. Hinton was carrying their purchases in a string bag, from the top of which poked out a copy of a weekly illustrated paper, given, among other matters, to discussing the doings of prominent persons in a somewhat flippant manner.

There was not very much conversation as they toiled up the exceedingly steep hill on the top of which is the real village of East Porthmouth, clustering round its old church.

" Here we are," said Hinton, at length. " This is our little hotel, you see."

" Don't mind him, Mr. Lake. It may not be very large, but I think you'll say it's comfy enough."

It was only an ordinary cottage, but Mrs. Hinton was right. If there was not very much room for furniture inside, such furniture as there was was artistic and good. Preparations for a meal were spread on a charming little oak gate-leg table, a genuine antique, and the four chairs matched it. A small, beautifully carved, oak coffer stood in the tiny bow window, with a great, blue jar of flowers upon it. There were only three pictures on the colour-washed walls, but they were signed etchings of note.

And the meal, if vulgarized by the name of supper, belied that name—simple as it was. The soles were exquisitely cooked, the cutlets particularly appetizing, the savoury unquestionable.

"We have a treasure," remarked Mrs. Hinton, between the courses, "do notice our maid. She does all the cooking—in fact, everything."

The Dean was feeling more at home than he had done since leaving Frattenbury. It was more like home—like his own home, and like the little dinners in the Close.

He drank sparingly of the wine, but his taste was sufficiently educated to know that the sauterne was no cheap brand. When the coffee made its appearance he was thoroughly comfortable.

"A cigar?" asked Hinton, pushing his case over the table, "or do you prefer a pipe?"

"Well—if Mrs. Hinton doesn't mind?"

"Not at all. Please light it."

She, herself, took a cigarette from a silver box which the maid had put on the table. As she lighted it she glanced quietly at her visitor.

"I hope you are not one of those people who object to women smoking?" she asked, with her slight drawl, smiling.

"I am too much accustomed to seeing my niece doing so," he replied. "One is not allowed to be old-fashioned in these days."

It was not a direct answer. Again she looked at him for a moment.

Hinton, meanwhile, had reached for the weekly paper he had brought home—and which he had laid on the oak chest. He turned over the leaves in a desultory manner, glancing at the illustrations. presently he stopped turning, and seemed interested. Then he began to chuckle, and finally burst out into a hearty laugh.

"What is it, George?" asked his wife, "you're horribly rude—reading that thing all to yourself."

"Sorry," he exclaimed, "look here," he went on, addressing the Dean, "this ought to interest you. We were only talking about him that morning I first met you."

"About whom?"

"The Dean of Frattenbury," replied Hinton, again indulging in a chuckle, "and you stood up for him—don't you remember?"

"Yes," said the Dean, putting down his coffee-cup, and wondering what was coming; "er—er—what about him?"

"Do tell us, George. What has the Dean of Frattenbury been doing?"

"Well," said Hinton, laying down the paper for a moment, "the very reverend Dean is on his holiday, it appears. And this is how he seems to be spending it."

The Dean's face grew a shade paler. His pipe had gone out—in fact, it lay on the table beside his coffee—and an anxious look was in his eyes.

"Listen," said Hinton, taking up the paper again. "I'll read it to you."

And he read the following, stopping now and again to laugh as he did so:

A Dean on Holiday.

There are times, apparently, when even eminent ecclesiastics catch the true holiday spirit, that spirit which joyously throws off all restraint. That jade, yclept "Rumour," has it that such a one is the Dean of Frattenbury, who is, seemingly, disporting himself on the Continent. When we say "disporting" we use the word advisedly, for his very reverence was recently observed in the Casino at the pretty little West Coast of France resort of Arcachon in merry mood—though attired as a dignitary should be. We would like to know the exact sum he won that evening by punting on the illusive pea, and we understand that his skill in forecasting lucky numbers was only equalled by that shown in his exhibition of the Terpsichorean art in an adjacent salon later on the same evening. Oh, Mr. Dean! Never mind. We love a touch of the sporting humour, in whomsoever it is manifest!

"There!" exclaimed Hinton, "what do you think of that?"

And laughed again. Mrs. Hinton had joined him, but, turning to look at her guest, suddenly checked herself. There was a look in the Dean's face, a pained, horrified expression, which was obviously not conducive to mirth.

"May I look, please?" he asked.

Hinton, still laughing, for he had not caught his wife's eye, handed him the paper.

Slowly and bewildered, the Dean read the terrible paragraph. For a moment or two his mind was numbed with the positive horror of it. Then he began to think. First the scandal of his own position, then the extraordinary action on the part of his brother. There must be some ghastly mistake.

"I can't believe it," he exclaimed, throwing the paper on the table and with the thought of his brother uppermost in his mind at the moment.

Hinton shrugged his shoulders.

"It is funny, isn't it? And awfully rough on

the Dean, poor devil! I dare say this rag has made the most of it. Probably he only risked a few francs and just looked on at the dancing. Why shouldn't he? Deans are only human, after all. There was no harm in it."

"Deans are only human, yes. I know that . . . But this is preposterous! Mr. Hinton, believe me. It is untrue. . . . It was not the Dean," for the horror of his own situation had now swerved on to his mind.

Mrs. Hinton glanced rapidly, but quietly, at him again. He spoke with such earnestness.

"No," she said, "I am sure it could not have been the Dean of Frattenbury. I don't know him," she added, "but I cannot imagine *any* dean—doing such a thing."

The Dean looked at her gratefully.

"Thank you," he said, with dignity.

"But who was it if it wasn't the Dean?" asked Hinton. "Surely this paper, rotten thing as it is, would not have dared to print this paragraph without a very good reason. They daren't."

"It was not the Dean," repeated his guest, emphatically. And again Mrs. Hinton looked at him.

"Then who could it have been?" He took up the paper once more. "'Attired as a dignitary should be.' Surely no one would be so unutterably foolish as publicly to impersonate a particular dean?"

"I'm afraid someone has—all the same," said the Dean, grimly, as the thought of his brother came uppermost again, "but I couldn't have believed it."

Hinton looked up at him abruptly.

"You were wielding the cudgel in his defence the

other day, I remember. Do you know the Dean of Frattenbury?"

"Yes," replied the other, shortly.

And thought. And might even have gone farther, for he liked these people. And the kindly judgment of the man of the world, when he really had thought it *was* the Dean, had appealed to him. But, just then, Mrs. Hinton broke in.

"If you know him" she said, with her quiet drawl, "we are sure it could not be he, aren't we George? And I am very sorry for the poor man and hope he will soon be able to prove—well—let us hope—that he was not at—what's the name of the place? Yes! Arcachon, at all."

The Dean sighed.

"It may not be easy to do that," he said.

Hinton, still blind to his wife's attempt at signalling with her eyes, blundered on:

"Whatever happens, it'll be a nine days' wonder at Frattenbury. Some gossip, eh? Lord, how I'd like to see some of the old geysers when they read this!"

And the Dean remembered the Bishop—and the Canon in Residence—and the Miss Brands—and Hurst, the Verger—and his own butler—and got up to take his departure. He could bear no more.

"Must you be going?" asked Hinton, cheerily, "have a whisky and soda first."

"Yes, do," urged Mrs. Hinton, kindly; "you have quite a walk before you."

"Thank you—I think I will," replied the Dean. And he needed it.

"Sorry it's upset you a bit," said Hinton, as he saw him off, "but I didn't know the old bean was a friend of yours or I wouldn't have read it out. But it *was* funny you know! Good night."

"George," said his wife, directly he re-entered the room, "I think you are really the most tactless man alive. I tried to stop you, but you *would* go on."

"Why? What on earth's the matter, dear? I didn't do anything. And when Lake wanted us to believe it was not the Dean, I agreed, didn't I? How was I to know he knew the blighter?"

"You might have seen that he was upset. George, do you know what I think?"

"What, dear?"

"That he is the Dean of Frattenbury himself," she replied, quietly.

"Good Lord, whatever makes you say such a thing? What nonsense!"

"Has he ever told you what he is?"

"No."

"What did you think yourself?"

"Oh, I don't know. It never occurred to me. I put him down as a literary chap. He said he was doing some writing here."

"Very likely. But to-night, when we called for him at his lodgings, a sudden idea struck me. It was seeing him in that black suit. It only wanted a clerical collar to complete it. My dear, he looked exactly like a clergyman. Then I began to study him a little more closely. He has the air of one."

"Well," grudgingly admitted her husband, "perhaps he has. What of it? A parson isn't obliged to parade his profession when he's on a holiday, is he? Where's the harm?"

"I never thought for a moment there was any

harm. I dare say he is glad enough to get a quiet holiday. But, for all that, you mark my words, George. I'm sure he's the Dean."

"But *why?*"

"Oh, you don't expect me to prove it. It's a woman's intuition. And yet—didn't you see how terribly upset he was when you read that paragraph?"

"Well—he says he knows the Dean."

"It was more than that, dear. He took it personally. I was watching him. I tell you the man is the Dean himself."

"But, suppose he is. Why doesn't he say so? What is he doing here? What's the meaning of the bally mystery? Who's the fellow that they saw in the Casino?"

"Oh, do stop, George. How can we attempt to answer a string of questions like that? All I know is that if he's the person I honestly believe him to be, he has some very good reason for keeping his identity to himself."

"What? Has he robbed the poor-box and bolted with the contents for a holiday?"

"Don't be funny, George. You might have the sense to see this is no laughing matter for the poor man. I don't want to pry into his affairs. I'm sure they are honourable, whatever they are. But I do want you and I—you especially—to be prepared to help him—if he needs help."

"How can we help him?"

"How long have you known him?"

"It's just about a fortnight ago that I first came across him—on the landing-stage."

"Very well, then. If he's the Dean of Frattenbury, you are probably the one person of any standing who can prove definitely that he could not have been at Arcachon. And he may be very glad of the proof. You thought the paragraph funny enough, I know. But there are others who will put a more serious construction on it."

"By George, yes," I suppose so, said Hinton, thoughtfully. "It would go against him. All right. I see what you mean, dear. Whether he's a dean or not, I'll prove his alibi—if he asks me."

"If he asks you. Of course, you must wait for that. Unless—well, you may find an opportunity for sounding him. But you will have to be careful. Only, just show him you're a friend, George. Make him see that."

"By Jove, I will. I'll look him up to-morrow. I said something about a sail in the afternoon—the tide'll be right for Kingsbridge."

Meanwhile the Dean was walking down the steep hill to his lodgings, much upset and confused. When he reached his little sitting-room he lighted his pipe and tried to collect his thoughts. What had really happened, and what was he to do about it?

He centred his mind, to begin with, on his brother. The latter had promised him faithfully that he would not attempt to assume his identity. He knew Edward Lake was a weak and foolish man—he had reasons for knowing it—but he could scarcely credit that, with all his foolishness, he would deliberately bring, what he must know would be a scandal, on one who had gone out of the way and had, in a measure, sacrificed himself on his behalf.

Besides, where was this place, Arcachon? Well, it was certainly somewhere near Bordeaux, and the *Sunflower* was to have touched at Bordeaux, but—

for he remembered the itinerary—only for a day, arriving early in the morning and leaving the same evening. There would have been no time for this night scene at the Casino—unless his brother had left the boat altogether. But why should he ?

Then there was the question of the suit-case. It bore his name and it held his dignitary's clothes. Had Edward taken it all the way with him ? Had anyone stolen it ? Oh, it was all very bewildering.

Then there came the aspect of the thing as it immediately concerned himself. What would people think of it ? What would "The Close" say ? The scandalous paragraph would be all over the place, and he knew enough of the world to be aware of the results. Even if friends were kind enough to think it was a mistake, or grossly exaggerated, there were plenty of people who would revel in placing the very worst construction upon it. He knew that, only too well.

What was he to do ? He could not allow the scandal to gain ground. And yet there was his brother to consider. What *was* he to do ?

Nothing, that night, at all events. It was late. He went to bed, but it was hours before he slept. In the morning he left his breakfast half eaten, and started for a walk, determining to make up his mind on *some* course of action, and then to carry it out.

He crossed the ferry to the Salcombe side, turned sharply to the left as he emerged into Fore Street, with the object of making for Bolt Head—a walk he had not yet attempted. Presently he had left houses and people behind him and was walking along the narrow path that led to the extreme point of the great headland, the sea far below him on the left.

With the clear, fresh morning air there came, slowly, the clearer vision of thought. He saw that, whatever happened, it was his duty not only to clear himself, but to clear the Church. If he could do so without dragging his brother into it he would. At all costs, not only for his own, but for Peggy's sake—he was genuinely fond of the girl—he wanted to avoid a family scandal. In less than a fortnight now, if he could conceal the whereabouts of his brother, there would be no scandal in that direction—no miserable police court proceedings.

At length he made up his mind what he would do. There was one man he felt he could trust—the Bishop of Frattenbury. The Bishop was a wise man and a personal friend. He knew that, just at this time, the Bishop was in London for Convocation. He ought to have been in Convocation himself, but his holiday had intervened. He would write to the Bishop, explain, as far as he could that he had had to alter his plans and had not left England at all. He knew the hotel where the Bishop always stayed. And he would follow up the letter by going to London himself the next day and taking counsel with the Bishop, whom he would advise of his coming.

He almost turned to go back to write his letter, now that he had made up his mind, but he was so close to the seaward end of the great headland that he thought he would just walk the couple of hundred yards or so, and see the view on the other side.

The path, at this point, narrows between rocks and boulders, a defile in the face of the cliff. Overhead, on the right, rises the sheer, upper part of Bolt Head, far down on the continuing slope, on the left, in the open sea. Just at the turn of the narrow path, at the extremity of its V-shaped track round the cliff, is a natural wall of rock, three or four feet in height, crossing the path. One has to scale it like a stile.

The Dean had just put one leg over the rock when, suddenly, there appeared a man, only a few paces away, coming along the path on the farther side. Owing to the peculiar formation of the track it had been impossible to see him until the corner was turned.

A tall, sombre-looking individual, in a dark suit and a hard billy-cock hat, pacing with slow and almost dignified step along the path, head well raised, eyes gazing straight in front of him, stick carried tucked under his arm as if from habit—a familiar figure, with that drooping moustache and solemn mien, a familiar attitude that—in which the stick was carried. Very much *too* familiar.

For it was Finch, the Dean's verger!

CHAPTER XV

WHEN Peggy went to work as usual on the day after the completion of floating the "Sapor" Company, she noticed, as she walked up the drive, that all the blinds in front of the house were down. She let herself in at the front door as usual, crossed the hall and went into the "office."

Stanniland was not seated at his usual place, working at his desk. At first she did not know anyone was in the room. She walked to the window to draw up the blind and then stopped as a voice said:

"Don't draw up the blind!"

It was an unaccustomed voice, yet with a familiar sound—a lazy, almost incoherent drawl. Not at all like the crisp, decided speech of Julian Bruce Stanniland. She turned in surprise.

One of the arm-chairs was drawn up in the darkest corner of the room. In it sat Stanniland, or rather reclined, for his feet were cocked up on another chair. He wore his Japanese kimono, his feet were encased in an old pair of carpet slippers, his throat was collarless, his hair dishevelled, and he seemed to be lying limp and helpless, one arm hanging straight down towards the floor.

Peggy gave a start.

"I beg your pardon, Mr. Stanniland," she said.

"I didn't see you at first. Is—is anything the matter? Are you ill?"

"Nothing 's'marrer."

She looked at him again. His speech was terribly thick, and his eyes were half closed. She made sure he was drunk—and it was only nine o'clock in the morning. She stood hesitating. He opened his eyes a little.

"'S all righ', Miss Lake. I'm resting."

"Resting?"

"Mind and body. Good thing, sometimes, eh? Habit o' mine—when job's over. Preparing f' fresh job. S' all righ'!"

Still she hesitated. He was so utterly different from the Stanniland she had been accustomed to. A little smile broke over his face.

"Don' be 'larmed. 'T isn't drink. Friends have thought I was drunk when they've seen me restin'. Ain't! Slacking, tha's all."

She glanced at the desk. A small batch of letters lay on it unopened. And he had always had the morning's post ready for her when she came.

"Shall I try to do the correspondence?" she asked.

"No. Let 't 'lone. It'll keep. Look here. You take a day off. Deserve it. Like the car?"

"What?"

"Take her if y' like. Go for joll' goo' run. Do you good. Lea' me 'lone, please. Rest cure."

"Oh," she said, excitedly, "do you really mean I may have the car?"

"'Course. Said so."

"It's topping of you. I'm ever so grateful. I shall——"

"Oh, go to—go 'way!"

She broke off, looked at him again, but he had closed his eyes and was apparently oblivious of her presence. She even found herself making just a little grimace at him. His manners were appalling. Then she moved towards the door.

"Thanks awfully," she said as she went out, darting one more look at him.

"'S all' righ'!" he muttered, in his thick voice, but never opened his eyes.

For this was Julian Bruce Stanniland's habit when he slacked from work. He never did things by halves. If he worked like a Trojan, he slacked like a lotus-eater. Careless of dress, food, and even speech, he rested his tired body and brain with a thoroughness that was truly characteristic. Top gear and high speed when at work. Neutral and dead stop when slacking.

Peggy, delighted with her day off, and the chance of a run all to herself, however, soon forgot and forgave Stanniland's extraordinary appearance and manners. She rushed back to her lodgings and asked Mrs. Finch to put her up a lunch to take with her. Then, back to the garage at Sapor House, and overhauled the car, filling her up with petrol. In half an hour's time she was leaving Frattenbury behind her, heading northward for the downs. It had always been a pleasure to her to drive Stanniland's small but high-powered two-seater, and now that she had it all to herself and could go exactly where she liked, it was a double joy.

"*Rather* decent of him!" she said to herself, as she accelerated up the sloping road out of Frattenbury; "he's really a dear old thing."

Every woman appreciates attention, and, in spite of Stanniland's brusque and strange behaviour that morning, she had the intuition to see that a kindly thought for her was in his mind. Most men, under the circumstances, would only have given her the day off, and have done with it. But, even in his lethargic state, he had thought of the car. Yes, it was really awfully decent of him. Rather a dear old bean !

Twenty — twenty-five — thirty — the speedometer needle mounted. She had marked out no fixed route. She would go whither the fancy led her

Up, on the main northward road, and out into the open country, the rolling downs in front, the vista broadening. Turning into an inviting-looking by-road, skirting a great wood, then up, ever up, the white track—she was off tarred roads now—that wound about the open downs with their crisp, short turf. Plunging into an avenue that led through the forest on the top, the trees just beginning to show the glow of autumn colour, out into the open again and on a level, hedgeless track, till a red triangle warned her the descent was at hand. She stopped, however, left her car on the road, and climbed the summit of a great, rounded hill on her right. Southward, far away over the tops of the trees through which she had come, just a dim grey streak on the horizon, marking the sea. To right and left the bare downs, northward an expanse of hill and plain bathed in the autumn sunshine. Her face glowed with health and pleasure as she gazed on it all.

Into the car again. Down a steep, curving road, into the village clustering beneath the downs, then away to the right through narrow, sinuous ways that ran parallel to the great range and were bathed in their shadow. Up once more, till she reached a spot far from human habitation, stopped the car, got out, and sat on a grassy bank, unpacking her lunch and admiring the view.

She had thrown off her hat, the wind played with her hair, and the sunshine threw a light upon it. The man who came swinging along over the turf caught sight of it as he drew near. He was dressed in loose, knickerbocker suit, and the pockets of his sports jacket bulged. He came from the direction behind her, down the hill, and the first sign to her of his presence was the scrunch of his footsteps as he left the grass to cross over the road. Then she looked up and caught his eye. He stopped. It was Donald Quarrington.

" Hullo, Miss Lake," he said. " I didn't guess it was you. Awfully glad to see you."

" Why—what are you doing here ? "

" I might ask the same question."

She pointed to the car.

" I'm taking a day off," she said, " all on my lonesome. Have a sandwich ? "

" Thanks," he said, " but I've got my grub in my pocket. I say, do you mind if I picnic with you ? "

" Not a bit. Especially if you've got any cigarettes. I've just discovered I didn't bring any."

He sat down on the grass beside her and took his lunch out of his pocket.

" You haven't answered my question," she said.

" Oh, what I'm doing ? We get a non-lecture day once a week at the Coll., and I often take a ramble like this. Trained out to Linderton, you know, and I'm making for Sidhurst—then train back."

"How ripping! Aren't these downs gorgeous!"

"I love 'em!"

Presently, as they ate their lunch, he said:

"I say, what's this tale about your very reverend uncle?"

"What tale?"

"Haven't you seen it?"

"No. What do you mean?"

"By George, you should have heard 'em last evening! I was having tea with my aunt—for my sins—and the three Miss Brands were there. They cackled about nothing else."

"*What* is it you're talking about, Mr. Quarrington?" asked Peggy, sitting upright and turning towards him.

"It's in *Sporting Echoes*—a bally rag of a paper. Says the Dean of Frattenbury's been seen at some French watering-place—I forget the name—betting and dancing in the Casino."

"What *do* you mean?" exclaimed the girl. "Are you making this up?"

"No. It's in *Sporting Echoes* right enough. I saw it myself. There's a run on the paper, I tell you."

"But it's absurd! My uncle would never do such a thing."

"That's what I said. I backed him up, Miss Lake. I'm going to be a parson myself one of these days, you know, and I hope I've got a sense of the decencies of things. I only know the Dean slightly, but I'm perfectly sure he wouldn't do such a thing."

"I know . . . but what can it mean?"

"Well, my idea is there's nothing in it at all. Lots of these Continental casinos are a mixture: there's a room for concerts, and others for roulette and dancing, and so on. You may depend upon it, the Dean simply went to a concert. Some unkind person with his knife into the Church saw him there and exaggerated. I told those old cats so last night."

"Frightfully decent of you."

"Not at all," he replied, looking straight at her. "I did it for your sake, too."

A tinge of heightened colour came into her face. His eyes were very admiring.

"Oh, that's all right," she said. "*I* don't care for myself. But I do about poor old uncle. It will worry him dreadfully if he gets to know about it."

"Have you heard from him?"

"N-no. I thought he might have sent me a picture postcard or something, but he hasn't. Mr. Quarrington, what am I to do about this horrid story? I feel, in a sort of way, I ought to do something about it."

He handed her his cigarette-case, took one himself, and lighted it.

"Don't know exactly what you *can* do. When will the Dean be back?"

"In about a fortnight's time."

"He'll be able to put it right, I'm sure. Meanwhile I'll back him up right and left. Not that *I'm* any good. Tell you what, though. Would you like me to horsewhip the editor—if I can get at him?"

She laughed.

"I think he deserves it—but it would probably only make matters worse."

"You've only to ask me. I'd do it with pleasure—for you."

Peggy laughed again.

"Don't talk rubbish," she said, "though, really, you're a nice boy to say so. Now I'm going to put the thing out of my mind. I don't want it to spoil my day."

She got up, put on her hat, and brushed a few crumbs from her frock.

"I say, take me for a run, won't you?"

"You're not one of Mr. Stanniland's business friends. Remember what I told you."

"But you're not out on business to-day, you see. It's a jolly old joy ride."

She had taken her seat and was pressing the electric starter.

"All right," she said, "jump in."

"Topping!" he exclaimed, as he did so. "Whither away?"

"Where would you like to go? I don't know any of these roads. It's all new to me."

"Let's run to Sidhurst first, and then on to Fittlebury. There's a quaint little fisherman's inn there, where we can have tea. Topping place—artists and fishermen go there, you know. And we can go back by way of Dunley Hill and the Fair Mile. It's one of the best bits of the downs."

So they went on to Sidhurst, explored the quaint, sleepy old town nestling in a hollow among the woods, then to Fittlebury, where they arrived with an appetite for tea, and in the late afternoon by a roundabout route back to Frattenbury.

It was about a couple of miles out of Frattenbury that they met the peculiar vehicle belonging to the Miss Brands, with the three ladies in question seated, in an inevitable row, in the only seat. The road was narrow, and Peggy had to slow up as they passed.

" There," she said, for the three ladies in question, after a prolonged stare as they approached the car, had bowed, " that'll give them something else to talk about."

" Oh, I say," said Donald Quarrington, " I hope I'm not getting *you* into a——"

" Say it," said Peggy, as he stopped short. " Scandal, eh ? My dear boy, old nineteenth century can say what it likes about twentieth century as far as I'm concerned. There's nothing in it."

" I wish there was," ventured Donald, who had been falling in love with his chauffeur head over heels.

" Don't be silly," retorted Peggy, " or you'll spoil the joy ride. What's the time ? "

He looked at his watch.

" Good Lord ! " he said, " almost time I was back at Coll. It's been perfectly topping ! I say—we'll have another, eh ? "

" Oh, I don't know," replied Peggy. " If Mr. Stanniland gives me another day off with the car—perhaps ! But not if you're going to be silly."

Meanwhile Stanniland had been doing nothing with both hands all day. He simply lounged and dozed. He did not even smoke. And he kept in a darkened room till late in the afternoon. Then he stretched himself in a deck-chair in his garden, where the boy brought him tea. Even then he was almost too lazy to take it. But a cup of strong tea with a slice of lemon in it freshened him up a little. He went back into the house, had a bath, shaved, and dressed himself for the first time that day. Then he put on his hat and started for an aimless stroll—still in his lazy mood.

He made his way outside Frattenbury, found a convenient stile by the side of the road, lighted a cigarette, and sat on the stile, idly swinging his stick to and fro, his mind a blank—for he had trained himself to keep his mind a blank on these days of slacking. He knew his brain would be all the more alert later on.

The souud of an approaching car broke on his ear. He looked up, lazily enough. As it came near, however, his eyes widened a little. Peggy and Donald Quarrington were in that car, and she was laughing merrily as she drove. Neither of them noticed him as they passed—they were too much engrossed.

Stanniland jumped off the stile, his languid body stiffened. He gazed after them as they ran down the road, a little frown knitting his forehead.

Then he softly gave vent to one word. And it was not the word which suited a restful mind.

" Damn ! "

He walked back to Frattenbury with considerable more alertness than he had shown when strolling out of it. And although he did no work that evening, he was restless. The boy got quite a wigging because he was slow in waiting at table.

The next morning he was in his laboratory soon after six, clad in a long white smock. And Bunsen burners and test tubes and putty and mortar were kept busy under his skilful hands. At half-past eight, after a hasty breakfast, he went into his office, still in his white smock, ripped open the pile of letters, read them, and pencilled notes. He had the telephone to his mouth as Peggy entered, and did not turn round.

"Got that? . . . Get busy with it, then. Ring up when you've done—yes? Right! Hurry now!"

Then he turned sharply.

"Good morning," he said, in the hard, business tone he had assumed when he first interviewed Peggy. "Type these answers, please. I want them got off by the morning post. When they're ready for signature, touch the bell. I shall be in the laboratory."

And, without another word, he strode out of the room.

Peggy looked after him as the door closed, and a rush of colour mounted to her cheeks.

"He might have asked me how I enjoyed my day off!" she said to herself. "What a beast! I hate him!"

And again she blushed as she applied herself to the typewriter and banged the keys with quite unnecessary force.

CHAPTER XVI

HOWEVER much Finch may have been surprised—and he certainly was—at meeting the Dean on that sudden turn in the path round Bolt Head, his features did not betray his feelings. He raised his hat with a dignified bow, and, just as if he had been accosting the Dean in the Close at Frattenbury, said :

" Good morning, sir. A beautiful morning ! "

" Er, yes—ah, good morning, Finch. I—er—hardly expected to see you here."

" No, sir ? I am taking my little holiday, sir."

" Yes, er—I see. And," went on the Dean, " I suppose you hardly expected to see me ? "

" No, sir, I did not," replied Finch, with imperturbable face and respectful accent. " I had understood that you had gone abroad, sir."

" Quite so. But I varied my route, you see. When I left Frattenbury I had no idea that I should come here."

" Just what I do myself when I take a holiday, if I may say so, sir. I generally set off with no fixed purpose, so to speak."

The Dean had seated himself on the rocky stile. Finch was standing before him, in dignified but semi-deferential attitude. He had, from force of habit, taken his stick from under his arm, and was holding it pointed at an angle, downwards, as though in readiness for the customary procession when it should please the Dean to make a start.

Bewildering thoughts passed through the Dean's brain. Had Finch read that terrible paragraph? Of course he was sure to hear of it sooner or later. But had he read it now? He dared not ask him. Still, he must say something

"Are you making a long stay here, Finch?"

"No, sir. I only came here yesterday, and intend leaving by boat this morning. I am making a little detower, as you may say, sir. To-morrow I hope to visit Exeter. The Cathedral there is unfamiliar to me, but I understand there are points of interest in it."

There was just that superior tone in his voice as he uttered this last sentence which implied that any cathedral, familiar or otherwise, was extremely inferior to Frattenbury.

"You will enjoy seeing it," remarked the Dean.

"Possibly, sir," replied Finch, as though there was a distinct doubt about it.

"All well at home, I hope?" asked the Dean, more for the sake of saying something than anything else.

"I believe so, sir. Mrs. Finch and my daughter were in good health when I took my departure, if I may say so, sir. Miss Lake has been a little perturbed, sir."

"Perturbed! Why? What is the matter?"

"Well, sir, the morning you left a strange man was observed in your garden—apparently coming out of the Deanery."

"Indeed!" exclaimed the Dean, a little rush of guilty colour rising to his cheeks. "Who—who saw him?"

"The man next door—at the 'Chantry,' sir"—it was his method of expressing disapproval on the advent of Stanniland to the Close—"he saw him crossing the garden and going out through the little door at the end of the garden, sir. He told Miss Lake about it."

"Oh, really. Mr. Stanniland did not recognize him? No—of course not."

"No, sir. But he telephoned for the police. Miss Lake told my wife all about it."

"The police! I see. What did they do?"

He was beginning to get alarmed. Now Finch had made inquisitive inquiries of his friend, Sergeant Stanton, anent the matter. But the police have a habit of not telling all they know—even to their friends. And Stanton had, apparently in a burst of confidence, informed Finch just as much as it was wise for him to know, and no more.

"Well, sir, I understand they searched the house——"

"Searched the house? But it was locked up. How did they get in?"

"I can't tell you that, sir. But there was nothing to arouse suspicion. And the police came to the conclusion, sir, that this Stanniland"—he *would* not give him a "Mr."—"must have been mistaken."

"You mean that he did *not* see—see—this man?"

"Not exactly that, sir, but that he was mistaken in thinking he had come out of the house—that he was simply prowling about the garden, probably for no good purpose, sir. Possibly he was aware the Deanery was empty—it was just after you had left, sir, and the police knew you had gone. Superintendent Walters saw you at the station."

"Oh, *did* he?"

"Why, sir he says he spoke to you.'

"Of course—of course. . . . I see. Well, what else, Finch?"

"Well, sir, they tracked the individual, whoever he was, to Fernley Station, where he took train. And they tell me they lost all trace of him there."

The Dean heaved a sigh of relief. The tension had been great.

"Thank you, Finch," he said, getting off the rock. "When do you return to Frattenbury?"

He was thinking rapidly. Finch, of course, would say on his return that he had seen the Dean at Salcombe. Very likely he would write home and tell his wife the news. And it would soon become known in Frattenbury. He could scarcely attempt to frustrate this. Fate had been against his concealment, but he had no wish to fight against Fate. After all, he had done no harm, or, if he had, it was only the question of conniving at his brother's escape. And, so far as he could see, this need never leak out. Certainly he was going to beg no favours of his own verger.

"I hope to get back in about ten days' time, sir."

"I see. Well, I hope you will enjoy your holiday, Finch. Good morning!"

And he made as though to pass him. Finch mechanically, and from sheer force of habit, lifted up his walking-stick till it pointed at an angle to the sky.

"I beg your pardon, sir!"

"What is it?"

"If I may say so, sir—with all due deferen sir?"

" Say what ? "

Finch cleared his throat, but never lost his attitude of respectful gravity.

" Is it your wish, sir, that I should mention I have seen you here, or would you prefer that I should say nothing about it ? "

" Now why do you ask me such a question ? " asked the Dean, backing towards the rocky stile and resting against it. " Explain, please ! "

" If you will pardon my saying so," replied Finch, with extreme dignity, " I have been connected with the Cathedral ever since I was a boy, and my—er—reputation, sir, is bound up with it and the Cathedral clergy. Never once, I am happy to say, has there been the slightest hint of any scandal in the precincts of the Close. Naturally, there has been gossip, but I am alluding to actual scandal.'

" I don't quite follow you," said the Dean.

" I have the privilege of being the senior verger, sir—the Dean's verger," went on Finch, still holding up his walking-stick as though to enforce the distinction and speaking with great pride, " and, in that capacity, the honour of the Dean touches my personal honour, so to speak. You may, or you may not have observed it, sir, but there have been occasions upon which I have ventured, with the knowledge that you were new to the office, to—er—in point of fact, to put you right with regard to certain details."

" I *have* observed it, certainly," replied the Dean, with a grim smile. " But—go on. '

" And I trust you have pardoned me, sir. It was not only out of consideration for yourself, but with a thought to my own position."

" I can well understand that."

"Therefore," went on the verger, emphasizing his remarks with his walking-stick, "any scandal which concerns the Dean reflects upon *me*, sir!"

"Now will you explain exactly what you mean, Finch?"

"I will, sir, gladly."

Slowly and solemnly he produced from the breast pocket of his coat a—to the Dean—too familiar object. The copy of *Sporting Echoes*. Slowly he turned over the pages till he arrived at the fatal paragraph, and handed it over to the Dean, pointing it out with his forefinger.

"Have you seen this, sir?" he asked, in a sepulchral tone of voice.

The Dean steeled himself.

"I have," he said, abruptly. "But before I discuss it with you, I must ask you for your own opinion of it."

"My opinion!" retorted Finch. "There can only be one opinion in my mind, sir. I have had considerable experience of Cathedral dignitaries, and I hope I know how to respect them. I do not believe it for a moment, sir!"

The Dean positively smiled. It was the first grain of comfort he had received for hours. His opinion of the pompous Finch went up by leaps and bounds. In his gratitude he extended his hand.

"Thank you, Finch!" he exclaimed. "Of course it is not true."

Finch took his hand in his own limp one, and made a courteous bow as he did so.

"I never thought for a moment it was, sir. You will, I have no doubt, be able to repudiate it. But until you do, sir, the Close at Frattenbury—not to mention the City itself—will naturally be—er—apprehensive. That is bad for you, sir, and for ME." And he repeated, " I have the honour to be the Dean's verger ! "

The colossal conceit of the man made him tilt up his head an inch higher. Yet, in spite of it, the Dean was grateful. For Finch's loyalty was equal to his conceit.

" That is what I meant, sir," he went on, " by asking you if you would like me to mention that I had seen you here. I do not wish to be inquisitive—far from it—but simply to do what is best to assist you—and myself. I believe," he added, with great pomposity, " that my word has no little influence in —er—the Cathedral circle ! And I——"

But the Dean cut him short.

" You can certainly speak the truth, Finch. I hope to make this wretched business clear on my return. Meanwhile I may tell you I have never been out of England since I saw you last."

For he had now quite made up his mind that this was the only reasonable course to take

" Thank you, sir," replied Finch. " I am exceedingly glad I happened to meet you, for I have felt much disturbed. You rest may assured, sir, that, as far as it lies in my power, I will do anything that you may wish to assist you. Good morning, sir ! "

He raised his hat with one hand, lowered his stick as if in salute with the other, bowed solemnly, and passed on. The Dean remained seated on the rock. He filled and lighted his pipe for solace, and he thought hard. Once or twice a smile broke over his face when he remembered Finch's pomposity and conceit. But gratitude was uppermost. The man

14

had positively refused to believe him guilty of such indecorous conduct, and had not asked for a single proof to the contrary. Magnificent faith went hand in hand with magnificent conceit—as it often does.

More than ever he made up his mind to write to the Bishop without delay. He finished his pipe, strolled round the farther side of Bolt Head for a glimpse of the view, and then made his way back to East Pouthmouth. It was lunch-time when he reached his rooms, but directly he had finished the meal he sat down to write his letter.

"My dear Bishop——"

He got no further, for a voice exclaimed:

"Hullo! May I come in?"

He looked up. Hinton was standing outside the open window. A shade of annoyance crossed his face. At the best of times he disliked being disturbed when engaged in correspondence. But he was nothing if not courteous.

"Yes, come in," he replied, with more geniality than he was really feeling.

Hinton entered in his breezy way.

"I thought you might care for a sail," he said. "There's a bit of wind outside the harbour. Won't you come?"

There was something very friendly about Hinton, and the Dean liked him.

"I was just about to write a letter," he replied, "which I am anxious to get off by the next post."

"All right," said Hinton. "There's no hurry. I'll wait while you write it, and you can post it as soon as we cross the ferry."

"Thanks very much."

He dipped his pen in the ink again, and went on:

"I want your advice, as an old friend, badly. I——"

There came a scrunch of heavy footsteps on the little gravelled path leading from the road to the door of the cottage. Hinton was looking out of the window.

"Hullo!" he exclaimed, "what does *he* want, I wonder?"

The Dean glanced out of the window. A uniformed policeman was coming up the path—a sergeant, by the stripes on his arm. They heard him speaking to the landlady as she opened the door to him, and the next moment she showed him into the little room. He stood just within the doorway, helmet in hand, and looked keenly first at one and then at the other of the two men.

"Good afternoon," remarked the Dean. "What is it?"

The sergeant answered with another question.

"Which of you two gentlemen is named Lake, please?"

"My name is Lake," replied the Dean, a sinking feeling in his heart. What *else* was going to happen?

"Can I speak to you in private, Mr. Lake?"

Hinton got up to go. But an appealing look in the Dean's eye made him hesitate. The Dean never felt so much in need of a friend, though the very next moment it flashed upon him that Hinton could not help him. Still he said:

"Don't go, Hinton. There is no reason why you should not speak to me in this gentleman's presence," he added to the sergeant.

"As you please," said the latter, "though you will remember I gave you the chance. I must ask you to come with me, Mr. Lake. There is a warrant out against you."

"Oh, really——" began Hinton. But the Dean stopped him, raising his hand.

"On what grounds, sergeant?" he asked, very quietly.

The sergeant consulted the invariable pocket-book of his order.

"Melford—alias Corney & Co," he replied, "charge of fraudulent company promoting—with intent to deceive." He added the words as if to explain that fraud *did* mean deception.

Hinton gave vent to an exclamation: "Good Lord! Melford! *I* know!"

But the Dean went on, quite calmly: "May I see the warrant, please?"

The sergeant shook his head.

"Scotland Yard holds it," he replied. "My instructions are to detain you until they send a man down with it."

"And suppose I tell you you are making a mistake—that I am not the man you want?"

"I can't help that," said the sergeant. "You may or you may not be. I am simply under orders to detain you. Of course," he added, with that touch of fairness and kindliness which is so often apparent in the police, "if you can prove you are not the man we want, your detention will only be a matter of a few hours."

"Oh, look here, sergeant," broke in Hinton, "I know this gentleman——"

"How long have you known him?" interrupted the sergeant. For although he had asked the official question as to which of the two men was named Lake, he knew Hinton very well, and astute inquiries had also made him quite aware that the acquaintanceship had only begun at Salcombe.

The Dean answered his question frankly, with a wan little smile.

" Mr. Hinton has, unfortunately, only known me for a fortnight."

" But, my dear fellow——"

The sergeant, however, was only alive to facts, not protestations.

" Is there anyone else you would like to apply to ? All the same, it's my duty to detain you."

The Dean thought rapidly. A wire to the Bishop—to Canon Burford—to—ah, Finch—his verger ! But Finch had said he was leaving by that morning's boat. He was well on his way to Exeter by this time.

Besides—a thought suddenly took root in his bewildered mind. Something that Superintendent Walters had told him weeks ago. And he wanted time to think it out.

" I will consider," he replied, with dignity. " Meanwhile I understand you to say that, whatever course I may take, it is your duty to detain me ? "

" Yes, sir—till they send from Scotland Yard. Then the matter will be out of our hands."

The Dean noticed that, for the first time, the man addressed him as " sir." It was quite involuntary, but the Dean's dignified bearing had induced it.

" Can I bail him out ? " asked Hinton.

" No magistrate would grant bail—with the warrant out," answered the sergeant.

" Lake," exclaimed Hinton, " you will believe me when I say that I feel this is a mistake ? "

" You are exceedingly kind," replied the Dean,

"but you must bear in mind that I have not *said* so myself."

For the thought that was in his mind was taking hold upon him. When he had his back up against a wall, the Dean of Frattenbury could be a very obstinate man. He had got himself into all this trouble with the idea of saving his brother and his family honour. And, even now, he did not feel inclined, somehow, to give in.

"No, you haven't *said* so," retorted Hinton, looking straight at him, "but *I* know it's just as much a mistake as that affair at Arcachon. There! And I shouldn't wonder if the two are connected. An alibi might be found in both cases. What?"

The Dean returned his gaze steadily.

"I prefer, just now," he said, "to keep matters in my own hand. But some day I may ask you to give an account of me—for the last fortnight."

"Now," said the sergeant, who was growing impatient, "there's nothing more to be said. I must ask you to come with me."

"May I pack my bag and bring it with me?"

"Yes; but be quick, please."

Hinton went with him to the police station, crossing the ferry to Salcombe. Few words were exchanged. Hinton arranged for a dinner to be taken to him that night, in his cell, for they insisted upon putting him into a cell, and for his breakfast in the morning. He promised to call the next day, and made one final effort to induce his friend to clear himself.

"No," replied the Dean, doggedly. "I shall neither assert my innocence nor my guilt. I have a very good reason."

In his cell he thought out that reason, which was this. Superintendent Walters had told him that if his brother were arrested there was no need for anyone to know that he was related to the Dean of Frattenbury, unless he said so himself. A policy of silence would preserve the family honour. In ten days' time at latest the *Sunflower* would have returned, his brother's innocence would be established, he could communicate with his brother, and nothing need ever be made public. He had had enough of publicity over that miserable Arcachon paragraph without his name being dragged further into the satirical humour of a ribald press. With Hinton's help he hoped to put that right in due time. Meanwhile, for the sake of the Church, for his brother's, Peggy's, and his own sake, he persisted more and more in his mind that he would remain silent.

Contrary to his nature? Not a bit of it. A secluded, methodical life often renders a man equal to facing an adventure when it comes, even if he deals with it with rather a foolish courage.

So, while the sergeant was informing Scotland Yard that he had caught one of the Melford group, and was receiving the answer that one of their men would start with the warrant to Salcombe by the first morning train, the Dean of Frattenbury sat in his cell, with a look of grim, if obstinate, determination on his face. He would see this thing through in his own way.

CHAPTER XVII

FRATTENBURY CLOSE was in a flutter of excitement. A copy of *Sporting Echoes* found its way into every house, including that of the Canon in Residence. The Dean was discussed from every point of view.

The report, emanating from Major Wingrave, that he had left the boat at Bordeaux, and that Bordeaux was in the vicinity of Arcachon, of course lent vivid colour to the paragraph and enhanced the scandal. It spite of this, however, some, loyal to the Cathedral tradition, tried to persuade themselves—and others—that it was either a mistake or a gross exaggeration. Others shook their heads sadly, and recollected—for the first time—that they had noticed little traits in the Dean's character, little indications of what he *might* be like if temptation assailed him, or if he were free from restraining influences.

Thus Miss Marshall declared that she had seen him, with her own eyes, playing bridge at the Westons' evening gathering. "Of course, my dear, he did not play for money—he *couldn't* very well. But he was at the table for quite two hours, and one could see he *liked* it! The gambling spirit, I'm afraid. I've told my nephew, Donald, it ought to be a warning to him *never* to touch cards."

"But it wasn't cards in this case," remarked someone; "it was roulette apparently."

"Quite so," replied Miss Marshall, "but all in the same category. If the Westons had had roulette, I've no doubt he would have played at it. It is all very sad!"

The Miss Brands, too, reminded their friends of the significant fact that the Dean had attended a dance in the Town Hall at Frattenbury. As a matter of fact, it was a very dull social evening, with a little dancing at the end to vary the monotony, got up by the local branch of the Y.M.C.A., of which the Dean was President. And he had looked in for half an hour.

"Did he dance *himself?*" asked a shocked auditor.

"N-no—not exactly," replied Miss Prudence Brand, "but he was *there!*"

"*And* the only Cathedral dignitary present," added Alethea Brand.

"I *hope* so, indeed!" exclaimed Monica, and they all wound up in chorus, "You see, we *know* he got off the boat at Bordeaux. We would *like* to think it is a mistake, but——!"

It was all very significant. They wondered what they would do on his return. They *couldn't* listen to his sermons, if, indeed, he had the audacity to preach after that escapade in the Casino. But, probably, he would resign. Far the best thing. Frattenbury had *never* had such a scandal before. The *Dean*, too! It was appalling—horrible!

Peggy had to put up with sudden silences when, on two occasions, she attended these afternoon teas. She guessed what they had been discussing before she entered the room. One or two friends commiserated with her point blank, and received their well-deserved reply. For Peggy could be a little spitfire when she chose, and was loyal to her uncle. Whether he had or had not committed an indiscretion—and she told herself it *must* be a mistake—she showed very plainly what she thought of discussing it.

And thereby incurred displeasure. The Miss Brands were not slow in retailing the news that they had met her driving out with Donald Quarrington, and the unfortunate Donald received a severe lecture from his aunt on the subject. It was hinted that she was a fast, designing girl—and what else could one expect when one knew what the family was like ? Living alone in rooms, too, and working in the house of a bachelor ! What could the Dean be thinking of to allow it ? But, there—— !

It was a pretty little scandal, but it did not affect Peggy or her work. And work she had to once again. " Sapor " had given place to " Jecinora " ; Stanniland was in his element. In his laboratory, in his office, interviews, telephoning, telegraphing, rushing up to his London premises, alert, brusque, and all the time sanguine.

It was this sanguine and enthusiastic element in his temperament which probably made him, now and again, break through the mask of the curt, business manner he had reassumed with Peggy the day after her car trip. He *had* to talk about the object he had in hand. Yet, Peggy noticed, all the time there was a subtle difference. And it baffled her. More, she was beginning to find, in spite of herself, that it—well, she would have said just then, annoyed her. He had begun to be so friendly, and she had had a glimpse of something very human beneath the business qualities of her employer. And now he seemed determined not to let her have that glimpse again.

She had just come into the office one morning to begin her day's work. As usual, he was bending over the correspondence. He turned round.

" Good morning, Miss Lake. Well, ' Sapors ' are at a premium already. They're not officially quoted yet, of course, but they're being dealt in. The fact that they were over-subscribed seems to have put them up."

" Oh, I say," she exclaimed, clapping her hands, " but that's topping! I *am* glad! "

" Are you ? " he said. " Yes, you'll get your profit for the Dean."

" I didn't mean that," she replied. " I'm glad for your sake, Mr. Stanniland. I wanted them to do well."

" Umph! "

He looked at her keenly for a moment. Then his eyes suddenly hardened.

" Now then," he said, " I advise you to take the premium while you can get it."

" You mean sell out ? "

" Certainly."

" How do I do that ? "

He glanced at the clock.

" I'll phone to my broker for you—after ten o'clock. Too early yet. Yes, sell out the lot—early as possible. They may drop a bit later on in the day if the stags are out for profit-taking."

" Are you going to sell yours ? "

He nodded.

" Yes. I want every penny I can lay hands on to float ' Jecinora.' But it won't do for me to sell my lot all at once. A block like that would send 'em down directly."

He turned round to his work once more. The typewriter started clicking.

A little after ten he took up the telephone and asked for his broker's number.

"Hullo-hullo! That you, Porlock? . . . Stanniland speaking . . . yes . . . yes. How are 'Sapors' this morning? No—I know there's no official quotation yet. . . . Right. . . . I'll hold on."

"What's your full name?" he suddenly asked Peggy.

"Margaret Beryl Lake."

"Right. . . . Yes . . . are you there? Oh, really! . . . That's good. Now, will you sell two hundred, please—no—not mine—Miss Lake . . . Margaret Beryl Lake—yes . . . two hundred. . . . I say, phone through when you've done it . . . and the price. Thanks. Now, I want you to sell for *me*—got that? Yes . . . yes. . . . I want to get rid of the lot . . . no, no—of course not. Work 'em off in blocks . . . don't overdo it . . . if they fall? Yes . . . I think so . . . anything up to sixpence premium . . . hope they won't go to that, all the same. . . . No . . . I don't care if you take a month about it . . . oh . . . that's all very well . . . but I've got something bigger coming along. Right! So long!"

Correspondence and typewriting went on for a time. Then the telephone bell rang.

"Hullo—yes—Stanniland speaking . . . oh . . . good . . . right!"

"That's all right," he said, "he's sold your shares at two shillings premium. That's twenty pounds for the old Cathedral."

Her eyes sparkled with pleasure.

" I'm most awfully grateful to you ! "

" That's all right," he replied, tersely, and turned again to his work.

After a time the second morning post came in—mostly parcels and circulars. There was among them a long roll. He cut the string and tore it open.

" Ah ! " he exclaimed, " here we are. The artist's proof. What do you think of it, Miss Lake ? "

For the enthusiasm of enterprise was on him once more, and he had to blurt it out to someone.

He held up before her a large coloured sketch. The artist had certainly carried out his instructions. The upper portion of a man, in coal-black coat with a flaring necktie, a serious, massive head, with flaming auburn hair, concentrated, determined countenance, piercing blue eyes that fixed one in a compelling stare, hand stretched out with forefinger impressively pointed straight at one as if to drive home an announcement upon which one's very existence depended, and the glaring message underneath,

IT'S YOUR LIVER I'M TALKING ABOUT !

TAKE JECINORA !

" That ought to fetch 'em, eh ? "

" Rather ! " said Peggy. " It's perfectly topping ! "

" Think so ? "

" Of course I do."

He looked at it critically.

" Hair a bit too short. Big fuzz on top of his head would look better—take down what I say, please—I shall want you to write at once. A little more white cuff to show on the wrist—got that ? . . . Not quite enough frown on his forehead . . . background to be worked up a little . . . the word JECINORA to be bigger than the others. That'll do."

She typed the letter while he opened the rest of the correspondence and glanced through it. Mostly waste-paper basket matter. When she had finished she found herself saying, almost to herself:

"Oh, I do hope it will be a success!"

"What? The picture's all right, isn't it?"

He wheeled round suddenly.

"I mean the whole thing—Jecinora."

"Why shouldn't it? It's a good thing!"

"I'm quite sure it is, Mr. Stanniland. Have you finished inventing it now?"

He laughed.

"I did that a long time ago," he replied, "before I came to Frattenbury."

"Oh! But I thought you'd been working at it in your laboratory all this week!"

"Finishing touches, that's all. Just a trifling alteration in the formula—and the flavouring of the stuff—for the public."

"*I* see! To make it taste nice?"

"Good Lord, no! Quite the opposite. Folks don't think half as much of medicines that taste nice. My trouble's been to make it a bit nasty, for its natural formula it's really rather pleasant."

Peggy laughed heartily.

"You do amuse me, Mr. Stanniland!"

"Oh, do I? But it's business, all the same. Yes," he went on, reflectively, "I've had the thing made up for a couple of months or so, and sent samples for analysis and report. Nothing like getting a few good notices beforehand in the technical journals.

It has to be done if you want to put it on the market for a boom."

"Have you had any notices yet?"

"No. But I expect there's one here," and he tapped a thick, wrappered missive which the post had brought.

He turned round to his desk again and tore off the wrapper. The contents were a monthly periodical of technical and trade interest, *The Chemical Journal.*

Turning over the leaves rapidly he suddenly paused. Peggy, over her typewriter, could see that he was reading intently. She stopped in her work.

"Is the next batch ready, please?"

He made no answer. There was a dead silence in the room. He went on reading.

Suddenly he threw down the journal on the desk, rose to his feet, said the single word "Damn!" turned on his heel, and went out of the room, banging the door as he did so.

Peggy, who had just finished a batch of correspondence, waited a minute or two. Then she leaned forward, reached over to Stanniland's desk, and took up *The Chemical Journal.* Her curiosity was aroused.

There it was on the page he had left open.

"JECINORA."

We have received from "Bruce & Co.", the firm which was instrumental in placing "Sapor" relish on the market, samples of a new preparation produced by them which, we understand, will shortly be before the public. One would imagine, from the multitude of "liver cures," good, bad, and indifferent, which are already within the reach of the confiding and bilious, that the advent of a new one from the enterprising firm of "Bruce & Co."

would bring with it special features for its recommendation. So we turned to the sample with interest. Frankly, however, we are disappointed. We are not saying, after careful analysis, that the preparation is not a good one. In many respects we think it excellent, and quite a safe remedy for those ordinary troubles of the liver which may not entail the expense or prescription of a medical practitioner. But, from our analysis, we have found little to merit its claim as a novelty among the thousand-and-one preparations of a similar nature. The inventors, by the way, seek to establish that claim by—what we have so often heard before—an ingredient in the formula which is new to this country, and not in the British Pharmacopœia. All very well, but we are under the impression that we have generally discovered, when analysing similar preparations, the usual trace of *calomel!*

As for the name, " Jecinora," well, we think it apt, and that it is probably better than the actual formula. We mean for advertising and selling purposes! The public loves a good name when it doses itself!

Peggy was still holding the paper when Stanniland re-entered the room. In his hand was a notebook.

" Ah ! " he exclaimed, " have you been reading it ? "

" I thought you wouldn't mind."

" Mind ? It's public property, isn't it ? Worse luck ! "

" It's a rotten shame ! " she exclaimed, indignantly. " Why have they done it ? "

" They've a perfect right to their own opinion . . . though they're sometimes biased enough to get their knife into one. Lots of influences behind the scenes in journalism. The beggar that wrote it may have been got at by the proprietors of some other liver mixture, for all we know. Worth his while. Calomel, indeed ! As if the whole bally thing was calomel ! Look here ! Here's the formula. See ? "

And he laid the notebook on her table and pointed at scrawled hieroglyphics with his finger.

"You won't understand it all, of course. But this shows the proportions of an ounce. There's just one-eighth of a grain of calomel in each ounce. See what I mean?"

"I think it's perfectly horrid," she said.

"Do you?" he echoed, suddenly looking up from the notebook at her.

"Why, of course I do!"

"Why?"

A faint colour suffused her cheeks as she replied:

"Because I believe in you, Mr. Stanniland. I don't think you're the quack they make out for a moment. You wouldn't do a mean action."

Again he looked at her. His hard expression softened a little.

"That's kind of you," he said; "but I'm afraid, after this, that there will be lots of people who won't believe in me—or rather in 'Jecinora.' It's the same thing."

"Of the two, I think I'd place 'Jecinora' a good second. Though I believe in that too," she said, quietly. "But what will this mean?"

"Mean? Well, this bally paper's got no end of influence in business circles. Take one instance. You've seen something of the ways of underwriters when we were working at 'Sapor.' They've got to be fished for carefully at times, when it's a question of a new undertaking. This won't make 'em bite any the better. Then there are the financial papers to reckon with. When the prospectus is out they may remember this notice, and hint that it would be wiser for the public not to subscribe. See?"

She leaned back in her chair, her forehead knitted. "What are you going to do about it?"

"Do?" and he banged the table with his open palm. "What do you think? Get on with it, of course. I've had to fight my own battles all my life, and, by George! I rather like a fight. D'you think this damned notice is going to stop me for a moment? Not much!"

She caught his enthusiasm, and smiled at him.

"Hurrah!" she exclaimed. "I call that splendid! Three cheers for 'Jecinora'!"

He began to stride up and down the room.

"No, by gad!" he cried. "It takes more than this to baulk Julian Bruce Stanniland. And I'll show 'em, too. I've got the goods, and I'll push 'em—even if I put my last dollar on it. 'Jecinora's' *got* to hum!"

She had seen him in many moods, but never so much in his capacity as a fighter. A few weeks ago she would have ridiculed the idea of a man fighting for a liver mixture. Now, however, she regarded him with admiration. The cause might be bizarre, but the faith and spirit of the man were fine.

He stopped short in his walk.

"It'll mean work—devilish hard work!"

"I don't care. I'm with you—if I can help."

"If you can help? Of course you can. That's what you're here for, isn't it?"

"And I'm awfully glad to be here—really, Mr. Stanniland. I *want* to help."

Again he looked at her intently. Her eyes fell before his gaze.

"Look here——" he began suddenly. And, as suddenly, stopped. And his eyes hardened.

"Yes?"

But whatever Stanniland meant to say at that moment he never said it. He snatched at the telephone, got on to his London office, and gave some hasty directions. Then he consulted a time-table.

"Hang it!" he remarked. "Just missed that fast train. There isn't another before three-forty. But I must get up—sharp. Miss Lake, I want you to drive up to London with me. There'll be some running about in the car while I'm at the office. So I want you."

"Righto!"

"You may have to stop the night there. Don't know yet" . . . he was ringing the bell . . . "we'll have a bit of lunch first. Ah!"—for the boy came in—"have some food for two on the table—anything—cold meat—whatever there is—in five minutes. Do you hear! Hurry! Stamp the letters, will you, Miss Lake. The boy can run round to your rooms to let 'em know you won't be there. We start in half an hour. Car ready?"

"Quite ready."

"Good! Yes, what is it?"

"If there is a chance of my having to stay the night, isn't there time for me just to run to my digs and pack a few things in a bag?"

He was in the act of opening the door to go out.

"You must have luncheon," he said.

"And I must have—a tooth-brush—and other things."

"Rot! Buy 'em in London—if you stay. You'll feed first."

She shrugged her shoulders.

"Jot down a list of what you want—now," he

went on, " and if you stay I'll send Jarvis out to get 'em."

She gave way to a peal of laughter. And when Peggy laughed she was certainly very charming.

" Poor Jarvis ! " she cried.

He looked at her again, hesitated a moment, and then threw a Parthian shot at her.

" It isn't going to be a joy ride ! " he said.

" I prefer it to a joy ride."

" Why ? "

" Because it's in the service of—' Jecinora,' " she replied, demurely.

" Now, what the dickens did she mean by *that ?* " said Stanniland to himself as he closed the door. " Oh, damn ! . . . Hi ! Charles ! Hurry up with that lunch ! "

CHAPTER XVIII

It will be necessary to go back a little to gather up one of the threads interwoven in the movements of the unfortunate Dean of Frattenbury.

Edward Lake, when he drove his bargain with that rascal Corney, by means of which the latter had been able to get out of the country, had found that, in one respect, the man who had duped him had got the better of the said bargain. He held certain documents which, while they fully established the fact that the Dean's brother had only been used as a tool by him and was innocent of any criminal charge, were considerably in evidence against his own defalcations. These he was quite ready to deliver up in exchange for the Dean's tickets and passports. But he made a condition.

"It's like this," he said. "I don't want to run any risks. And the fact that I've given you these things—when you show them—will prove that you've been with me pretty recently. And you'll be sharply questioned about my movements."

"I'm not likely to say anything."

"That's just what you *are* likely to do. You're a blundering fool. Look at the way you've come to me to-day—in broad daylight, when you knew you were being shadowed! And you get the wind up so jolly soon, too. If they once begin to ask you questions, you'll give the show away, and I shall be arrested at the first port where the *Sunflower* touches."

"I assure you I won't give you away."

"You may not mean to—but I'm not going to chance it. Here, let me have a look at this," he consulted the itinerary of the voyage. "Bordeaux, Lisbon, Marseilles. Now, look here, if I have luck I shall go as far as Marseilles and get off there. She's timed there for Thursday week. I believe you call yourself a gentleman, don't you?"

Edward Lake fired up indignantly.

"I hope so," he said.

"Not much in it, so far as I know of you. But it's the only thing I've got to go on. Will you give me your word of honour as a gentleman that you won't make any attempt to clear yourself till I get to Marseilles?"

"Oh, but, I say. That's too much, Corney. What am I to do?"

"Do nothing—for ten days."

"But suppose they arrest me?"

The other shrugged his shoulders.

"I must take that chance, I suppose. Why, then, of course you'll have to give up the papers. But there's no bally reason why you should be arrested—if you show a little horse-sense."

"I can't do it, Corney. I'm sick of wandering about—with the eternal thought of the police on my track."

"Don't wander about then. Stay here."

"Here?"

"Why not? It's safe enough."

"Why don't you stay here yourself, then?"

"Don't be a fool! I *must* get out of the country

—or do five years. *You* needn't. Look here. I took this house a couple of months ago—for three months, in case anything happened—not in my own name, of course—and paid rent in advance. The safest hiding-place is always in a crowd, and they swarm here. No one knows or cares about his next-door neighbour. So long as you keep indoors all day, and slip out at night to buy a bit of food, it's all right. Call it a bargain, Lake, and give me your word."

Edward Lake expostulated, but was ever a weak man. Finally he gave the required promise, and for ten days hid in the empty house. There were a few books lying about, which he read through and through. He longed for the Thursday that was to clear him, and the days passed slowly enough.

As luck would have it, on the Wednesday evening, when he was returning from his foraging expedition with sundry provisions, tinned meat, bread, and so forth, he met with a slight accident. He was crossing a road when a taxi came rushing round a corner. To avoid it he stepped suddenly backward, caught his foot against the curb of the pavement, and fell heavily. When he picked himself up he had an excruciating pain in his ankle. He managed to limp home with difficulty, and could only just force his boot off. His foot swelled rapidly. It was a badly sprained ankle.

For several days longer he was kept a prisoner, carefully eking out his little stock of food. At length he managed to get his boot on once more and hobbled out, taking the nearest bus to the city. There were two firms which had laid information at Scotland Yard about Bruce & Co.

The senior partner of the first firm received him in his inner office. As soon as he realized who he was, he scribbed something on a bit of paper and rang the bell on his table.

"I know what you are doing," said Edward Lake. "You are sending out for the police."

"I am," replied the other.

"Do you mind waiting first—and hearing what I have to say?"

A clerk entered. The senior partner hesitated.

"Very well," he said. "Jenkins, take this. If I ring again go straight to the nearest policeman and give it to him. Lock the outer door as you do so."

"Now," he said, turning upon the other, "what is it, please? I have very little time to give you."

Edward Lake selected some papers and laid them before the other.

"Will you look at these, please?"

The other scanned them rapidly. And then looked up.

"H'm!" he said. "You seem to have been a damned fool!"

"I was," replied Lake, and explained further.

The senior partner handed him back the papers.

"If they're correct, you're deuced lucky. That's all I can say—or do. The matter is in the hands of the police, and must take its course."

"But you can withdraw the charge, sir."

"I shall do no such thing. Warrants are out for all you people in 'Melford & Co.' You ought to have consulted a solicitor—not me."

And he held his hand over the bell.

"Don't!" implored Lake. "Give me a chance. Let me see Bruce & Co. first. They're in it too."

"Bruce & Co!" said the other, with a short laugh. "You're not likely to get any change out of *them!* They're not the people to stand any nonsense."

He looked at Lake for a moment or two. The latter was haggard and emaciated. He had had little food for the last few days.

Then he wrote something on a sheet of paper, put it in an envelope and sealed it.

"If you think you can do yourself any good by seeing Bruce & Co.," he said, "you can go there. But you won't get any farther, I fancy, my friend!"

He opened the door and called Jenkins in.

"Here," he said, "go round to Bruce & Co. with this gen'man. Give them this note. If he tries to bolt, stop him and hand him over to the police."

"Poor devil!" he ejaculated, as the two went out of the office. "Only a dupe, evidently. But he'll have to go through with it. Pity they can't lay hands on his boss."

Julian Bruce Stanniland was seated at his desk in the inner office of "Bruce & Co." And Julian Bruce Stanniland was making things hum in the office. He had come up post haste from Frattenbury in the car with Peggy. The latter he had already sent on an errand. It was half-past four in the afternoon, but Jarvis was feeling there would be overtime that day.

"Eh, what's this?" asked Stanniland as Jarvis brought the note in. "What? Melford & Co. again—one of that rascally gang. Oh, yes. I'll see him for a minute—and—Jarvis?"

"Yes, sir?"

"Go and get a policeman, sharp."

He bent over his table for a moment to sign a letter—he was wasting no time. He heard the man come in. Then he looked up.

" Good Lord ! " he exclaimed. " What the dickens ! "

He leaned back in his chair and gazed at Edward Lake, whom he had never seen before, though correspondence had passed. Something extraordinarily familiar had struck him. His thoughts flew to Frattenbury—to the Close—to the Deanery.

" What's your name ? " he asked, abruptly

" Lake."

" *Lake !* "

" Yes."

And Stanniland muttered to himself: " I'd forgotten there was a Lake in it. That's queer, though ! "

" You're one of the Melford lot ? "

" Yes."

" What do you want ? Out with it."

Edward Lake explained, and handed over some papers. Like the other business man, Stanniland glanced through them rapidly. And came to the same conclusion.

" Well ? " he rapped out.

" I hoped—you'd withdraw the charge—when you'd seen these."

" I see you've been to Shalford Brothers ? "

" Yes."

" And they mean to let things take their course ? "

" I'm afraid so."

" Serve you damn well right, too. Even if you're only a fool."

Edward Lake sighed. " It's rather hard," he said.

Stanniland looked at him closely again. " Same

name," he was saying to himself, " and the likeness—but it can't be ! "

" Look here," he suddenly blurted out, " tell me the truth now. Are you any relation of Lake, the Dean of Frattenbury ? For you're devilish like him."

Edward Lake's wan face blushed crimson. " I'd rather not say," he hesitated.

Stanniland banged the table with his fist.

" Out with it, man—if you want me to help you ! "

" For God's sake don't make it public—he's—he's my brother. Don't drag him into the mess."

" Drag him into the mess ? Not much, poor old buffer. I happen to know him. You're a rotten disgrace to him."

Edward Lake hung his head.

" Does he know what you've been up to ? " went on Stanniland, remorselessly.

The other nodded.

" He's been most awfully good to me," he said.

A sudden thought struck Stanniland. Peggy had told him once that she had a father living—and he had noticed her reticence when she said it. He went to the point at once, as usual :

" Have you got a daughter ? "

Edward Lake looked up in surprise.

" Yes," he admitted, " but I haven't seen her for a long time. And she doesn't know of——"

" What's her name ? Now ! "

" Why—why do you want to know ? "

" Never mind ! What is it ? "

" Margaret."

" Any other name ? "

" Beryl—Margaret Beryl."

In an instant Stanniland made up his mind—as he usually did.

" Sit down ! " he ordered. " Here—have a whisky. You look as if you want one." He reached to a cupboard and took out glass and decanter. Then snatched up the telephone.

" Hullo—yes . . . Number 1854 City—right. . . . Eh—hullo . . . are you Shalford Brothers ? . . . Mr. Howard Shalford—yes—Bruce & Co. speaking. Look here . . . about this rotten Lake . . . Yes ? . . . I want you to withdraw the charge . . . I will. . . . It's no use prosecuting . . . he's only a damn fool. . . . There's nothing to be got out of it. . . . Let things take their course ? . . . But what's the bally use ? It only means time—giving evidence . . . and they won't convict. You owe me a favour. . . . Let the thing go . . . will you ? . . . Right. . . . Good. . . . Thanks. . . . You'll communicate with Scotland Yard ? . . . Yes . . . so will I. . . . I . . ."

As he held the instrument he was sitting exactly opposite the door, his gaze abstractedly wandering in that direction. It opened . . . slowly . . . and he saw. . . .

He threw down the instrument, started upon his feet, made a flying leap over the table and rushed for the door. Peggy, who was opening it, gave a gasp of surprise, for he caught her by one shoulder, turned her round, pushed her back into the outer office, and banged the door behind them.

" Mr. Stanniland ! Whatever is the matter ? "

" Sorry ! " he exclaimed. " I was busy—private interview—see ? Don't mind me. Everything's on the rush to-day. Sorry ! Look here—do you mind running out again "—he was racking his brain for an errand for her—" here "—and he thrust some notes into her hand—" go and buy those things you want—Jarvis wouldn't choose 'em so well—and book yourself a room somewhere—Liverpool Street Station Hotel's all right."

She looked at him, a little indignantly at first.

" For the sake of ' Jecinora ' ! " he urged.

And then she broke into a merry laugh, and went out. Stanniland heaved a sigh of relief. Then turned, and saw the policeman.

" What the—oh, yes ! Of course ! Look here, constable, it's a mistake. Not the man I thought he was. Here—take this and drink my health. Sorry to have bothered you."

The policeman took the five shillings, saluted, and departed.

" And, Jarvis, get a taxi, sharp ! And when Miss Lake comes back tell her to wait here for me."

" By George, but that was a close shave ! " ejaculated Stanniland as he retreated into the inner office. " Now then, Lake. Come along, please. I haven't any time to waste."

" Where are we going ? " asked Lake.

" To Scotland Yard. Buck up, man. I'm trying to put things right for you."

" It's exceedingly kind of you."

" Don't thank *me*," snapped Stanniland, as he struggled into his overcoat.

The Inspector of the Criminal Investigation Department looked up sharply from his desk as the two men were shown into his room. Stanniland had already sent in his card—" Bruce & Co."

" Yes ? " said the Inspector.

Stanniland explained his errand briefly. When he mentioned that his companion was Lake, of the Melford gang, he eyed the latter intently, a curious little smile playing around the corners of his mouth.

"You want to withdraw the charge. Yes, I see," he said, thoughtfully, when Stanniland had finished. "Wait a bit, please."

He rang a bell.

"Send Harris to me—with the depositions in the Melford case—yes—Corney. And send Sergeant Langston too, if he's in."

"I see," he went on presently, having glanced at the depositions, "that 'Shalford Brothers' are in it."

"Yes—but they, too, are willing to withdraw the charge."

"They haven't done so yet. May I look at those papers, please?"

The papers in question were those Corney had given up to Lake.

"Yes," said the Inspector, "I don't think any charge could be substantiated, in any case. But there are certain formalities that must take their course. Ah, here's Langston. Sergeant," he said, "pointing to Lake, "do you know this man?"

A puzzled expression swept across the sergeant's face as he looked at Edward Lake.

"Yes," he said, "he's Lake—of the Melford gang. Corney's lot. But I don't understand, I——"

"All right!" interrupted the Inspector, raising his hand. "We'll see about that in a minute. Now, Mr. Lake, when did you see Corney last?"

Edward Lake gave the date.

"Ah! Do you know where he is now?"

"I do not."

"Have you any idea?"

"I can't say."

"Or won't, eh?"

"Look here, Inspector," blurted out Lake. "Corney's no friend of mine. He got me into a nasty mess. But he's paid, partly, for that by giving me the means to clear myself. I give you my word of honour I don't know where he is now. Need I say more than that?"

"You are not obliged to answer any questions unless you like," replied the Inspector, dryly. "And perhaps it doesn't matter. We have a very shrewd suspicion, sir," he went on, speaking to Stanniland, "that we're on the man's tracks at last. I can't tell you any more—but I hope we shall get him. Now, Mr. Lake. I shall have to detain you till we've seen Mr. Shalford. But I hope it won't be for long. But tell me first, have you been in Salcombe lately?"

"I've never been in Salcombe in my life."

"It's queer. But we had a phone from Salcombe this afternoon telling us the police had detained you there."

"*Me!*"

"That's so, isn't it, sergeant?"

"Quite right, sir. I was going down to Salcombe by the first train in the morning to serve the warrant."

"Ah, well, perhaps you'd better go, all the same. It may be another of the gang. We can't chance letting him slip away."

"May I ask," said Lake, "how they came to arrest a man in my name?"

"You may tell him, if you like, sergeant," said the Inspector. "The sergeant," he explained, "has had the case in hand from the first."

"I don't know, sir. They didn't explain. But, of course, every police station has had his description —weeks ago."

"Ah, mistaken identity very likely," said the Inspector, lightly. "All the same, you go down there in the morning and see into it."

"May I say a word in private to Mr. Bruce"—Stanniland went by that name in the firm—"before he goes, Inspector?"

The Inspector shrugged his shoulders.

"Oh, if you like—but in this room, please."

Edward Lake drew Stanniland aside, and said in a low tone of voice:

"I'm very much afraid they've mistaken my brother for me. We are rather alike."

"Who? The Dean?"

"Yes."

"Nonsense! I happen to know that the Dean of Frattenbury is on a Mediterranean cruise."

"But he *isn't*," retorted Edward Lake. "I can't explain."

"Now—please," broke in the Inspector.

CHAPTER XIX

WHEN Stanniland returned to his office he found Peggy had completed her purchases, and had arrived there before him. For some little time he kept her and Jarvis hard at work, and then prepared to close down for the night.

When he had finished he turned to her: "You've booked a room for the night?"

"Yes—where you told me."

"Right! We'll finish this job in the morning, and then run back to Frattenbury. Now, Miss Lake, I've rushed you about a bit to-day. Will you come and dine with me?"

He was putting on his coat. She looked up at him. This was the first time since that day off that he had dropped his business attitude towards her.

"Thank you very much. I should like to."

"All right, then. Come along."

He locked the outer door of his office and they came downstairs together. In the street he hailed a taxi, and directed the driver to a West End restaurant. He consulted her tastes over the menu, and finally ordered the dinner. During the meal he talked easily enough, but with a certain constraint which Peggy could not help noticing. Presently he said to her:

"I want to ask you a question, if I may. Have

you heard from your uncle since he left for his holiday ? "

" No, not a word."

" Are you sure he went abroad ? "

" What makes you ask that ? "

" Oh, nothing much."

" You've seen that horrid thing in the paper about him ? "

" No, I haven't. I don't know what you mean."

" Why, everybody in Frattenbury is talking about it ! "

" Very likely. But, you see, they haven't talked to me. I'm not exactly in with the Frattenbury set. But what about this thing in the paper ? What is it ? "

She had her little dispatch case with her. She opened it, and produced a newspaper cutting which she handed to him across the table.

" Read that," she said.

He read it, and burst into a laugh.

" It's very funny," he replied, " but I don't believe it, all the same. Do you ? "

" I can't believe it of uncle."

" Exactly. Well, look here. Somehow I fancy the Dean never went abroad at all. No, don't ask me what makes me say so, but I have a reason."

" But—it's most extraordinary. I don't understand you."

" No ? But I want to set your mind at rest. Don't worry about your uncle. You'll see he'll turn up all right with an explanation. This thing's all a mistake, depend upon it."

" There are some nice, charitable people in the

Close," she said, with a shy smile , " who will never believe it's a mistake."

" What does it matter what people say ? " he asked. " I never care what anyone says about me."

" Except when they pitch into 'Jecinora,' Mr. Stanniland," she replied, with a mischievous twinkle in her eye. " Then you hustle around, don't you ? "

" Oh, *that !* " he exclaimed, lighting a cigarette, for they had reached the coffee stage. " I'm not going to talk about 'Jecinora' just now. We've finished business for the day."

" What do you call this, I wonder ? " she asked demurely, leaning her chin on her hand and looking at him across the table. He met her gaze for a moment, and then took up his cup and drained it. And she noticed the sudden hardening which came into his eyes as he glanced aside.

" Oh, one must eat," he said, " and it is bad to worry the brain while one eats."

Peggy gave an almost imperceptible little pout.

" I wonder you asked me to dine with you," she said.

" Why ? "

" Because having to eat with your secretary opposite to you might make you think of business—and worry your poor brain ! " she replied.

" Rubbish ! Look here——"

" Well ? "

She did look there. And rather prettily. The dinner had taken away her tiredness. Her eyes were sparkling with animation. But, whatever he may have had in his mind, he checked himself abruptly. The old, hard look came into his eyes ; the old, dictatorial business manner showed itself.

"You've had a hard day," he said, "and I have some one to see before I get a room at my club. I'm going to put you in a taxi now, and send you to your hotel. You won't mind going alone?"

"Why should I?" she replied. "I always try to obey orders cheerfully. Thank you ever so much for a topping dinner."

And, as she got into the taxi, and said good night to him, she added: "Try not to think of 'Jecinora' till to-morrow, now you haven't got me to remind you."

"That was horrid of me," she said to herself as the taxi drove off. Presently, after prolonged thought, and with knitted brow, she exclaimed, "I wish I'd refused his invitation to dinner—feeding me up because I looked tired, I suppose! Ugh! I hate him!"

As for Julian Bruce Stanniland, he, too, seemed to be in a bad temper as he made for his club.

"Wish I'd never come across her at all," he muttered, "or that I was ten years younger. Confound it all! He's a lucky young dog. Jove! He's a lucky young dog! Damn!"

They were both back in Frattenbury by a little after one o'clock the next day. He let her drive, or, rather, told her to do so. And spent most of the time looking over letters and papers. When he spoke, it was only a curt remark or two, and that about business. Distinctly a case of employer and employed.

After garaging the car Peggy went to her rooms to get some lunch, and found Mrs. Finch bursting with news.

"I've just had a letter from Finch, miss."

"Have you? I hope he's enjoying his holiday."

"Very much so, miss. He writes from Exeter. He attended afternoon service at the Cathedral, miss, and he says the way they do things there is deplorable. But what I wanted to tell you is that Finch has seen the Dean."

"Oh! In the Cathedral, I suppose?"

"No, miss, he met him at Salcombe."

"*Who* do you mean, Mrs. Finch? Are you talking about the Dean of Exeter?"

"Good gracious, no, miss. *Our* Dean—your uncle, miss!"

"Seen him at Salcombe?"

"Yes, miss. He had a long talk with him. He said—the Dean, I mean—that he'd changed his mind and hadn't gone abroad at all. Finch had read that disgraceful piece of news in the paper, and wouldn't believe it. Now he knows it isn't true, and he says I'm to tell people so."

"I'm very glad to hear it," replied Peggy. She was very much puzzled as she ate her lunch. Why had her uncle changed his mind? Why had he not told her about it? And what made Stanniland say that he had reason to believe the Dean had not gone abroad?

She could not make it out at all. Just before she left the office that afternoon she told Stanniland about Finch's letter.

"That's all right," he said. "I told you there was an explanation somewhere."

And refused to discuss the matter further.

But Stanniland had shrewd suspicions. His active brain had been piecing things together. Edward Lake had told him that the Dean had not gone on that Mediterranean cruise, and had said that he could not explain. Also that he thought his brother had been arrested in his stead. The more Stanniland turned it over in his mind, the more he guessed at the truth. Not that it mattered to him what the Dean had done. But the Dean's brother was Peggy's father. And Peggy—well, he told himself that one would naturally try to shield a girl from an unpleasant scandal. But he hesitated to tell himself, all the same, that if it had been any other girl than Peggy he would not have troubled to act the knight errant so readily.

Anyhow, that evening he called at the police station and asked to see Superintendent Walters.

" I want a word or two with you in confidence," he said.

" Certainly, Mr. Stanniland."

" Well, then, tell me. That man whom I saw leaving the Deanery by the back way that morning. Who do you imagine he was ? "

The Superintendent put on an absolutely blank expression.

" I can't say, sir. We lost all trace of him."

" Rubbish ! I know who you suspected him to be."

The Superintendent arched his eyebrows in well-feigned surprise.

" Really, Mr. Stanniland ? "

" Oh, yes. You needn't try to fence with me. You see, I happen to be one of the prosecutors in Melford & Co. You thought he was Edward Lake, Superintendent."

" What makes you say so ? "

" Because I happen to know he is the Dean's brother. see ? "

The Superintendent threw down his cards.

"Well," he said, with a short laugh. "I suppose I may as well own up, sir. Yes, I had very good reason for believing he was the individual you mention. And I don't mind telling you now that I was right. He *was* Edward Lake. We traced him to Southampton, and then he gave us the slip. But the Hampshire police got hold of a clue and, after a good deal of trouble, he was tracked down. I had a telephonic message from Salcombe, in Devonshire, last evening, saying they had taken him there."

"Oh, indeed," said Stanniland, with a smile.

"Now, look here, sir," went on the Superintendent. "As you're concerned in the case, I want to tell you something. It isn't known publicly that this Lake is a brother of the Dean, and, unless he gives the show away himself it need not come out. Lake is a very ordinary name, and people are not likely to couple the two. I like our Dean, and I'm anxious to spare him, if possible."

"In spite of the fact that he connived at his brother's escape—as he must have done?"

The Superintendent smiled.

"Oh, come now," he said. "I've no grudge against him for that. A bit natural, wasn't it? It need never come out. We've got the man. That's the main thing. He was to be taken up to London to-day, and you'll probably hear from Scotland Yard asking you to go and identify him before he is brought before a magistrate."

"I think not," said Stanniland, dryly.

"Why?"

"Because I was at Scotland Yard yesterday afternoon with Edward Lake."

"But you couldn't have been, sir. He was only taken yesterday afternoon at Salcombe."

"So you think. But he wasn't."

"Then who did they take, sir?"

"The Dean!" replied Stanniland.

The Superintendent stared at him, his eyes opening with astonishment.

"What!" he exclaimed at length.

"I think you'll find it's true. You've been tracking the Dean all the time. It was *he* I saw leaving the house."

"But that's impossible," exclaimed the bewildered Superintendent. "I saw the Dean getting out of his taxi at the station that morning."

"Not you!"

"Then who was it?"

"His brother, most probably. Was he dressed as a dean?"

"N-no. But——. O Lord!"

Stanniland burst into a hearty peal of laughter.

"But—but——" went on the Superintendent. I saw his suit-case: 'Dean of Frattenbury' was painted on it."

"Exactly," said Stanniland. "Oh, it was a pretty little game. That Dean's a cute hand, Superintendent. Don't you see? He sent his brother off on the sea trip and did the vanishing trick himself. Good old blighter! And, if any question had arisen, *you'd* have proved the alibi. It's perfectly Gilbertian."

"It's all very well for you to laugh, Mr. Stanniland," said the Superintendent, ruefully. "Why, I even helped him to make his get-away. Scotland Yard knew there was a passenger named Lake booked for that trip, and I informed them it was all right—he was the Dean of Frattenbury. Good Lord!"

"Yes, it *would* be funny if they got you in the witness box, eh? A superintendent of police conniving at the escape of the very man he was after and then sleuthing the Dean! That's why I think you'll do what I want. Hush the thing up. There's no need for it to get out. Now, you see what I mean. This Edward Lake went off as the Dean of Frattenbury. It was he who played the giddy goat in his brother's clothes at Arcachon. You've seen the paragraph in *Sporting Echoes*?"

The Superintendent nodded. His face broke into a grin.

"I have," he said. "It's the talk of Frattenbury. Yes, I see now."

"But," he went on, "you say you were with Edward Lake yesterday? I don't understand,"

"Nor do I. The thing was this. Lake came to me of his own accord, and produced pretty plain proofs that he'd been a damn fool—just made use of. There was nothing—after those proofs—in the way of a criminal charge against him, and he's probably free by now. He must have got off the boat, stayed at Arcachon, and then come back to England. The only thing that puzzles me is that if he had those proofs—why didn't he produce them before? Why did he try to escape?"

"Just a minute, sir," said the Superintendent, opening a pile of correspondence. "Ah—yes, here it is. Perhaps this will explain. We have reason to believe that the man Melford—Corney's his real name—has been seen in the south of France. Scotland Yard has applied for an extradition warrant on the chance of it. Now, Lake may have come across him there and got those proofs out of him. Then he'd come straight back—naturally."

Stanniland nodded. "It may be so. But now, what are you going to do about it?"

Superintendent Walters thought for a minute or two.

"Well," he replied, at length, "so far as I can see the case is pretty simple now. You tell me Edward Lake has cleared himself—there'll be no prosecution. As a matter of fact, his name has never been before the public. It only appears, in connection with the Melford fraud, in our private advices. And by this time the Dean isn't being detained at Salcombe any longer, I should imagine. He may not have told them who he is. But if he has told them, only the police would know. And we're never very anxious to admit mistaken identity."

Stanniland grinned at him. "You speak feelingly, Superintendent!"

"I do. I own it. I should look a bit of a fool if it came out. But it needn't. *I* shan't say anything. But I shall have a little private talk with the Dean when he returns," he added, grimly.

"Don't be too hard on the poor old buffer! Remember, you've given him a pretty bad time of it."

"He deserves it!" said the policeman. "A night in a cell won't do him any harm—after the trick he played me."

"All right, then," said Stanniland, getting up to go. "That's settled."

"One moment," broke in the Superintendent. "That girl—Miss Lake, the Dean's niece. She's in your employ?"

"Yes, what of her?"

"I think she must be Edward Lake's daughter. The Dean has only one brother, I believe. And it's a pity to drag her into the thing if it could be avoided. I've got a daughter myself, and I know how upset she'd be if I got into trouble. Don't say anything to her about it, Mr. Stanniland."

A softer light came into Stanniland's eyes. He had his hand on the door. Now he took it from the door handle and extended it to the Superintendent.

"I'm glad you take a human view of things. No, I won't say anything! Good night. Many thanks!"

CHAPTER XX

THE unfortunate Dean of Frattenbury, having once made up his mind as to his course of action, set himself to see the thing through with that same doggedness which he portrayed when he began to write a new book on the somewhat abstruse subject for which he was so well renowned for his scholarship. The strange adventure which confronted him served to put him on his mettle.

He passed a not uncomfortable night, partly due to the fact that the sergeant of police in charge of the station had received a message in the evening to the effect that a mistake had apparently been made. Unaccustomed as he was to the ways of a police cell, he was not aware that the extra bedding with which the sergeant provided him, together with permission to smoke, was due to this message, as also was the fact that the sergeant placed his own " best parlour " at his disposal when the morning came.

Meanwhile, Hinton and his wife had talked the matter over, and it was not without reason that the former packed a small bag which he took with him to Salcombe a little while before the first train from London was due. He was determined, in the kindness of his heart, to make the journey to London if necessary, and to do anything in his power to befriend this man whom his wife still persisted in believing was no other than the Dean of Frattenbury.

Detective-Sergeant Langston duly arrived, clad in plain clothes, and made his way to the police station. After a brief interview with the sergeant in charge, he was shown in to the Dean, who received him very stiffly. For, among other things, the Dean's back was strictly up.

Langston subjected him to a keen scrutiny, without saying a word except to give the other good day, and to state who he was.

" Well," said the Dean, " I presume you have come to take me to London? I should like to see your warrant, please."

Langston ignored the question.

" Your name is Lake?" he asked.

" It is."

" Hm! I think I ought to tell you, sir, that you resemble very closely an individual of that name for whom a warrant has been out for some weeks."

" Very well," replied the Dean, " I admit nothing. Please remember that. You had better proceed to do your duty."

For the first time the detective-sergeant smiled.

" It is a very pleasant duty, so far as we are both concerned, sir. I see that a mistake has been made. We thought so at the Yard last evening, but my orders were to proceed to Salcombe to verify matters. I am exceedingly sorry that you have been put to any inconvenience, and glad to be able to tell you that we need not detain you any longer."

The Dean heaved a sigh of relief. It was better than he had expected. He had quite made up his mind to endure a very unpleasant week.

" Thank you," he replied, with great dignity. " It has certainly been a novel experience to me, and I am thankful that it is over. May I ask a question ?"

"Certainly, sir."

"You say that I resemble this—er—individual you—er—want ?"

"Well, you *do*, sir. A description of him was circulated to the police. And I understand, from what the sergeant here tells me, that your own movements rather helped to convey the impression that you were the same man."

"Perhaps they *did !*" replied the Dean, a grim little smile twitching the corners of his lips as he remembered the part he had played, "but the question I want to ask you is *this*. You tell me you conjectured at Scotland Yard that a mistake had been made. Why did you think so ? And why are you so sure I am not the man you want ?"

Langston gave a light laugh.

"Because we had him at the Yard last evening, sir. He was still detained when I left this morning."

"You had my br—— this man Lake last evening !" exclaimed the Dean in astonishment. "Why, the boat——" but he checked himself in time. He was doing some rapid thinking. The *Sunflower* was not due for a week at the earliest.

The detective looked at him curiously.

"Yes, we had him, sure enough," he replied quietly. "He gave himself up, you see. But," he added slowly and deliberately, watching the other intently as he spoke, "by this time I expect he is free. He produced documents which have led to the prosecutors withdrawing the charge as far as *he* is concerned in the matter of Melford & Co."

"Thank God !" exclaimed the Dean, fervently, leaning back in his chair. It was the moment when he felt he had the reward for all that he had gone through. His brother was an innocent man. *How* he happened to be in England at all was a mystery yet to be solved. But the paramount fact in the Dean's mind was that the family honour was saved. His sacrifice had not been in vain. For the moment he had forgotten the Arcachon affair.

The detective-sergeant, still watching him shrewdly, now observed:

" Will you allow me to ask you a question, sir ? "

" What is it ? "

" If it is not impertinent, how is it that you have made no attempt to prove that you were wrongfully detained ? My experience is that innocent people, arrested by mistake, are only too anxious to prove their identity as quickly as possible."

" I am a stranger here," replied the Dean, shortly, " on my holiday. No one here could prove who I am."

" And may I ask who you are, sir ? "

" That," retorted the Dean, with extreme dignity, " is *my* business."

The other nodded his head slowly.

" I see," he said.

So he did, in a vague way. He knew very well that the man he had been after was, according to the description, " reported to be related to the Dean of Frattenbury, whom he is said to resemble slightly." And he felt, though he could not make out exactly what had happened, that there was an element of self-sacrifice in the situation. And self-sacrifice is always heroic.

Instinctively he put out his hand.

" I quite understand, sir," he said, " that you

would rather I asked you no further questions. And, indeed, there is no need to do so. The unfortunate matter is entirely at an end, and will never be referred to. I hope I've got a human side to my nature, and while I assure you that we much regret your detention here, may I congratulate you, not only that the thing is cleared up, but, if I may say so, sir, without offence, on the extremely plucky attitude I—I think you have assumed?"

The two men looked straight into each other's eyes for a moment, and then the Dean took the detective's proffered hand and wrung it warmly.

"Thank you very much," he said, simply. "I appreciate the human side of your nature, even if I have been inconvenienced by the professionalism of your calling. And now I suppose I may go?"

"Certainly, sir."

"By jove!" said Langston to himself when the Dean had departed. "Whoever he is, he's a game one! Worth ten of that silly fool we had last evening!"

"Hullo, hullo!" cried a cheerful voice, as the Dean came out of the room. "My dear chap, I'm awfully glad! The sergeant has been telling me it was all right. Come along, come along!"

Hinton was shaking him heartily by the hand as he spoke. For the life of him the Dean could not help a little lump coming into his throat as he thanked him. In his secluded unadventurous existence he had lived a little apart from the world of ordinary men. In his office and work he had not had to rely on the ordinary kindness which ordinary men so often show. And the fact that this comparative stranger, who knew nothing about him, should have stuck to him so loyally in his trouble had touched him more than he cared to say.

"Now then," said Hinton, as the two men walked out of the police station, "what are you going to do? What are your plans?"

He gave a sly little look at him as he spoke. But the Dean, who did not notice it, replied, hesitating slightly:

"Well—er—the turn of events has been so rapid that I have hardly had time to make any plans. But I think—yes—I shall go to London to-morrow. In any case, I had determined to do that. To-night—yes—I'll get a bed at an hotel. My landlady," he added, with a grim touch of humour, "might not be willing to receive me back after my having been taken away by the police."

"You'll do nothing of the kind, my dear fellow. Whatever you do to-morrow—and we'll see about that—you'll come home with me now and stay the night. Yes! My wife insisted upon my bringing you if you were set free. It will be a pleasure to us, really!"

Again the Dean felt that little lump in his throat. He could hardly answer at first. When he did so, he said:

"I don't know how to thank you both. It *is* good of you."

"You'll come, though?"

"Yes," said the Dean, "I'll come—with great pleasure and gratitude," and, as he said the words, he was making up his mind as to a certain course of action.

"Righto!" replied Hinton. "Let's make for the ferry. We'll try to give you something better than bread and skilly to-night."

"Thanks to you," laughed the Dean, "I didn't have bread and skilly. But the sergeant's wife was infinitely inferior to your excellent domestic as regards the culinary art. She did her best, doubtless, but she can't cook eggs and bacon—er—tastefully!"

* * * * *

It was after dinner—or supper as Hinton insisted upon calling it—that evening that the Dean launched out. They were sitting over their coffee, Hinton with his cigar, the Dean with his pipe, and Mrs. Hinton with a cigarette. One of those little spaces of silence which so often follow a lively conversation had fallen upon them. The Dean took his pipe from his lips and broke the silence.

"There is something I want to tell you," he said.

Mrs. Hinton looked up quickly and across the table at her husband.

"Ye—es?" she drawled.

The Dean hesitated a moment, reddened a little, and then plunged.

"I have never told you who I am. You see—er—I am really the Dean of Frattenbury."

Mrs. Hinton turned towards him with a smile.

"Yes," she said, "we knew that all the time."

"You knew it?"

"My dear fellow," broke in Hinton, "my wife ought to have said that *she* knew you were the Dean. *I* didn't, till she made me think so. She's got a habit of making me think what she wants me to, you know."

"What made you think so?" asked the Dean of Mrs. Hinton.

"Well," she said, with a little laugh, "you stuck

up for yourself over that Arcachon affair, didn't you? The rest was my prerogative--a woman's intuition. We said nothing to you about it because, you see," she went on with her pleasant drawl, "we guessed you were here for a quiet holiday and didn't want to be bothered.

"But whatever did you think of me when I was taken to the police station yesterday?" he asked Hinton.

Hinton laughed.

"Well," he replied, "of course I knew at once it must be a mistake."

"What we *did* wonder at," said Mrs Hinton, "was why you did not inform the police who you were. But we imagined you must have had some good reason"

"Yes, I had a good reason," replied the Dean, "and I want to take you into my confidence and tell you what that reason was. I owe you that for your extreme kindness to me."

"If you would rather not——" began Hinton, but the Dean interrupted him.

"Really, I would rather tell you. My arrest was the result of extraordinary circumstances—and entirely my own fault."

And he told them the whole story. Once or twice they smiled, especially when he described his surreptitious escape from the Deanery. And when he recounted his sudden meeting with his own verger at Bolt Head they had to laugh outright.

"There," he said, when he had finished, "it's been a relief to tell it all, and it's very kind of you to have heard it so patiently. I suppose I have been foolish."

"But you don't regret it?" asked Mrs. Hinton, quietly

"No—I *don't!*" he replied, emphatically.

"I think it is just splendid of you," went on Mrs. Hinton.

"By Jove, yes!" exclaimed her husband. "There's only one thing I regret."

"What's that?" asked the Dean.

"That I ever said a word against the Dean of Frattenbury when I first met you that day—don't you remember? But I didn't know you then."

The Dean gave a little laugh.

"I hope you have a better opinion of me now?"

"It's a real pleasure to know you, Mr. Dean!" replied Hinton, warmly.

"You have been through an unpleasant experience," drawled Mrs. Hinton, with her kind eyes regarding him closely.

The Dean lapsed into thought. Presently he said slowly:

"Do you know I am glad of the experience. I have been learning much. Yes," he went on, leaning back in his chair and half closing his eyes. "You see, I have lived a rather secluded life, with my books and in a quiet little parish. My friends have been those of my own calibre. I can't say I have mixed with the world very much. Certainly I have had no striking adventure—until now. But there is one thing that has been borne in upon me impressively."

"May we ask what that is?" said Mrs. Hinton.

"The extreme kindness—kindness of judgment, perhaps I should call it—of people whom I have not, I suppose, had the opportunity of understanding before. First there was the Superintendent of police at Frattenbury. Nothing could have exceeded the refinement and kindly feeling of the man who, knowing he had an unpleasant duty to perform, was human enough to let me understand that he would have condoned with me if I had attempted to frustrate his purpose, which, indeed, I did. Then there was Finch, the verger. I had written him down in my mind as a pompous ass. Yet he showed, beneath his pomposity, a loyalty and faith that touched me very much—and which is, perhaps, greater than I could even find in some of my fellow clergy. To-day, again, that detective from Scotland Yard—I almost think he guessed who I was—it was the kindliness and generosity of the man that surprised me. And you, my dear friends, if I may call you so—I hope I may—you have shown me—a stranger to you—such friendship and sympathy that I shall never forget."

"It was nothing," said Hinton.

"It has meant very much to me," replied the Dean, earnestly. "I trust I have always tried to exercise a humane judgment myself. But I know now that I shall return to my work at Frattenbury with a wider outlook than—than—I should probably have gained had I taken my projected trip round the Mediterranean. No, I do not regret my enforced holiday here—not for a moment!"

There was silence for a moment or two. Hinton broke it abruptly.

"The only thing which remains to be done is to clear up the mystery of that Arcachon affair. I hope that'll come out all right. And now, what are your plans?"

And he looked at his wife with a smile as he spoke. They had already had a talk on the subject.

"Well," said the Dean, "I shall go to London to-morrow and consult the Bishop. He is up there this week for Convocation. I was actually writing to him when the sergeant of police came in yesterday. Then I think I shall remain in London for the short time left to me of my holiday. I can't go back to the Deanery because it is shut up and my servants will not have returned. Besides, there's my brother. I must see him. I ought to have asked that detective how I could get at him. By our arrangement we were to meet at the Western Hotel when the *Sunflower* returned from her voyage—about the middle of next week."

"Now, may I give you a bit of advice?" asked Hinton.

"By all means?"

"Well, look here. Write to the Bishop, if you like. But I don't see that anything is to be gained by seeing him just now. And you can't clear up that Arcachon affair till you have met your brother. He may take it into his head to come down here. Very likely he knows of your false arrest."

"I don't think he would do that."

"Very well, then. Why not enjoy the remainder of your holiday? Be our guest here. We shall be awfully glad if you will."

"Yes *do!*" pleaded Mrs. Hinton. "My husband is quite right. There's nothing to be gained by leaving just now. We should love to have you if you'd stay with us."

"Pot-luck, you know," broke in Hinton.

"*And* the boat!" added his wife. "My husband

will be only too glad of a companion. He likes to have someone with him—and I can't always go."

"Really," exclaimed the Dean. "You overwhelm me with kindness."

"Rubbish, man! Now, you'll stay with us, won't you?"

The Dean thought for a moment.

"On one condition—I will."

"What is that?"

"That you return the compliment, and come and have pot-luck with me at the Deanery after I return."

"By Jove, yes—we will, won't we, dear? It will be a new experience for us."

"It will be very quiet, I promise you that," said the Dean.

"Oh, I don't know," laughed Mrs. Hinton. "It may be melodramatic—you may want us to escape by the back way, with the police on our track. But of course we'll come."

"That's settled, then," said Hinton, genially. "Us for the briny to-morrow morning! We'll make the coming week a real holiday for you, Mr. Dean, and then I'll tell you what I'll do."

"What?" asked the Dean.

"I'll come up to London with you, if I may. You may be glad of a layman if there has to be an interview with the editor of the *Sporting Echoes*. For we've got to make him apologize for that paragraph, somehow, and I can use language that you can't."

"Though I might like to!" retorted the Dean, with a twinkle in his eye and a smile twitching the corners of his lips.

CHAPTER XXI

THE Dean and Hinton duly arrived at the Western Hotel-and took rooms for the night. The next day was the one appointed for the rendezvous. In the morning Hinton expressed the intention of lunching at his club.

"Very well," said the Dean, "I shall remain here. My brother may arrive at any moment."

"All right," replied Hinton, "I'll be with you early in the afternoon."

Before luncheon he went into the smoking-room of his club and opened the morning paper, scanning it leisurely. Presently a paragraph caught his eye:

THE "MELFORD AND CO." CASE.

ARREST OF CORNEY.

A SMART CAPTURE.

James Corney, *alias* Melford, was arrested at Marseilles yesterday in the act of embarking on a steamer bound for the Argentine. He has been wanted for seven or eight weeks, during which time all trace of him was lost. Corney" was the principal instigator of the firm known as "Melford & Co." and is charged with alleged fraudulent company promoting. The arrest will arouse interest in the City, more than one well-known business house being involved in the prosecution.

From information supplied to us we understand that for several weeks the police have had reason to believe that Corney had managed to effect his escape from this country. It is owing to the patient and assiduous work of Inspector Miles, of the Criminal Investigation Department, Scotland Yard, that he was ultimately tracked to the Continent. He will be extradited immediately and proceedings will probably be taken against him at a magistrate's court early next week.

Hinton put down the paper and looked up as a hand smacked down on his shoulder.

"Hullo, old man! What the devil are you doing here? I heard you'd retired on the wealth you'd made at the House and were swanking around somewhere in a yacht."

"Hullo, Marsden? And I'd heard that you——" But he suddenly stopped short.

"Go on. You'd heard I was barmy in the crumpet. So I was. Mad as a hatter, old bean. Chained to a keeper and let out into a yard for exercise. My word, I led 'em a life!"

"And how are you now?" asked Hinton, laughing; "all right again, I hope."

"Not a bit of it. I've ceased gnawing bones and putting straw in my hair. But I'm still more or less dotty. Have a Martini?"

"Thanks."

"Here, garçon!" cried Marsden to a passing waiter, "apportez-moi deux queues de coq—— Oh, hang, I forgot—two Martinis, please!"

"Been abroad," he explained; "only returned last night."

"Having a holiday?"

"Well, didn't I want one? They thought I was cured, you see. I humbugged 'em into it and got away on my own."

"And what are you going to do now you're back?"

Marsden lapsed into sanity for a moment.

"Oh," he said, "I'm not really so bad as I'm kidding you. I shall be all right, I expect, in a few weeks' time and get to work again. Mustn't overdo my poor old brain, though, any more. You see," he added, gravely, but with the wicked look in his eye, "it was the rubber boom. I got the idea in my head that I was a balloon tyre and wanted to roll along the street. I wasn't *really* dangerous. I'm not now. Lunching here?"

"Thought of doing so," replied Hinton, sipping his cocktail.

"Lunch with me, then. Let's go and see what they've got. I hate being by myself, and I'm safer when I've got anyone with me. Come and keep me in order."

"All right," laughed Hinton, and they made their way to the dining-room.

The waiter came for orders. Marsden, who was talking to Hinton volubly, broke off, and again began:

"Que-ce-que c'est que vous avez pour manger——? Damn! There I go again. Silly old fool, ain't I? Told you I was still mad. Soup? All right. Bring some soup, waiter, to begin with."

"Where have you been?" asked Hinton.

"Oh, all over the place: Paris—Lyons—Bordeaux—Biarritz—San Sebastian. I say, I've been nicely swindled, too. I'm going to Scotland Yard after lunch. Blighter regularly took me in. Damn parson, too. Look here!"

He took a cheque out of his pocket-book and unfolded it.

"Seventy-five quid, my boy. That's what he got

out of me. And gave me this in exchange. I called at the Bank just now—I'd posted it there, you see—and they handed this back to me: 'Signature differs.' That's what they've written on it. Won't pay it. Damned fraud. But I'll show up the old swine."

He handed the cheque across the table to Hinton. The latter took it and looked at it. The first thing he noticed was "Westminster Bank, *Frattenbury*," on the top. Then he glanced at the signature: "E. Lake."

"Gad!" he exclaimed, "who the deuce gave you this?"

"I told you. Damn parson. Who d'you think he said he was?"

"Who?"

"Bally old Dean. Had his full rig-out with him, too."

"Dean of *what?*" cried Hinton.

"Name on the cheque: Frattenbury."

"By George! I say, *where* did he give you this, Marsden?"

"I picked him up at Bordeaux. Then we went to that place where they sport red trousers. I say, Hinton, talk about Oxford bags, you should see my crimson ones. I'm going to wear 'em——"

"Oh, damn your red trousers. What's the name of the place, you blighter?"

"Arcachon."

"That's it!" exclaimed Hinton, "we've solved the riddle. Look here, he wasn't the Dean at all."

"The dickens he wasn't! Well, I had my doubts about him afterwards. I was sane enough for that. When he gave me the slip after getting the seventy-five quid out of me."

"Look here," said Hinton, "I want to know this:

did this chap who called himself the Dean of Frattenbury make a fool of himself at the Casino—roulette and dancing, and all that sort of thing—eh ? "

Hinton grinned wickedly.

" That was *me*, old buck ! " he said, with disregard for grammar.

" You ? "

" Rather ! You see, the Johnny left his full rig-out behind him. I put 'em on, and had the evening of my life. You ought to have seen me dancing the can-can in apron and silk breeches and stockings. They chucked me out," he added, as if recalling a pleasant reminiscence, " otherwise I might have made a night of it there. I was particularly dotty that evening." And he gave vent to a series of chuckles. " I fetched 'em ! "

Hinton laughed too, in spite of himself, but regained seriousness and said :

" You *are* a bally fool, Marsden ! "

" Why, of course I am."

" Do you know what you've done, you ass ? This escapade of yours got written up in *Sporting Echoes*, and the unfortunate Dean of Frattenbury, whom I happen to know, is standing the racket of it."

Marsden burst into a peal of laughter.

" Oh, I say," he cried, " but that takes the biscuit ! If I'd only known they were going to write it up I'd—I'd have kissed my partner. By George, I would ! "

" You damned idiot ! "

" Well, I can't help it, can I ? I told you I'd been off my head. Don't blame *me !* "

" Very likely. But you've got to put things straight, all the same, or you may find yourself in Queer Street over this affair."

" How ? "

" Well, for one thing, the Dean might bring an action against you for impersonating him. But we won't discuss that. Look here, I'm going with you straight away to Scotland Yard. You want to find out about that cheque, and I want to find out something, too, if I can. And then you're coming with me to the editor of *Sporting Echoes*. This thing's got to be put right, and I'll jolly well see you do it."

" Righto ! " said Marsden, cheerfully ; " I'm in for it. My fault. I asked you to take charge of me.

" But," he added, chuckling again, as he got up from the table, " it was a topping spree, old chap ! I heard 'em talking about the dancing dean at Biarritz, even ! "

" You dance along with me, now," replied Hinton, grimly.

The same Inspector who had interviewed Stanniland and Edward Lake received them at Scotland Yard. He listened to Marsden's story with a smile on his face, for Marsden told it in his mad way.

" Let me see the cheque, please," he said.

Marsden produced it.

" Yes, I understand. The Frattenbury Bank returned this to your bank—with the endorsement. Now, Mr. Marsden, can you describe this man who gave it to you ? "

" Clean-shaven Johnny, not quite so tall as I am, sort of fairly dark hair and the usual eyes, nose, and mouth."

The Inspector laughed.

" Not very adequate," he said. " Where did you say you picked him up ? "

" At Bordeaux."

" And then you went on to Arcachon ? "

" That's right."

" Um ! Should you know this man again if you were to see him ? "

" Of course I should."

The Inspector was pulling a drawer out of his writing-table.

" Did he show his teeth a good bit when he laughed ? "

" Yes. I noticed that, because of the gold stopping on one of 'em."

" Ah—well, look through this," and he handed him a copy of the *Police Gazette*. " See if he's there ! "

The Inspector leaned back in his chair, rubbing his hands together softly. Marsden turned over the pages of the *Police Gazette*, that carefully edited publication consisting of short, but lurid, illustrated biographies, for private circulation only.

" Here he is ! " suddenly exclaimed Marsden. " That's the blighter, right enough."

" Let me see—Ah, I thought so ! "

" Who is it ? " asked Hinton, bending over the table.

" Corney, sir—the Melford & Co. case. You may have heard of it ? Yes ? He was arrested at Marseilles yesterday. We haven't been quite sure about all his movements. We don't know how he managed to give us the slip here and get over to the Continent, but we traced him there, and we know he was in the neighbourhood of Bordeaux. Well, sir," he went on, turning to Marsden, " he'll be here soon, on another charge. You can prosecute him if you like, of course, but I fancy in any case he'll get five years at least, and I don't think you'd get your money back. We know him. He's a clever scoundrel."

"Damned clever," retorted Marsden, "it was I who suggested I should cash a cheque from him. But then, how was I to know he was not the Dean of Frattenbury?"

"What's that you say?" asked the Inspector, sharply.

"That's who he said he was."

"What? The Dean of Frattenbury?"

"Yes."

"Oh! And what made you think so?"

"Well, his name was on his suit-case, 'Dean of Frattenbury' and he had his glad rags with him, apron and so on, you know. Besides, there was his cheque-book on the Frattenbury Bank—I had an opportunity of looking through it. And it seemed all right. Anyhow, if you think it isn't worth while, I shan't bother to prosecute."

"I see," replied the Inspector, thoughtfully.

Then Hinton broke in:

"I happen to know the Dean personally, Inspector. With the exception of clearing up a little scandal about him which has arisen over this matter, and which I think I can easily do, I suppose there is no occasion for his name to appear publicly?"

"Oh, I think not, sir," replied the Inspector, "especially if your friend here is not going to prosecute. We've got Corney. That's the main thing. I haven't quite fathomed the affair myself, but I fancy if Corney happened to be still at large we might have wanted to interview the Dean. Oh yes, that will be all right!"

"Now," said Hinton to Marsden, as they left the office, "you come along with me to the editor of *Sporting Echoes*. That's all I want of *you* now!"

"Oh, I say. You know the jolly old Dean, eh? Won't you introduce me to him and let me explain. It would be just topping!"

"Not much I won't," retorted Hinton, emphatically, "I'll explain myself."

"But I should like to hear the old geyser swear at me. I've never seen a dean in a rage."

"You won't see this one. You'll bally well keep clear of him."

As soon as they had gone out of his office the Inspector rang up Frattenbury Police Station over the telephone and asked for Superintendent Walters. But, even when he had heard all the Superintendent had to say—and the suit-case formed part of it—and had chaffed him roundly, both men remained a little mystified. It was only afterwards, in the Dean's study at Frattenbury, that Superintendent Walters quite understood.

* * * * *

Hinton, when he returned to the hotel, found the Dean closeted with his brother, a very subdued brother. The Dean introduced him:

"You need not mind Mr. Hinton," he explained. "He has been a very good friend to me, and knows the whole story—so far as I did until you told me the rest just now. I want to tell him, unless you would like to?"

"Go on, please," said Edward Lake.

"One moment first," broke in Hinton, "I've had a stroke of luck since I saw you. I've solved the Arcachon mystery and put it right. The editor of *Sporting Echoes* is going to put it right in his next issue. I had to threaten him, in your name, with an action for libel, before he would quite see my point. But he caved in. It will be all right."

"Really, Hinton," said the Dean, "I don't know how to express my gratitude to you. It was this man —Corney—I suppose? My brother——"

"No, it wasn't Corney at all."

And he explained. Even the Dean could not refrain from laughing at his description of Marsden.

"I've known him for years," Hinton said. "He was always a happy-go-lucky sort of fellow—some of us are, on 'Change, you know—then his brain gave way from overwork, and I think he's right when he insists upon saying that he's not quite sane yet."

"Poor fellow!" said the Dean. "I hope he'll make a complete recovery. He's caused me some anxiety—but I forgive him. Now let me tell you what happened to my brother after he left me at Frattenbury."

When he had finished, the Dean went on:

"My brother is thinking of going abroad at any rate for a time. And I agree with him."

Hinton nodded.

"I hope you will find something to do there," he said to Edward Lake.

"I shall try," replied the other quietly. "I've had a pretty severe lesson over this affair."

"I don't want to interfere in family relationships," remarked Hinton, bluntly, "but I should like to tell you, Mr. Lake, that you've had a close shave. And to add that you've got a brother you ought to be grateful to all your life. There aren't many men who'd have done what the Dean has done for you—and who would be prepared to suffer still more if necessary."

"Nonsense!" muttered the Dean.

"I know," replied Edward Lake, hanging his head. "And I hope I'll be able to show my gratitude. I've been a fool and a bit of a beast."

"Every bit of one——" began Hinton. But the Dean held up his hand.

"I think we'll say no more, please. And it's nearly dinner-time," he added.

"Allow me to be the host," replied Hinton, breaking into his customary geniality. "And I think the occasion demands Veuve Cliquot; or perhaps you prefer Pomeroy?"

"I am not a judge," said the Dean, with a smile; "I leave it to you. But, in either case, I shall not refuse a glass. I must have something in which to drink the health of the *deus ex machina*."

"Meaning?"

"*You*, my very good friend."

"Rubbish! If it comes to that, there is the villain of the piece. What would you call him? The *diabolus ex machina*?"

"Who do you mean?"

"Why, Corney," replied Hinton.

The Dean laughed.

"As far as I am concerned," he retorted, "I should name him Marsden. But the relief is so great that I would willingly act as the *advocatus ex diaboli*"

CHAPTER XXII

Curiosity with regard to the Dean's holiday was beginning to die in the Cathedral Close. There was still a vague feeling among some that it was not quite clear why the Dean had changed his plans at the last moment and preferred to stay in England. But it had been substantially proved, to the satisfaction of most, if not quite all, that the Arcachon incident was a mistake. *Sporting Echoes* had published a semi-humorous apology and thrown the blame upon "Our Correspondent." The explanation, so the paper stated, lay in the fact that one of the guests at a *bal masqué* who had adopted the costume of a Church dignitary had visited the Casino without troubling to change and, in a mood of facetiousness, had declared himself to be the Dean of Frattenbury.

The manager of the bank was a little puzzled over the matter of the cheque, but then, he never gossiped about business affairs, and when the Dean explained to him that his cheque-book had been stolen, thought no more about it. That model of discretion, Superintendent Walters, wisely held his tongue, and no word about the Dean's brother ever came out. Finch's assertion that he had met the Dean at Salcombe helped considerably to allay all suspicions.

Except, perhaps, those of a few denizens of the Close who revelled in conjectures. The Miss Brands, seated in a row on a minor canon's sofa at an " At Home," considered that, " after all, it was very strange," " there was *something* at the bottom of it," " men in the position of the Dean ought to be more careful," and so forth. Miss Marshall exhorted her nephew to beware of deception in his future career, winding up with the admonition that, however the Dean might have cleared himself, the fact remained that his niece was one of those designing personages distinctly to be avoided by a young man with a clerical career before him.

Donald Quarrington felt, a little bitterly, that the admonition was unnecessary, or, rather took the form of a reversal. For he made no advances with Peggy. She was quite chummy with him when, on rare occasions, he met her, but showed him plainly, to use her own expression, that he was " not to be silly."

Once, on her Saturday afternoon off, he came across her taking a country ramble and joined her. She made no objection. Peggy was an independent modern young person who saw no harm in the frank companionship of a nice boy. They had tea together in a quiet little hostelry in one of the villages northward of Frattenbury nestling among the downs. As they came out a two-seater car was bearing down on them along the road. The driver glanced at them as he passed, and raised his hat.

" Who was that ? " asked Donald.

" My employer, Mr. Stanniland," replied Peggy, and the colour mounted a little to her cheeks as she spoke.

" Queer sort of chap, isn't he ? "

" He's a very decent sort," she said; and immediately changed the subject.

Peggy, of course, had seen her uncle. She thought him a little reticent over the matter of his holiday, but accepted his explanation quite naturally, chaffing him a bit over the Arcachon incident, and he took her chaff quite good humouredly. When she touched on the subject of the strange man in his garden he brushed it aside lightly—the police had settled that matter quite satisfactorily.

The Dean was extremely busy, too, on his return. The matter of the restoration found him plenty to do. Money was coming in as the result of the appeal, and Peggy presented her twenty pounds.

"My dear child," he said, "this is very generous of you. But you can't afford it, Peggy."

"Oh yes, I can. I've had a little gamble."

"You haven't been betting on horses, I hope?" asked the Dean, a little shocked.

"No—nor even playing roulette!" she retorted, with a smile. "It's a deal on the Stock Exchange. Purely business. Even *you* could have transacted it without a breath of scandal, uncle!"

"I don't understand."

"'Sapors!' Mr. Stanniland advised me to buy some. They went to a premium, and I sold out. This is the result——"

"But—I hardly like——"

"Look here, uncle dear, Sir Francis Skindles sent you a cheque for two hundred guineas, didn't he?"

"Well?"

"Are you going to ask *him* whether he made it on the Stock Exchange or not, eh? Well then, why bother about me? By the way, has Mr. Stanniland sent you a donation yet?"

"I haven't heard that he has done so."

"Oh, but he will, I know. He's frightfully busy just now, though."

Julian Bruce Stanniland *was* frightfully busy. All his energies were concentrated in floating 'Jecinora.' And it was becoming a battle. There were more adverse notices in the trade journals; the *Chemical Review* seemed to have set the pace, but the more he was thwarted, the harder he fought. "Jecinora" was already on the market—sold by "Bruce & Co." —done up in queer-shaped little bottles—he believed in the bizarre. Flaming advertisements were appearing on hoardings throughout the country, and people were being silently exhorted to take stock of their livers and then to seek for safety in "Jecinora."

And all the time preparations were being made for attracting the subscriptions of the public. It was the same as "Sapor," only more so. Interviews, correspondence, phones, wires, rushing journeys by train and car, agents, prospectuses, alluring advertisements, *and cheques*—cheques for various payments flying all over the place. Stanniland spared no expense. Like the general of an army, he knew he had to spend much in ammunition, as well as evolving tactics, before the battle could be won.

He kept Peggy at it, and Peggy responded cheerfully. It was "Jecinora" on the brain. The girl had never worked so hard in her life before. Stanniland himself was at it early and late, and Peggy more than once noticed the anxious lines on his face, the growing hollowness of his cheeks, and the darkening rings around his eyes. Once she ventured to remonstrate with him on doing too much, but he answered her sharply and curtly, telling her to mind her own business.

"If you think you can't stand it yourself—if that's what you mean," he added, sarcastically, "you'd better knock off and go!"

Peggy was genuinely hurt. He had his back to her, or he might have seen the paling of her cheeks and the moisture that gathered in her eyes.

"Don't!" she said, quietly. "I want to help you. I like doing it."

"Oh, all right. Sorry!" he growled. Don't take any notice of me."

"I—I know you don't mean it."

But he went on with his work and made no answer.

At length all was finished—prospectuses sent out, the last advertisements inserted in the press. Every shot had been fired. The actual fighting was over. There only remained the result.

On Saturday morning he said to her:

"You can take it easy the first three days next week. I'm going to. Drop in about ten and see to the correspondence, and be ready to answer the phone. That's about all. You can leave early in the afternoon. Don't ask for me if you can help it. I want a rest."

"You need it," she replied.

"Umph!"

On Sunday, Monday, Tuesday, and Wednesday he did absolutely nothing. Clad in his kimono, unkempt, unshaven, he lounged in his darkened room like a drunken man, scarcely even touching food. He would see no letters, not even the daily papers. The prospectus was issued to the public on the Monday; the subscription list closed on the Wednesday morning. He had worked with concentrated energy. He rested with concentrated inertia.

On the Thursday he went to London, and Peggy saw little of him before he started, but enough to convince her that he was once again the keen man of business. On the Friday he was at his desk, as usual, when she came in the morning at nine o'clock. She asked him how things were going. He only replied that it was too early yet to say. But she noticed that he was very silent all day, and that he kept all important correspondence and messages to himself. And she contrasted it, in her mind, with the buoyant expectancy he had shown when floating "Sapor."

On the Saturday morning, however, she noticed a change had come over him. He looked more cheerful; his eyes flashed with their accustomed alertness; his face had the old confident expression. He greeted her quite affably, much more as he used to in the early days before that strange reticence seemed to have gripped him.

"Good morning, Miss Lake," he said. "I hope you are feeling more rested after all this rush of work?"

It was the first time he had alluded to her personally. She smiled with pleasure.

"I'm very well, thanks very much, and I hope you are."

"First-rate," he replied, cheerfully, returning her smile.

"'Jecinora' gone all right, I hope?"

"I'll tell you—presently. One or two things I want done first. Take this down, please. Er—you know the right way to address your uncle, of course—eh? 'Dear Mr. Dean'—exactly. Now, please:

THE VERY REVEREND
THE DEAN OF FRATTENBURY,
The Deanery,
Frattenbury.

DEAR MR. DEAN,
I have much pleasure in enclosing a cheque for £1,012 8s. 3d. for the fund for the restoration of Frattenbury Cathedral.
Yours very truly,

"Mr. Stanniland!" exclaimed Peggy, "but how splendid of you!"

"All right, eh?" he said, with a little laugh. "'Sapers' went up well after you sold out. I wish, now, I'd advised you to wait a bit. I said I'd give two thirds of any premium I sold at—and that's the exact sum."

"You sold all yours?"

"Every one of 'em," he retorted, grimly. "I had to—for 'Jecinora'."

"Oh, won't uncle be pleased. It's just topping"

"Here's the cheque. Give me the letter to sign. There—put it in an envelope and direct it."

The typewriter clicked for a few moments. He sat still, looking at her, a queer little smile on his face.

"May the boy take it to uncle now? He's got a Chapter meeting this morning, and he'd love to have the cheque first."

"In a few minutes," replied Stanniland. "I want you to take down another letter for him, then we can send the two. Are you ready?"

She nodded, and he dictated:

DEAR MR. DEAN,
If you are still desirous to purchase my house, I am ready to entertain an offer from you, either direct or, if you prefer it, through the medium of Messrs. Pegg Brothers. An early answer will oblige.

Peggy looked at him over the typewriter, round-eyed and astonished.

"What do you mean?" she asked.

"What I say," retorted Stanniland. "Give it me, please. He may also like to have *this* in time to lay before the Chapter," he added, grimly, as he signed it.

"Oh!" exclaimed Peggy.

"I'll explain in a minute," replied Stanniland. He rang the bell, and the page-boy came in.

"Take these two letters and leave them at the Deanery. Sharp!"

The boy left the room. Stanniland wheeled round and faced Peggy.

"The next item is an unpleasant one," he said. "Please believe me when I say it is no fault of yours. I am grateful to you for your services, but I must give you a week's notice—from to-day."

"What does it all mean, Mr. Stanniland? I don't understand."

"It means that 'Jecinora' is a failure, and that I'm smashed," he replied, in a steady tone of voice.

"'Jecinora' a failure! Oh! After all your work?"

He nodded.

"Those notices damned it, I'm afraid. We can't go to allotment. Only about seven per cent. of the capital was subscribed and none was underwritten, so subscriptions are being returned. You see," he went on quietly, "I planked down all I had on it. And there won't be much left. I must sell the house. I want cash badly. And, of course, I couldn't afford to live here now."

Peggy had her elbows on the table and her chin in

her hands. She was looking at him intently, and the tears were standing in her eyes.

"Oh!" she exclaimed again, with the suspicion of a sob in her voice. "I *am* sorry! It's absolutely rotten luck."

"There it is, though."

"But—but," she said, "you say you want money, and you have just sent uncle a cheque for over a thousand pounds. Surely——"

He held up his hand.

"That was a promise," he replied. "I said I'd do it, and I've never broken my word yet."

"But I made you do it. It was my fault. Oh!"

"That's all right."

"But you did it to please me!"

A sad look flashed into his eyes as he answered:

"I don't regret it."

"But what are you going to do? Are you *quite* ruined."

"Pretty well. I may have a little left, but it won't be much. What am I going to do? Why, start again, of course!" and his eyes grew steady as he threw back his head a little and squared his shoulders. "It isn't the first time I've played and lost. I've been in a worse hole than this and come out of it—so I shall again."

Peggy's cheeks flushed with admiration.

"I think you're simply splendid!" she said, in a low voice. "Can't I help you?"

He looked at her in silence for a few moments, then slowly shook his head.

"I wish you could—but it's better not; and I aan't afford a secretary now—nor a chauffeur," he cdded, with a smile. "The car must go too."

"Let me work for you for nothing," she cried, impulsively. "I've saved a little money, and I can afford it. I'd love to. I want to see you start again. I want to help you."

An almost tender expression came into his firm, determined face.

"Why do you want to?" he asked. "Last time I asked you that question, you said it was for the sake of 'Jecinora.' But 'Jecinora' is done for now."

"Yes. But *you* are not done for," she answered.

"Is that why?"

She nodded her head.

His lips parted a little. He drew a sudden breath.

"May I ask you a question?"

"What?"

"It is a very personal one."

"Go on," she said. But her face crimsoned, and she looked down on the table.

"Are you engaged to young Quarrington?"

She started in genuine surprise and sat up in her chair.

"Whatever makes you ask me that? Surely you don't listen to the beastly tittle-tattle of the old women in the Close?"

"I don't know any of the old women, and don't want to. Look here. I always speak plainly. You know it. Twice I've seen you out with him—first time on a joy ride, then, last Saturday, on the downs. Why? That's what I want to know." And he leaned forward in his chair eagerly.

She tried to look severe, but a smile insisted upon breaking over her face.

"Well," she said, demurely, "you see, *you've* never

asked me to go for a joy ride with you. You've only taken me out—on business! "

"Would you have gone?"

His eyes were fixed on hers. She took a pencil off the table and fingered it, looking down at it.

"I—I should have preferred it—to—a silly boy—who tried to make love to me——"

"Yes?"

"Only I wouldn't let him!"

"Peggy!" He jumped up, bent over her and took her hand. "May I try?"

"Do you think—you know how to?"

He stooped still farther, putting his arm round her.

"I've never tried before, but I generally do what I've a mind to—and——"

"'Jecinora!'" she murmured, mischievously.

"Damn 'Jecinora'! I'm not talking business."

Then she looked up to him with a roguish smile.

"In a way—I hoped you *were!*" she whispered.

"Peggy—is it true? Do you really love me?"

"Why—I—don't think I can help it, dear!" and she raised her lips to his.

"Oh, Peggy dear, and I thought all the time it was somebody else—and tried to steel myself——"

"You were rather horrid, sometimes!"

"I'm sorry, dear!"

"But," she went on, her eyes shining with joy, "you're rather—nice—now!"

He drew her to him and kissed her, then suddenly stood up.

"Peggy dear," he said, "a few weeks ago I was in a position to offer you a home; now I'm a poor man. I want you to be my wife, but it isn't fair to ask you yet. Only, will you believe in me? I haven't gone under. Will you wait till I've pulled round again —for pull round I *shall!*"

Peggy's breath came fast; her bosom heaved. She looked up at him.

"Why should I wait?" she murmured.

"Won't you?" he asked.

"Can't I help you best if I don't wait, dear? Can't we pull round—*together?*"

* * * * *

"Peggy," said Julian Bruce Stanniland half an hour later, "I hope your uncle will be satisfied now he can have the house, for I owe him a debt of gratitude. If it hadn't been for the Dean I might never have met you."

"And 'Jecinora.' Oh, I'm so sorry it is a failure."

"But it isn't a failure at all," he replied with a light laugh. "It was because I was going to bring out 'Jecinora' that I wanted a secretary. It brought me *you*, dearest. I don't care a damn because I've lost my money. I can get that again. But I couldn't get another Peggy. There isn't another Peggy in the world."

"So," said Peggy, slipping her arm round his neck, "what it's all going to mean is like the story-books: 'They lived happily ever afterwards'—thanks to the Dean and 'Jecinora'!"